THE WRONG SIDE OF PARADISE

By
RAYMOND F. JONES

I0616755

ARMCHAIR FICTION
PO Box 4369, Medford, Oregon   97501-0168

*For more information about Armchair Books and products, visit our
website at…*

www.armchairfiction.com

Or email us at…

armchairfiction@yahoo.com

WAS IT ACTUALLY HEAVEN—OR A HELL OF A PLACE?

Somewhere out in a forbidden area of space it lay—a Utopia, a promised land usually found only in one's wildest dreams, with every man a strutting king, and every woman a beautiful princess. There was just one little drawback: Lovers of freedom usually went straight to hell!

This grand sci-fi adventure takes you on a trip into a "paradise" that doesn't really fit the normal stereotype. The guide for your journey is the man who gave us "This Island Earth," sci-fi veteran, Raymond F. Jones.

FOR A COMPLETE SECOND NOVEL, TURN TO PAGE 73

CAST OF CHARACTERS

BILL SCOTT
When he decided to fly his spaceship into "Derelict Sea," little did he know the dangers that were in store for him.

LETHA JERGENS
The most beautiful Princess in all of Paradise. She could love you one moment, then call for your blood the next.

DOC HODGES
This crusty old space dog had a secret dream: a cottage next to a lake with a flowerbed to tend to!

MA JERGENS
She and her daughter ran an old freighter on planetary runs. What was the deep space secret she guarded so closely?

GREG LAWSON
He figured out a way to escape from the parasites' mind control—and it almost cost him his life.

MUNSON
He was old and frail. So why did he want to take a rocket ride into a forbidden area of outer space?

CHAPTER ONE

"THERE'S NO use kidding ourselves." Doc Hodges paused and spat a brown tobacco stream onto the immaculate concrete apron of the spaceport. "It isn't much of a ship, but it's a shoestring to start on and we'll work it into a whole boot before this summer is out or my name ain't Doc Hodges."

Bill Scott grinned wryly. That wasn't much of a risk for Doc. He had changed his name so many times in the course of his spotty career that even he had forgotten which one he started out with.

"No, it isn't much of a ship, as freighters go, but a busted up soldier back from the wars can't be choosy," said Bill.

The two men walked slowly beside the red hull of the little cargo-carrier, the *Mote*. Even its fifty-foot length seemed long to Bill, whose limping walk was still painful after an unlucky ray shot had put him out of commission the day before peace was signed to end the four-year Venusian war.

Doc himself managed a pretty lively pace on a wooden leg gained an unknown number of years before because of some private space battle.

"The thing we've got to do," said Doc, "is concentrate on the carriage trade until we can get a bigger ship. Luxury stuff like this cargo of orchids from Venus and pearls from Pluto— that's where the real dough is. Leave the big muscle work of hauling fifty-ton beams and machinery to the hefty boys who like that stuff. While they wear out their muscles, we'll be making the dough."

"I only hope you're right," Bill said.

The *Mote* represented every cent that he owned in the world. After his medical discharge he had taken his bonus and put it with the meager savings he had hoped to get married on before the war. He put all of it into the *Mote*. The marriage plans had vanished when his fiancée had married someone else two months after he left. He knew that he would never plan and save again for such an event.

No, the rest of his life was going to be spent on the starways. The war had given him a taste of it, and he knew it was in his blood to stay. Earthbound jobs and clock punching—and coming home every night to dinner were all right for the guys who liked that sort of thing—and who had someone to provide the dinner.

The *Mote* was a fast little express ship that had been sold by the government as surplus. Because he agreed with Doc's theory of trade, Bill had bought a small, fast ship, rather than a large one. They would concentrate on small express shipments that had to get places in a hurry.

BUT ANOTHER idea had been brewing in his mind for days. He said suddenly, "Doc, what do you know about Derelict Sea?"

"Nothing—except that it's a good place to stay away from. At the last count there were about one thousand ships milling around in there, and no one has ever come out of it. You aren't thinking of adding the *Mote* to the pool, I hope."

"Somewhere off between Jupiter and Uranus, isn't it? I've never had occasion to be near it, you know."

"Yeah, that's about it. Say, listen, you—"

"Ever stop to think what a wonderful salvage haul that would be?"

"You idiot. Every salvage outfit in the System has at least one ship in there—permanently. Cargo is our line not harebrained salvage projects. Now just forget about Derelict—"

"But we aren't making enough money. We've got to make a lot of dough if we ever expect to build up a business that amounts to anything. This hauling daisies across the Solar System isn't going to do it for us."

"They ain't daisies," Doc exploded. "They're rare orchids and we get a nice fee for hauling them—enough to suit me."

"Maybe it's old age," Bill said musingly. "Funny that you'd get cold feet just thinking about those thousand ships milling around in Derelict Sea with their ports hanging open and no sign of life."

"Why, you young pup!" Doc's false teeth clattered loudly with his excitement. "I walked barefoot across Pluto's mountains before you could even crawl around in three cornered pants. I've got guts enough to supply seventeen men like you and leave enough over for three boys. Cold feet—!"

"Okay, Doc. That's all I wanted to know. By peculiar coincidence I find in checking our course to Pluto that we go smack through the region of Derelict Sea. Just wanted to know what you thought about sticking to that one before figuring a new one."

"But we don't know anything about salvage! That's a highly specialized business these days."

"The *Queen of Mars* alone ought to net us half a million, don't you think? She's one of the newest liners in there."

"The best outfits in the business have given up long ago." Doc's forehead was beaded with sweat. He realized he had been dragged into the most fateful argument of his career and he was losing fast.

"Listen, Doc. This isn't a problem of salvage. Salvage is going out, grabbing a beat-up ship, and dragging it back to a port. As far as we know, every ship in Derelict Sea can still move under its own power. All we have to do is go in there and fly them out."

"Oh is that right?" Doc exploded. "Then why the hell hasn't someone done it long ago?"

"Well… There's something keeping them in there, obviously. Our problem is to find out what that something is. Now, I've got an idea—"

"An idea? I should tie up with a daydreamer like you and lose my hide for an idea!" Doc's teeth clattered loudly.

"The *Mote* is one of the series of ships on which the Sherman-Hagerman drive was installed," Bill said. "Now, this drive is no good at all on a large heavy ship, but it has worked wonders on the little fellows. Have you ever wondered why no ship with an S-H drive was ever lost in Derelict Sea?"

"I didn't know that there hadn't been."

"Well, I do, I've been thinking of this for a long time and I've looked up the records of the ships lost in there. It's logical that, with all the ships there are in space, at least one S-H drive should have been lost. But there isn't even one in there."

"So what?"

"So I think there's some kind of natural force field in space that is holding those ships and preventing them from getting loose. But the properties of the S-H drive make it immune to that force."

"Yes, and if that's so, why is the port of every derelict open? Why has there been absolutely no sign of life?"

"There are some questions that my theory doesn't answer right off, of course. But the point is, we *have* an S-H drive and no S-H has ever been caught in Derelict Sea. That fact alone makes me think it would he a safe gamble to go in and investigate. In fact, I'm determined to do so. You don't have to if you'd rather not, Doc. Seriously, I'm not trying to egg you on. I know there's risk, but it's the kind I like to gamble against."

"So you're trying to keep me from going, now?" Doc sputtered under his breath. "Listen, you just *try* and keep me from coming along. I'm going to prove what a damn fool you are, and when we're stuck and helpless in Derelict Sea I'm going to sit there and laugh and laugh—before I figure out how to get you out of the jam you're getting us into."

AS THEY entered the flight office of the spaceport, their ears were assailed by the clatter of teletype machines and the static crashes from a dozen open receivers. The sound poured out of the communications room, making a bedlam in the vicinity of the counter.

The counter was a long wall on which were posted flight notices and information and regulations for the benefit of spacemen. Usually three or four pilots were scanning the clip files carelessly, but today no less than twenty-five were competing for space in front of one particular notice.

Bill halted a pilot just leaving the crowd, "What's up?"

"Derelict Sea—they've forbidden the entire area. And just when I was getting a hankering to see how close I could brush it with my tail flaps and not get caught."

Bill whistled softly and Doc grinned smugly. "Shall we see if we can pick up another order of daisies around here before we leave—or would you rather plot our new course first? The one dodging Derelict Sea?"

Bill made a reply. Doc could see his lips moving, but the words were inaudible because of a sudden thunderous roar that broke somewhere in the sky above the port.

The pilots rushed to the door and Bill followed. Outside, in the shining summer sky, a black freighter was weaving drunkenly towards Earth, a long trail of thick smoke behind it. The roar of its erratic rockets was like the sound of battle.

"Doc—why aren't they getting out the emergency squad? That ship's going to crash…"

Doc looked up lazily at the crazy twisting of the freighter. "Naw, she's all right. Watch and see."

"Anybody can see it's going to crash!"

"That's Ma Jergens' ship," said Doc. "There's a saying among spacemen that when Ma's on the throttle there's thunder on the starways. And that's no lie. You can practically hear that old crate of hers in the dead vacuum of space. Good old Ma. If she'd been a fighter pilot we'd have won the war in a week. The only trouble is that she couldn't get inside anything smaller than a medium freighter."

By now the black ship had made a semblance of an attempt to level out for a landing, but the tail was spinning in a circle as if all the tubes on one side were dead.

"She'll never make it," Bill said. "The fire squad should be out there."

"You'll see," Doc said.

AT THAT moment the thunder died as the motors were cut off. The nose of the ship dropped sharply, then the tail kicked down to level it out, and the ship banged and squealed against the surface of the field. Slowly it rolled to a stop not far away.

Every pilot who had been watching gave an unconscious sigh of relief. One of them wiped his brow. "Ma's a chiseling old deadbeat," he said. "But she can sure fly with the best of us."

They always hoped, but never quite dared believe that Ma Jergens would make it down in safety. Bill had heard of Ma and her ancient crate, the *Dartmoor*, before. Hardly a spaceman from Mercury to Pluto had not heard at least the name of Ma Jergens and her rusty tub—and her daughter Letha, whose beauty was as far famed as her mother's piloting skill.

Abruptly the port of the *Dartmoor* banged open. From where he stood Bill had supposed it to be a decent-sized opening, but the figure that emerged had trouble squeezing through.

Then Ma Jergens was on the ground, waddling forward with a gait that would make a duck seem as graceful as a ballet dancer. She smiled broadly and waved to the pilots, who gave her a brief cheer.

"Hi, boys—how was that for a landing? Not too bad with fourteen rear tubes burned out. That shows what kind of a ship the old *Dartmoor* is. Anybody want to buy her?"

"What d'ya mean?" said one of the pilots standing nearby. "Don't tell us you and the old tub are parting ways."

"Yep." Ma replied. "This old hulk and that old hulk are separating. That was the last set-down. From now on I'm riding in style." She raised her arm and pointed in the distance. "There she is, boys, the *Packet.*"

Everyone glanced down the field where a great shining new freighter almost dwarfed the *Mote*. For days it had been a matter of speculation who the *Packet* belonged to. Now they stared at it incredibly.

"I'm in the money, boys," Ma said, laughing a little. "If any of you has money coming from me, now's your chance. Line up and present your bills."

In the back of the crowd Doc muttered through his teeth, "Now where do you suppose that old biddy got the cash to buy a ship like that? She hasn't hauled enough cargo in the last year to pay for even a coat of paint on that new ship of hers."

Bill watched her bulbous, overalled figure disappear into the flight office to file her report.

Doc was cursing softly, "She hasn't had enough jobs in the last year for anything—"

Bill laughed, "Don't let it get you down. Maybe we can find where she struck the pot of gold and get one ourselves."

"But she never had enough to pay her fuel bills," Doc insisted, "Joe Evans used to carry her a thousand gallons behind all the time, then it got to be two, and he finally crossed it off the books. Half a dozen other dealers have done the same. Incidentally—look! There's what most of these guys are hanging around to see."

Bill's eyes followed Doc's gaze back to the *Dartmoor*. A second figure, one with proper proportions, stepped gracefully to the landing field.

"That's Letha, the daughter. She's mechanic and co-pilot for Ma. Never misses a trip with her."

IN SPITE of his avowed lack of interest in women since his recent experience in being thrown overboard, Bill could not refrain from staring a long moment at the girl who came running toward the office.

Her head was graced with a mass of tumbled auburn hair that was blown back by the gentle breeze in the air. She could not be more than twenty, he thought, and the white overalls did little to hide the loveliness of her figure.

Then, disgusted with himself, Bill turned away. "Better get our cargo checked for takeoff," he said. "I want to recheck our trajectory."

"You mean work out a new one? That's a long job."

"I said 'recheck.' We're not changing."

In the flight office, Bill stood at the counter, copying the coordinates of the area now closed to flight. It not only included the actual space known as Derelict Sea, but a large margin on all sides. It was a sizable chunk of space. Even if he were going to obey the order—which he wasn't—it would require considerable change of plans and more fuel.

As he stood there, a creeping aura of delicate perfume enveloped him. It was so faint that for a moment he thought the wind had blown a gust from the patch of blooms outside the building. Then he glanced aside and saw Letha beside him.

"Hello," she said pleasantly. "Any news?"

Mentally he cursed the sudden confusion within him. Hadn't he learned his lesson well enough to keep a pretty smile and a dainty figure from doing this to him?

"Not much," he growled with more unpleasantness than he planned. "Just roped off Derelict Sea to keep crazy fools out of it."

"Dere—" The girl's face went suddenly white and she stared at the notice.

Bill stared curiously at her agitated face. "It's a big spot," he said. "Kind of changes your plans if you had a trajectory through that part of the System."

"Yes—yes, it does," she said. Her smile was nervous now. She turned abruptly away and hurried into the chart room.

Bill watched her go, his eyes upon her in frank admiration. It seemed incredible that Ma Jergens could have been the mother of such a slim beauty.

He wandered on into the chart room to check the coordinates he had copied. He glanced about expectantly for Letha, but she was not visible in the aisles between the racks of maps and star charts that he could see.

HE WAS moving down the length of a rack to find the chart he needed when he suddenly heard the muted, contralto voice of Ma Jergens in heated argument on the other side of the rack. She was with Letha and an old man.

"I don't give a hoot what the brass hats say," Ma Jergens whispered hoarsely. "I've been flying when and where I wanted to for forty years now, and if I want to keep on going into

Derelict Sea, I'm going to do it. I don't intend to let any man tell me what to do at this late date. Your father was the last one that tried that—and he ended up full of regrets. We're not changing our plans!"

"But, Mother, there'll be patrol ships all over the region. We can't possibly get through them. They'll turn us back if we approach too close—and they'll fire on us if we don't. It's illegal now. We've got to give this up…"

"And lose the *Packet*? I've worked forty years to get a ship like her. Any time you think you've had enough of space tramping you can quit. I've tried a thousand times to get you to settle down with one of these goggle-eyed pilots and raise a bunch of kids. That's the job for a woman, not this chasing around the stars."

"Speak for yourself, Mother. Why don't you give up with tramping and go back to Dad?"

"That's *different*," Ma said with finality. Then she turned to the old man who had been standing next to them during their entire conversation. "You can tell your friends to meet me at the abandoned copper company's field at Dakar Point, Mr. Munson. We'll pick you up there and continue with plans according to our previous agreement."

"That will be satisfactory, Mrs. Jergens." The older man's voice was wheezy and cracked. Bill could not see him clearly through the bars of the chart racks. Then he realized he had no business listening at all, but he could not force himself away. The mention of Derelict Sea was a magnet that held him.

"I do hope this prohibition will cause no trouble with the flight," said Mr. Munson. "We are so anxious to make the trip."

"There won't be any hitch," said Jergens. "You be there and we'll get you where you'll never have to worry again."

There was a sudden shuffling of feet, and Bill Scott moved hastily away. From the seclusion of a chart table he watched the shrunken creature, who was evidently Mr. Munson, shuffle away. The man appeared to be about seventy-five and in a bad state of repair. Bill wondered where in the System he wanted to go and why he didn't go on one of the regular liners instead of Ma Jergens' freighter.

But the voices of Ma and Letha were raised again indiscreetly.

"You're going to land us in jail!" the girl stormed.

"At least we'll be able to eat well when we get out."

There was the sound of rustling bills over there, and then Ma continued, "Twenty head at ten thousand apiece. That's not bad, I'd say. It beats hauling cement and bricks in the old *Dartmoor*. The *Packet* will be paid for in six months at this rate. We're leaving tonight so let's get our gear transferred to the *Packet* before it gets any later."

Ma Jergens waddled out of the chart room, Letha following determinedly in her wake, like a graceful sloop behind a lumbering tug.

CHAPTER TWO

BILL REMAINED over the charts for several minutes. Their trajectory would take them directly into Derelict Sea all right. But his mind was busy pondering over what he had heard. Finally he rose and went out to the *Mote*.

Doc was busy with last minute touches to make things shipshape. Bill said, "There's someone who knows how to get in and out of Derelict Sea."

"Yeah? Who?"

"Ma Jergens."

Doc straightened with a jerk. "Ma? What does she know about Derelict Sea?"

"She's flying old men in there for ten thousand dollars apiece. What do you make of that?"

"You're crazy. Where'd you hear that?"

"Eavesdropping."

"It doesn't make sense. Ma doesn't know anything about science—not enough for her to figure a way in and out of there. Besides, what is she hauling old men in there for?"

"That's what I'm asking you."

"Aw—I don't believe it. Anyway, the ban on flights through that area will fix that."

"On the contrary, Ma's planning on defying the ban. I heard her assure one of her customers that she'd get him where he'd never have to worry again."

"What did she mean?" Doc scratched his head. "I don't like the sound of it."

"Neither do I. I don't like the sound of the whole thing. Neither does Letha. She wants Ma to give it up, but Ma loves the rustle of folding money too well."

"Yeah—she would," Doc said moodily. "Well, as I see it it's no skin off our noses. But Letha—"

"Yeah, Letha," Bill said slowly, "I hate to see her mixed up in a thing like this."

"We couldn't—I mean—" Doc looked at Bill. "Letha—"

"Sure we can. You've still got an eye for feminine pulchritude haven't you—you old codger? We won't let a pretty young thing like that get caught in a jam because of an old harpy of a mother, will we?" Bill put a hand on Doc's shoulder.

"I knew—Letha's father," Doc said slowly, "He was a fine man. He'd want me to do this because I was his friend."

"Okay. They're taking off tonight We can postpone our takeoff until about the same time. And it may be helpful to us to know just how Ma gets in and out of Derelict Sea. The *Dartmoor* doesn't have an S-H drive, so it could be that my theory's all wet."

IT WAS midnight when they actually filed their time of departure. The *Packet* had left an hour before, but they wanted to give Ma time to pick up her mysterious passengers.

As the *Mote* rose swiftly and Earth dropped away beneath them, Bill and Doc sat back comfortably in their inertia control chairs. Life seemed suddenly very good again as the old thrill of space filled them. To some pilots it became mere commonplace after the first few times, but never to Doc Hodges and Bill

Scott.

They set the course graphs into the automatic pilot and got up from their seats. Bill stepped to the tiny bar, "Like a drink?" he asked.

"Sure," Doc said.

Bill drew two tall glasses of tomato juice. This was the strongest stuff allowed in space. Spacemen had long before learned that liquor and spaceships didn't mix, and Doc had been taught so severe a lesson in his youth that he never touched anything stronger than milk either aboard or on land.

They turned up the radio for last minute news from Earth, for soon the broadcast channels would be too feeble and all they would get would be the high frequency stuff necessary to keep them in touch with the planets and patrol ships.

Some dance music filtered out; Doc snorted impatiently, "Let's see what the news in the System is."

Bill adjusted the receiver, "Just in time," he said.

The blare of an announcer's voice filled the room, then a commentator's voice took over. "The biggest news today is the tragedy that overtook the greatest and newest of Earth's luxury space liners, *Empress of Titania*, late this afternoon, Earth Eastern time.

"The *Empress* radioed that a ship-wide revolt had broken out, in which the passengers overpowered the crew and took control. We know nothing of the purpose behind this unprecedented action. No communication was received after the mutineers took over."

"Greg Lawson was aboard that ship," Bill said.

"Almost at once," the commentator said, "the course of the great vessel was changed and it was driven directly towards the heart of Derelict Sea. This was after Director of the Space Patrol Cummings had issued orders prohibiting flight near or into that area. The Patrol was called and a boarding attempt was made, without success. So today the greatest ship yet trapped by Derelict Sea lies in its treacherous clutches. The fate of its thousand passengers and crewmembers is unknown. Perhaps we never will know, for the *Empress of Titania* hangs in space, her great ports open, her hatches swinging wide, air and life gone from her—a helpless derelict, wandering through time and space like the ship of the Flying Dutchman, guided by ghosts."

"Pleasant fellow," Doc said.

"I saw Greg Lawson just once after he got out of the army," Bill said, "He was already signed up for radioman, third, on the *Empress*. He was as proud as a kid with a new bicycle. This must have been his first flight, poor devil."

THEY MADE no attempt to contact the *Packet*, but midway in the flight they got a radar identification and location of her coordinates. She was behind them, so they slowed to let her pass. By alternating watches and slowing their time senses alternately with the drug, *Tempora,* which made an hour seem like a minute, they shortened the apparent length of the two-week journey. On the thirteenth day they began tracking the *Packet* in earnest.

Doc picked up Ma's new freighter on the plates. "There she is—heading straight for the middle of Derelict Sea. I don't see any patrol ships."

"There's one—off to starboard. And he's spotted the *Packet* too. He's signaling Ma to stop."

"Check her speed. She's accelerating at a blackout pace. She's going to try running the blockade, all right."

"And we're right behind her—but we stand more of a chance of running into that Patrol ship. Hang on, I'm adding more Gs."

Automatically, the inertia control increased as the acceleration of the little *Mote* mounted to a terrific figure. But the *Packet* maintained its lead and even increased the distance between the two ships.

An alarm suddenly rang within the ship.

"The Patrol!" Doc exclaimed. "They're signaling us to stop."

Bill stepped to the communicator panel. "Freighter *Mote* responding. Go ahead."

"This is Patrol Cruiser *Sybellus*. You are ordered to stop and proceed no further on your present course. The area of Derelict Sea is forbidden to any closer approach."

"We're not going in," said Bill.

"We're trying to halt the freighter, *Packet*. They seem to be out of control, and we're closer than you are. This is an S-H drive we're using. We can reach the *Packet* if anyone can."

"Interception is the job of the Patrol. You are not authorized to go nearer."

"The hell with you, then. You can stew in your own red tape. We're going to overtake the *Packet*," Bill said curtly. He then cut off the transmission.

Doc's face was a pitiful thing to see. "Bill...do you realize that was a patrol cruiser that you just told off? We'll never see daylight again once they catch us."

"They've got to catch us first," said Bill grimly. He stepped the acceleration to the maximum limit and their senses suddenly wavered and the room grew fuzzy.

From somewhere there came the distant sound of the alarm again, then a coruscating blast exploded near the ship, sending its blinding light through the port. Dully, Bill realized the Patrol was firing upon them.

He glanced at the screen. The *Packet* was even farther ahead. It was surprising how powerful the inertia controls were that she mounted. And now the dim graveyard of space was visible. The myriad of occupants of Derelict Sea stood out like faint ghosts in the ever darkness of space. A thousand of them milling eternally in the void, derelicts drained of life by some unknown property of this area of space. Their ports were open like blind eyes and their ramps were down as if the passengers had simply walked out into space and vanished.

Somewhere in the *Mote* a plate creaked as it twisted against its neighbor, and Bill wondered dully if the ship were falling apart. Another blast—much closer this time—came from the cruiser.

Then blackness possessed him as consciousness fled.

CHAPTER THREE

AT A PRESET time the automatic controls cut down the tremendous acceleration of the ship to allow the men to return to consciousness.

It returned to Bill suddenly, as always, as soon as the blood circulation was restored to his brain. But what he saw as light swimming back into his eyes made him doubt that consciousness had returned.

The ship was flooded with golden light streaming through the ports as if from some warming sun in an atmosphere of Earth or above the red and yellow sands of Mars. He put out a hand and shook Doc who was still groggy from the flight.

"Hey, Doc! Wake up. Look—!"

"Huh—?"

Doc stirred and opened his eyes wearily, and then his upper plate dropped with a clatter as he gasped. "Bill—what's happened? Where are we?"

He stared, speechless, out the ports and into the vision plates. The *Mote* had slowed; was almost motionless now. The acceleration control was at zero and power was off, though Bill couldn't remember cutting it.

They were coming to rest beside other great ships of space—small cruisers, great freighters, mighty liners. They stopped beside the *Empress of Titania!*

"Bill—is this—? It can't be!"

"No, we're not dead. But this is something new all right. Where's the *Packet?*"

Doc shook his head. The freighter of Ma Jergens was not to be seen.

Bill came up to the port window beside Doc and stared out toward a distant golden city where tall spires reached to a golden sky and silver motes danced in the sunlight. Birds soared gaily through the air and trees with green and crimson leaves moved as if nudged by summer breezes.

"It isn't real?" Doc whispered hoarsely. "I've heard of

mirages in space but I've never seen one before."

"Mirage? It looks like pretty solid substance that the *Mote* has settled on."

"But if it's real, where *is* it? Nothing like this was visible a few minutes ago."

"Another dimension, another space, a twisting of Time—who knows what it might be?" Bill said. "It could be anyone of a thousand things. I've an idea we're going to find out before we're through, but the important thing is, what has become of the occupants of all these ships?"

"There's some of 'em, I suppose." Doc pointed towards the gardens beyond the field where the ships lay. Groups of people idled in the park or lay on the grass. Others were moving along the avenues, "You know, I'm beginning to form a theory," he said. "About this coming back business. Wherever this is, consider it—look at that city! Remember Earth and its filth, the sand and dirt of Mars, the terror and death of Heliopolis. Maybe *we* won't want to go back, either."

Bill sent him a sharp look, "Don't let it throw you, Doc. Maybe it's real and maybe it isn't. Either way it's only a dose of hashish for us. It's not for Earthmen."

Why he said that, he didn't know. It was only that a sense of terrible alien forces at work about them settled upon his mind. Yet, in a moment he felt he was wrong. He felt as if a blanket were being thrown about his mind, protecting his thoughts from despair and dissatisfaction. Perhaps Doc was right—they might not want to leave this golden city.

"Let's go out and have a look around," he suggested.

"Better test the air—if any. Doggone it, I still think it's all imaginary. We're in the middle of Derelict Sea. We know what it looked like before we blacked out. There was nothing like this here then."

"Is that a mirage too?"

DOC STARED in the direction of Bill's pointing finger. A long avenue led through the center of the gardens and ended at the field. It was lined with waving trees, and coming down along it was a procession out of some wild dream of Bacchus. It was a scene out of ancient Greece with the gods and goddesses come to life.

Dancing flower girls spread blossoms upon the avenue of gold. Behind them, prancing elves tootled high-pitched melodies on silver flutes, and gay unicorns drew a lavish carriage of purple and gold.

But it was the figure, within the open carriage that brought gasps to the throats of Doc and Bill.

"Letha!" Bill exclaimed hoarsely. "Doc, look—"

"Letha…" Doc whispered under his breath. "But how could she—?"

Bill remained speechless before the vision that slowly approached the *Mote*. The procession wound about the corner of the avenue and turned directly towards the ship.

The fairy princess, clad in gossamer veils, lying on the carriage drawn by unicorns, was unmistakably Letha. The worried look that Bill had last seen in her eyes was gone now. Her face was not merely relaxed; it was joyous, as if she were experiencing the greatest happiness a mortal could know.

The faces of all in the procession seemed to share the same exhilaration, as if this were a world of happiness, a city of joy.

"Let's get out there and see what this means," said Bill. He whirled and strode to the port.

Doc said, "I've got the feeling that we're going to wake up and find this is a nightmare that'll leave us with the screaming meemies."

"There's only one way to find out. Come on."

There was no hiss as he unscrewed the clamps and threw open the port. The air outside was at Earth normal pressure. It was filled with the scent of flowers that made the interior of the *Mote* seem stagnant and foul by contrast, though the conditioner kept the air pure within the ship.

Following Bill, Doc jumped to the ground as he put his hand to his mouth to keep his plates in.

21

The procession halted and Letha rose to a sitting position and waved a slim, white arm, tossing them a handful of flowers, "Welcome to Paradise, starmen. Welcome to the city of happiness."

"Letha!" Doc blurted, "Letha—it's me, Doc Hodges. Don't you know us? Here's Bill—you saw him in the flight office before takeoff."

Letha's laugh was a merry tinkle, and it brought little tears to her eyes that made them glisten like stars, "Of course I know you. That's why I'm so happy to see you here. I was hoping so much that you would come. That's why we led you here, knowing you were trailing us."

"But where are we? What place is this?" Doc persisted.

"Paradise—Paradise of Derelict Sea. Do you wonder that the ships that find their way here never return? Who would want to leave this golden city of gladness and joy for the dirt and filth and unhappiness of the planets they have known?"

"But *what* is it? Why can't it be seen from—from outside?"

"All your questions will be answered in due time," Letha said. "But come with me. A celebration has been prepared."

She sat up straight and made room in the carriage. "Come and sit with me. One of you on each side. Bill, you haven't said a word. Are you speechless?"

"Very nearly," Bill admitted. He smiled, but somehow deep within him he didn't feel like smiling. A nameless oppression seemed to bear upon him. He could give no reason for it. There was just that sensation of a blanket that seemed to be smothering his thoughts, But even that dwindled and faded as he mounted to the carriage and sat beside Letha. On the other side, Doc took his place and the elfin driver set the unicorns in motion.

Now the elfin flutists took up their melodies again and the flower girls sang a gay song of love and springtime as they walked before the slow procession.

THE DIAPHANOUS veils that Letha wore were of

uncertain design and seemed merely draped about her. Whipping slowly in the light breeze, they hid little of her charms and Bill was uncomfortable so near to her. Her perfume mingled with that of the flowers in the gardens and surrounded him with an aura of sensuous delight.

But the intellectual part of Bill's brain, which he felt was being submerged in a flood of sensuousness, was coldly appraising the change in Letha. She appeared the same—but she was not the same girl he had seen in trim space overalls on Earth two weeks ago. She acted as if she had been released from all strain and tension and was perfectly free of inhibitions. As a matter of fact, Bill reflected, he rather felt that way himself. He felt that within this golden city of Paradise he could achieve all that he had ever dreamed of.

Doc's voice penetrated his consciousness. "Give me a little white cottage with a green roof and a garden by the sea, and I'll never set foot on a spaceship again. I've spent a lifetime of rough and tumble on the starways, but the dream of every starman is a little cottage in his old age."

This was the first time Bill had ever heard Doc admit he was old. Bill looked sharply at him. Doc's face was utterly relaxed too, as if the strain and tension in the scramble of living in modern civilization had been removed.

Paradise...this city was called Paradise of Derelict Sea.

Bill wondered.

They were moving slowly along the avenue now. In the distance, forests, gardens, fountains and houses of all descriptions covered the landscape. There was a lake of glorious blue a couple of miles distant.

The variety of architecture astounded Bill. There were tiny cottages nestled in quiet gardens; there were palatial mansions with stately, formal landscapes; there were tremendous structures like ancient feudal castles. All were placed indiscriminately over the whole landscape, yet the entire effect was not displeasing. There was an air of peace and satisfaction that enveloped everything.

Letha pointed toward the golden spires of the great city. "My palace is there," she said. "We shall feast and be entertained in honor of your arrival."

"I don't understand this at all," Bill said, "You are Letha of Earth, but now you are Princess Letha of Paradise of Derelict Sea. How did it happen?"

"Doesn't the dream of paradise exist in the lore of every nation of Earth? Not only that, but we find it in the lore of other worlds as well. The ancient Martians dreamed and talked of Paradise—Verheeda, they called it. Is it surprising, then, that such a legend should have a foundation in reality?"

"But paradise has been associated with the concept of life after death."

Letha's glorious laughter tinkled upon the sparkling air. "I assure you we are not physically dead, but we are dead to the old things of Earth. It is rare for a man to return to Earth from Paradise. Those who do, leave traces of what they have seen in the legends of which you speak. Rather than death, Paradise is the only real life in all the universe. Life, freedom; happiness, the chance to realize every great dream you have ever dreamed is here for you."

Bill felt that there was much she was not telling him; however, as this thought entered his mind it seemed immediately to fade. It occurred to him that there was little use in pursuing the question. Here he was. He had achieved a place in Paradise. Why not be satisfied without further questioning?

But another part of his mind would not put the question down, and suddenly with a cold flood washing over him, he realized that two parts of his brain were warring against each other, and that the questioning part was slowly but surely losing the battle.

THE HOUSES and gardens gave way shortly to the spires and palaces of the golden city itself. Immaculate streets glittered but did not blind with their golden splendor. Life was leisurely. The only vehicles on the streets were carriages drawn by gaily-prancing unicorns.

The buildings varied. There were low structures. Then there were some a dozen stories high, topped by reaching spires. There was none of the darkness, noise and filth of an Earth city.

But it was the people moving through the market places that struck Bill most forcibly. Serene and unhurried, they were like true princes and princesses, yet they deferred to Letha with short bows as the carriage passed. Impulsively, Bill felt that he would be truly content to remain here for the rest of his days.

Of the great public buildings he saw, none were so lavish as the magnificent palace of Princess Letha. The singing flower girls led the way between massive wrought iron gates into a garden of grandeur. The path turned in a semicircle around a blue pool with a fountain of shining water that arced into the sunlight. Then the procession brought up before the palace of glass and gold.

Doc tumbled out on his wooden leg. Bill stepped down rather stiffly and offered Letha his hand. She led them to the carpeted walk that led between wide doors into the great hall of the palace.

Narrow pools lined each side of the walk and glowing fish played in the depths. On the broad lawns on either side were other people, among them at least a score of exquisitely lovely girls, lightly clad as was Letha and surrounded by attendants.

Letha noticed his glance. "They are princesses, too," she said. "But don't forget—you are *my* cavalier." There was still laughter in her eyes, but a fierce possessiveness lay behind it that touched off a chill within him.

"How can there be so many princesses?" he said.

"Oh, that does not matter. Anyone who comes here may be a princess if she wishes, but not so many do. When the palace becomes too small for all of us, a new one is built."

"But who runs things around here? You can't all do it."

"Oh, none of us care to be bothered with government and things like that. Can't you guess who is in charge of affairs of the golden city? Mother is."

Bill swallowed hard to stifle the explosive surprise within him. Mountainous Ma Jergens in charge of Paradise! Then gradually the impulse to laugh at this grotesque incongruity faded, as had so many other impulses since he came.

He said, "She ought to do well. She likes to boss things."

"Oh, she does, and this is—well, Paradise for her, as it is for all of us. It is true when I say that every person may become exactly what he wishes here."

"And you wished to be a princess."

"Always."

CHAPTER FOUR

THEY CAME into a great hall surmounted by a high glass dome that let in the golden light of the city. The walls were composed of a thousand panels of vari-hued material. In the center of the hall was a large pool, and surrounding it was the great banquet table. Already the meal was in progress and Bill estimated more than five hundred diners were seated.

"Serving never ceases in the great hall of the princesses," said Letha. "Here we bring those who come in from the ships and who are to be our subjects and fete them with a great feast. In days to come you will learn who all these people are."

"And we are to be *your* subjects?" asked Bill.

Letha smiled a tantalizing, promising smile. "Would you find that so terrible? You don't have to if you don't wish to. In Paradise no one is under compulsion."

Bill felt his mind warring with itself again. He knew he was being utterly ridiculous when he said, "There is nothing I would like better than to devote myself to the service of Princess Letha."

"You shall have the opportunity. But come, our places are waiting."

She led them to the far distant head of the table where three places were waiting in reserve. Her attendants departed then and serving maids approached with the wines.

The wine was excellent, but to his surprise Bill observed that they didn't bring Doc any. They brought a glass of milk.

"Hey, did you tell them that you never drink wine?" he said.

Doc shook his head. "They must've read my mind. But this is the best milk I've tasted in a long time. Better have some."

"Doc—look, this place is wonderful, but we've got to get—"

The criticism vanished maddeningly from Bill's mind and he turned to answer Letha's sudden question. "What kind of music would you like?" she asked.

"Music—music—" He tried to get his thoughts back to what he was going to say to Doc. But it was gone. "I'd like some of the ancient Victor Herbert songs if they know any."

"Of course. Listen."

Almost instantly, the orchestra broke into the strains of "Sweet Mystery of Life." But never before had Bill heard it played as the ancient melody was being played by these musicians. The exquisite throats of the violins were almost human in their singing tones. Then, as if by pre-arrangement, Letha and five of the other princesses rose and stood together on the low dais beside the orchestra to sing the words.

"Ah, sweet mystery of life, at last I've found you—"

The ancient song of life and love floated out over the assembly. Bill watched their faces intently. There were men and women from every walk of life, officials of states, artists, mechanics, just plain vacationers— and universally their faces were suffused with that overwhelming feeling of satisfaction that fought for mastery of Bill's mind. Only a very faint nostalgia for Earth was apparent in the faces of some of them, and when a burst of applause broke the spell, even this dropped away.

The orchestra took up a new strain now as serving continued. Bill received a dish of golden brown meat that looked like some unknown fish. It was boneless—and delicious.

The music grew wilder like some frantic Gypsy air of a long distant and almost forgotten Earth. The dancers came forward again and whirled about the circle of the table in an intricate pattern of motion. Their costumes were a whirling mass of color: gold, brown, yellow, green, blue, and red. They spun and darted until the whole room seemed to partake of their motion and became a mad haze of color that was exhausting to the emotions.

Then, abruptly, on a wild, discordant note, the music ended and the dancers stopped.

"That gets you," said Doc, "I feel like I had been out there with them. I'm winded."

"You were out there," said Letha. "Not physically, of course, but you were undergoing every sensation of motion and exhilaration that you might have experienced had you been dancing. That's the essence and wonder of our "art" here in Paradise."

"I don't understand," said Bill. "Unless it's a sort of mental control."

"I suppose you might call it that." she replied. "Minds are more attuned to each other here. Men understand one another and there is little confusion. All of it is due to better mental harmony than is known outside of Paradise."

"Then there is definitely an unknown power acting upon our minds." Bill got the words out before that blanketing influence closed over his thoughts.

"I don't know," said Letha. "But whatever it is, it is good."

Bill didn't say, "I wonder." The words were clamped in his throat as if a hand had been laid upon him before he could utter them. And through the pain of the repressed words he sensed a warning—indefinite, intangible, and completely gone within an instant, so that it seemed only a figment of his imagination.

FINALLY Letha said, "Shall we leave—or do you want to see more of the show?"

"When does this end?" said Bill.

"Never. The feasting and the entertainment have never been interrupted since the beginning of Paradise. It will go on until the end of time."

Doc said, "Let's not stay until the end."

He grinned at Doc's joke, but Bill's mind struggled mightily as he tried to put double meaning into his words, "No, let's not stay—for the end."

The fairyland carriage was still waiting when they left the palace. They went now without the accompaniment of the flower girls and flutists. Letha said, "I will show you your estates in Paradise. Each of you shall have that which you have always desired."

"Me for the little white cottage by the sea," said Doc. "But I suppose we get shoved in some two by four apartment, proving that Paradise is as 'civilized' as the rest of the universe."

"You'll see," Letha promised.

"I'd like to see your mother," said Bill. "Can that be arranged?"

"I'm sure it can," said Letha, "She will be glad to grant you audience, I'll arrange for it tomorrow."

"Grant us audience—!" Doc spluttered. Then he subsided as if the same forces were at work on his mind as on Bill's.

The carriage moved across the city and back down the avenue, but turned off before they got to the field where the spaceships lay. They turned towards the blue lake they had seen before. As they approached, Letha stopped the carriage and stepped down. She motioned towards the shore.

"For Doc Hodges, for as long as he shall remain in Paradise."

Doc stared, his eyes bulging. By the shore was a small white cottage with a green roof. There were flower gardens and chicken coops.

"It's the way I've always pictured it!" Doc gasped quietly.

"It's a rather easy model to prepare," Letha said. "The dream of every old time spaceman is usually the same, with only minor changes."

"That's not for me," Bill said. "You've guessed wrong if you think you will settle me in a two-by-four chicken coop like that."

"Oh, no—we've prepared for you, Bill. There are many of your kind, too. Yours is on around the lake."

DOC WAS paying absolutely no attention to Bill anymore. He walked slowly and lovingly towards the flagstone walk that went around the house. As he came to the shaded porch overlooking the water he took out his pipe. Then he sat down and put his feet on the rail as if that was to be his spot for the next thousand years.

Bill watched him in bewilderment. The spell of this place had completely overcome Doc. He had forgotten Bill Scott existed.

"Come," said Letha to Bill.

"I think I ought to stay with Doc." He knew he shouldn't become separated from his older companion, but at the same time he knew he was helpless to prevent it.

"Let's look at your place, anyway," Letha said. She smiled knowingly as if she had absolute knowledge of what Bill was going to do for the rest of his life.

They left Doc without a word and the carriage took them along a narrow road that wound by the shore. Bill soon observed that the opposite side of the lake was far different from this. High rocky crags reared up from the water and a miniature storm seemed to be bursting with ferocity upon the cliffs. Black thunderheads reared into the sky, and vivid lightning flamed from sky to ground. Instinctively, he thrilled to the display of nature's forces. The sun had set before they left Doc, and swift darkness made a fit setting for the terror of the storm.

"Is this not for you, Bill Scott?" said Letha quietly. She seemed sobered, but not frightened by the storm into which they were coming. "Here are forces of nature, and there are forces of men, too, that you may battle. Is that not what you want? You have sought conflict and adventure on the starways. In Paradise you may do daily battle with the forces of man and nature and when you seek release from the struggle, there is the golden city—and me."

Bill looked at her dubiously. And then he knew how truly

his inner purposes and most secret thoughts had been invaded by the mysterious powers of this place. It was conflict that he had sought all his life, the thrill of conflict on the starways. It had been satisfied during the war by the fierce space battles, but in the days of peace it was hard to satiate that urge. It was this very thing that had led him to defiance of the ban on flight into Derelict Sea.

But this—this was a wholly artificial thing. These crags and this toy storm. It was only a stage setting, mere props.

As if in refutation of his opinion, the storm roared through the sky over them and burst with a painful tide of sound about them. Water flooded from the sky and washed over the gay carriage, drenching the occupants.

Gradually, the road turned away from the lakeshore and mounted the high crags. Then in the distance, nestling like a dull filling between jagged teeth, Bill spotted a building. It was like a castle in the crags, an ancient feudal castle complete with spires and minarets about which the lightning played with deadly purpose.

"Is that—?" Bill gasped.

"Isn't it lovely?" Letha said. "Here the very fires of Heaven and Hell play and challenge the soul of a man who is brave enough to meet that challenge. The House of Flame is yours."

"A man may like something other than an eternal thunderstorm…"

"Of course—and in the morning you shall see it. There will be the peace and quiet after the storm. And such a sight of the rising sun as you have never before witnessed—when it breaks through the blackness of the night and the clouds and bursts upon the golden city of Paradise. Yes, there is peace and quiet here when you want it. The House is staffed with servants who will serve your every need or will fight to the death for your amusement."

That would hardly be his type of amusement, Bill thought. He viewed the House of Flame with mingled feelings. The ancient castle was forbidding and inhuman, yet Letha was not mistaken. It challenged him—the surroundings, the storm beating about their heads, the harsh landscape.

Yet he felt that he was being played upon somehow by the hands of a skilled and merciless musician—a surgeon musician who was touching the nerves of his body at will, playing a harmony of strange emotions.

But it was only a fleeting thought that was quickly smothered.

The little unicorns halted the carriage at the top of the low rise. Bill looked questioningly at Letha, for the castle was yet high up in the jagged teeth of the mountain.

"This is as far as we can take you," she said. "You must go the remainder of the way on foot."

Unwillingly, Bill jumped down into inches of mud and water. Thunderheads rolled in the crags and swirled about the turrets of the House of Flame at the top of the hill. This was not Paradise; this was Hell.

"I'll see you again, soon," Letha said.

"The meeting with your mother tomorrow—" Bill reminded her.

"Yes. It will be arranged. Now, take these."

She handed him a pair of Flamers hidden somewhere in the carriage. Bill looked at the weapons with a start, then took the ugly cylinders from her.

"You'll need them on the way up," she said, "and afterwards."

Then she leaped back into the carriage, her thin garments clinging like wet gauze, the rain droplets sparkling in her hair. She gave word to the unicorns and the carriage vanished in the blackness of the night that descended upon them.

CHAPTER FIVE

WHILE lightning cast flares into the heavens and thunder shattered the silence, Bill stood staring through the rain. The wind rocked him and chilled him with its blast.

Paradise, he thought.

Then he considered Doc sitting by his quiet little house by his quiet little lake and his quiet little chickens—and nothing to do. And suddenly he laughed into the storm. Whoever was running this Paradise—and he didn't think for a minute that it was actually Ma Jergens—certainly had his number. Sure, this storm and this mountain crag with its mysterious House of Flame were his meat. And wild animals and unknown dangers on the trail to the castle—he hoped they were there. This was beauty. This was life—not the pale splendor of the golden city of Paradise.

He turned and began to fight his way up the muddy, rocky trail. It was literally a riverbed now with great, tumbled boulders to surmount. Where there were not rocks, there was clinging, sucking mud.

He wished he had a light. Though the sky was intermittently cut by flame, the intervals between left him in blinding darkness through which the forces of nature seemed to strike with new fury.

He left the remains of the old trail and struck out over the rocks. The going was somewhat easier there because the water ran between the crags and the sharp surfaces, which gave him a surer foothold than the slippery mud. He could only move, however, by waiting for lightning flashes, then photographing the scene on his mind and taking a step or two, and waiting for the next flash.

The rain was slackening somewhat, but the rising wind made his steps upon the rocks more precarious. It blew against him in gusts and whistled and whined among the rocks. He paused and tried to look ahead for the silhouette of the House of Flame, but it was invisible behind the overhanging rocks ahead and above him. He felt he must be nearly there, however.

The whistling of the wind was almost a shriek that tore at his senses. It rose and fell in a moaning challenge to his very right to live. It whined through the rocks and spun melodies of hate upon the water-laden air.

And then the fierce reality that his mind had refused to believe forced itself upon him. The whines and shrieks that tore the night were not of the wind—it was only a low moan that whipped gently about his ears. But this other sound—the sound of hate and challenge was the sound of a voice.

As if to punctuate this realization the skies lit suddenly with sheeting flame. The rocks stood out in livid white and their wetness was like slime. Not far away Bill saw the towers of the House of Flame glowing with purple fire.

Then he saw the moving, writhing coils and heard the voice, "I am Master of the House of Flame."

IT WAS not human or anything remotely similar to a human voice. It was a snarl of hate echoing out of some long forgotten tomb. Those great, shiny coils writhed and lashed about, and a head reared up bearing eyes of scarlet fire.

Without thought, by instinct alone, Bill brought up the twin flamers that Letha had given him. His fingers crooked around the familiar controls and blue radiance lit the night.

It touched the great serpent and the smell of burned flesh fumed upward. But the blow was far from fatal. The foot-thick body of the reptile lashed high in the air and crashed to earth. The blow landed within a yard of Bill, displacing boulders that crashed and rolled toward him. He leaped aside, throwing himself into the mud.

That voice came again, "I am Master of the House of Flame."

Bill knew it was the serpent who had spoken. There was no time to consider the evil miracle of this, however. One of the flamers was gone, lost in the mud as he fell. Holding tightly to the remaining one he crouched in the slime behind a rock, waiting for the next lightning flash to disclose the beast.

Then he saw it. The great scaled head was staring directly at him, and Bill rose and screamed back at the monstrous thing, "I am Master of the House of Flame!"

He poured the terrible radiance of the flamer into that face and almost insanely cried his defiance into the night.

The serpent reeled back from the blast and seemed almost to bury itself in the mud. The fearful hiss of its motion between the rocks and through the mud vied with the howl of the wind and the rain, Bill looked desperately ahead, straining in the darkness, blinded by the lightning flashes. Then he realized the reptile was gone. He waited a long time in the darkness for the sound of its coming, expecting the sweep of those great coils to enfold him.

But nothing came—nothing but the nerve-wracking absence of any clue to the serpent's presence.

By now the rain was reduced almost to a drizzle, and the wind had died. The turmoil of clouds in the sky permitted an occasional star to be seen.

Bill moved cautiously from his position. The talking serpent monster seemed like some long forgotten nightmare now, but he felt it still remained to challenge his mastery of the House of Flame. He would have to come back in daylight and search for clues to its presence. If he had struck a fatal blow, the body might be somewhere on the hillside below.

He surmounted the crest of the ridge immediately above him and found himself at last before the House of Flame. Only a narrow, walled courtyard surrounded the castle. Its gate hung dismally open and creaking in the light wind.

No lights appeared within, but the structure seemed intact. Great, intricately patterned windows behind heavy iron grills were unbroken. He strode up to the castle door and lifted the massive knocker. He would have sworn it weighed ten pounds.

The falling knocker sounded hollowly and boomed with the force of a cannon shot into the great building. Almost instantly, the door opened. A solemn, barrel-chested individual, nude to the waist, stood there.

"No one comes to the House of Flame," he intoned:

"The Master comes," Bill Scott said.

"The serpent, and only the serpent, is the Master."

"The serpent is dead."

Weariness was creeping over Bill. He could not recall when he had last slept, but it seemed as if a great draining of his life's energies had taken place. He had to have rest and sleep soon. But the ignorant brute in the doorway was adamant.

"The serpent warned of your coming," he said. "I shall throw you back down the valley from whence you came."

Hidden fires of anger blazed anew within Bill, and he leaped. That was his mistake. The man swung huge logs of arms and enfolded Bill in their grasp. Bill's arms were pinned to his sides, and though his fingers touched the flamer he could not bring it up to do any good.

The arms increased their pressure and the breath was driven from him. His vision grew spotty. The arms tightened.

The arms—

He fought back the blackness in his vision. There were no arms about him—only the thick, slimy coils of the serpent he had seen on the hillside.

Its bloody eyes looked into his, and evil laughter rang in his ears as the life was crushed from him.

He fell to the ground beside the door, the serpent wrapping fold after fold of itself about him.

GUIDED by instinct rather than thought, Bill touched the control of the flamer and set off the weapon at his side. His own clothes were impregnated against the effects of the radiance, but at this close range he felt the searing pain of its blast as it glanced against his leg.

The effect on the serpent was more telling, however. A momentary shudder went through the thing as a reflex of pain shot through it. The enormous folds loosened perceptibly.

Bill kept the flamer on despite the pain in his own leg where the glow touched. It was almost directly upon the sensitive spot of his old war wound.

The contest was entirely a question of which of the opponents could endure the most and which was getting the greater effect from the weapon.

The serpent was getting most of it, Bill knew. That was what kept up his own endurance, but if the material of the pants gave way, exposing his flesh to the full force of the radiance it would cost him his leg. That was worth the gamble, for now his life was at stake.

The bloody eyes of the serpent were still opposite his own, but in them Bill saw a weakening. They were not so bright, and they rolled as if in pain.

Then the voice of the serpent spoke, and there was indeed pain there, "I am the Master of the House of Flame."

In that instant the terrible coils fell away from Bill. With his remaining energy he twisted over as he spun on the floor and fired the flamer directly at the serpent vanishing through the doorway of the castle into its dark interior.

But it was gone before he could gauge the great speed of its slithering motion.

As he rose, he reflected that if this was Paradise he would gladly take its opposite. The light wind was cold on his wet body and a chill shook him. He didn't relish sleeping in the same building with the monster serpent who dogged his trail, but he had no intention either of sleeping out in the mud and rain.

He entered the hall that opened from the doorway. No one was in the spacious place, musty and deserted as a waiting tomb. Bill wondered about Letha's statement that there would be attendants to serve him. Surely the incredible serpent-man could not be one of them.

He was too utterly weary, however, to consider any of the mysteries of his situation. There was far more mystery here than he could fathom now, and his energies seemed to be more greatly depleted than his exertions warranted.

He supposed that sleeping quarters would be on the second floor, so he mounted the huge stairway at the end of the hall, a stairway that once had been a noble structure of stone and precious metals, but which was now dusty and neglected.

A long hall at the top of the stairway was lined with doors, all of them closed. And locked, too, Bill discovered after trying at least a dozen. But at last he found one that was open, a massive bedchamber. There was a huge, wide bed and ornate furnishings in the room, with thick carpeting covering the floor and heavy drapes at the windows.

Everywhere was evidence of long disuse. Though the bed was made up it was covered with dust, and as Bill drew back the covers they ripped to shreds. Then he noticed that the carpet was powdering beneath his feet.

In his weariness he concluded that Doc had got by far the best deal out of Paradise. But that was of no importance now. He fell across the bed and slept.

CHAPTER SIX

HOW LONG he was there he didn't know. But it was not yet light when he was roused by a disturbance within the room. The bed was shaking and a small voice was screaming shrilly.

"Bill Scott! Bill Scott—wake up!" He roused and blinked, then leaped to his feet in sudden alarm as recollection of his surroundings returned. He recognized no one who could have spoken, then he caught sight of a small glowing light in an elfin hand. It was the tiny driver of the carriage of Princess Letha.

"Wake up!" he screamed excitedly.

"What's the matter?" Bill demanded. "What are you doing here?"

"The Princess Letha is in danger. You failed to slay the serpent. Now they've got her. You must come at once to save her."

"Who? Where?"

"They have taken her to the Flame Pits." The elf darted away towards the door and Bill raced after him. He felt strangely refreshed even though he knew his sleep must have been short.

Somehow Bill felt he understood the implications of the elf's words. Somehow Letha was in danger and she had brought him to the House of Flame to avert that danger. She had called him her cavalier—and until now he had failed to understand the significance of the words. He was not only her subject; he was her guardian from some impending evil.

He was hard put to follow the racing elf with the miniature lantern. The creature led the way to the grand stairway and into the main hall. He fled on to the back part of the castle and halted at a wide stone stairway opening into depths below the castle. As Bill stumbled towards him in the darkness, his guide held the lantern high.

"Down there," he said. "You will find her there, and they already are preparing her for the chains."

"Lead the way," Bill ordered.

"I cannot. Only the demons who inhabit the place can go there, or those who challenge the demons for mastery of Flame House. This is the way it has always been. Go—and save the Princess Letha…"

Bill knew it was useless to argue with the little creature, its kitten-like face adamant in the glow of the lantern. He snatched the little light and—leaping into the opening—raced down the broad stairway, its steps worn and pitted as if by the feet of thousands through the centuries.

He held the light high to peer into the depths, but though he continued his wild pace downward, the end of the stairway was not yet apparent. On he raced until the opening behind him was lost in the dimness and the figure of the waiting elf a mote that he could no longer see.

Fatigue in his war-wounded leg forced him to slow his pace, and fear began to crawl upward within him as he halted on the stairway to look back. There was nothing there now. Only blackness above and below him, and this stairway like a segment hanging in outer space.

The lantern was almost useless, not illuminating more than a dozen steps, but he held it out and resumed the descent. He must find Letha if she was in this dungeon chamber.

After what seemed another thousand steps, the darkness

began to lift and a subtle crimson glow took its place. The stifling odor of smoke was in the atmosphere and Bill recalled the name the elf had used—Flame Pits.

The light was yet too deep in the infra red to permit any accurate vision of his surroundings. It was literally visible heat that assailed his senses.

Descending into the glow was like being lowered into a bath of blood, and the smell of death seemed to rise from the foul pits. The light increased rapidly now into the visible range and he glimpsed far below him a turn in the stairway.

AT LAST he reached the turn and left the steps behind, only to halt before the scene that lay open before him. He shuddered before utter fear struck all his senses at once.

The red glow over everything was like the heat of an annealing furnace. It came from pits of molten lava that bubbled and spumed liquid rock into the air. The sulphurous smell was overpowering.

But it was the sounds that came to his ears that assailed his soul, a cacaphony of hideous wailings in unison. He looked toward the sound and saw beyond the pits, a great open plain of sand where hundreds of humans were chained. They writhed grotesquely and from their throats came that unison of agonized chanting.

He swore feverishly. Like Dante's Inferno—this was Inferno!

Paradise!

Watching the wretches on the sands, he saw moving among them girls like the princesses, who were bringing water and caring for the chained ones, giving them sympathy and attention.

But Letha was nowhere visible. His eyes darted about, searching for verification of the elf's words.

At last he saw her. She was on the far side of the cavern, running wildly, dashing between the pits, slipping perilously close to the molten lava. Behind her—

It was the serpent-man of the castle.

Bill recognized him immediately, the assailant he had driven off at the door of the House of Flame.

His steps were less lithe than those of the girl. But Bill gasped as Letha paused to look back at the serpent-man, who brandished a spear. She was on the brink of one of the widest of the pits, trapped, unless—

She backed off a few steps, then ran forward and hurled herself through the air. She landed in a heap on the far side, only to begin slipping back as the sand slid into the pit. Wildly she clawed her way up as the flames seemed to touch the flimsy covering that was her only clothing.

As Letha struggled to safety, the serpent-man gave a cry of hate and frustration and seemed on the point of hurling the spear. But apparently he wanted to capture Letha unharmed.

Instead of hurling the spear, he backed off to duplicate Letha's jump. As he hurtled through the air, Bill's flamer caught him in mid-flight. Without a cry, the serpent-man crashed to the edge of the pit and rolled back into the lava. He disappeared as the pool erupted with a fearful, burbling sound.

There was sudden silence in the Flame Pits. Then the chained unfortunates began a new chant, a paen of welcome and joy. Bill, deaf to their words, rushed to where Letha lay in exhaustion on the burning sands.

"Letha! Are you all right?"

He raised her tenderly in his arms and her eyes opened slowly. She smiled up at him.

"Now I am," she said meaningfully.

"I wish you'd tell me sometime what's going on around here!" Bill began to revile the kind of paradise he had found, but the gate of his thoughts closed again and the words would not come out.

"Don't you see that Paradise is not *too* different from the world you've known?" said Letha. "There is good and there is evil here, and there is need of men like you to fight against the evil. That is why men whose whole aim in life is adventure and fighting, are brought here. Is that not Paradise for you?"

HE FOUND himself nodding in agreement. She was right. This was Paradise for him. Adventure and conflict—these were the things by which he lived. He felt a surge of exultation as he held Letha there in his arms, knowing he had saved her life. She was watching his face as though she knew his innermost thoughts.

"Of course it's Paradise, Bill Scott—and always at the end of adventure there is—Letha."

It didn't quite ring a bell, but he felt too tired now to make an issue of it. His sleep had been insufficient, he realized, and now that the urgency of his mission was gone, the weariness was creeping back over him.

Carrying Letha, reluctant to let her out of his arms, he started towards the great stairway with its endless steps leading out of the Flame Pits, "I'll get you out of here, and then free these people," he said. "Then you can tell me what it all means."

But as he turned, a voice shouted his name from a dark ledge at the side of the cavern.

"Bill! Throw her into the pool!"

Bill whirled at the sound of his name and Letha struggled in his grasp. She pointed a slender arm at the emerging figure and commanded Bill, "Kill him, Bill. *Kill him!*"

UNABLE TO comprehend the situation, Bill drew his flamer slowly and watched the advancing figure. It was a man, naked except for shorts. His body was wounded and scarred.

On his head a strange mesh sack that looked as if it were woven of copper wire hid his features. He spoke again. "Don't shoot, Bill! It's me, Greg—"

Greg?

Greg!

The name seemed to roar in his ears and long forgotten memories clamored in his mind for recognition.

Greg. There was once a face that went with that name, but there was no face now. The sack hid it.

No, he knew no one named Greg. Slowly, he lifted the gun and Letha screamed hysterically, "Kill him, Bill. Oh, kill him. Quickly!"

It seemed as if his own mind had dwindled to nothing and he was lifting the weapon automatically, almost impossibly, in the face of a great weariness overwhelming him. When he had the stranger in the sights, he pressed the control.

But the man was not to be disposed of so quickly or easily. He flattened against the sand floor of the cavern as the radiance, black in the red light of the cave, fanned harmlessly over him. Moving with great haste, he crawled and rolled and scrambled across the sands until he reached the spear dropped by the serpent-man.

Bill tried to keep the flamer trained upon him, but his hands seemed too weak to hold it and the control of his muscles could not guide the weapon.

The stranger in the mask leaped to his feet, the spear in his hands. He drew it back and hurled with all his might. The bright shaft sailed through the air. Bill saw it coming, but his senses registered only dimly and his reflexes were too sluggish to respond. The weapon caught him, piercing the flesh of his thigh with agonizing fire.

Then the fire slowly burned out in his brain and unconsciousness came.

CHAPTER SEVEN

A SHATTERED dream, a lost world. These lay before Bill's, slowly recovering senses. Paradise had proved to he a house of broken dreams—that was the first thought to pierce his wearied mind.

He opened his eyes slowly—then recoiled in sudden alarm. He was trapped, bound. He jerked fiercely, and the wound in his leg sent pain smashing through him. But he could move.

He wasn't tied, after all. Yet—

His head was in a sack, a sack of copper mesh like that of his assailant. The stranger—!

"Greg!" he cried.

"Bill! Are you all right? That spear in the leg—I'm as sorry about it as I can be. You would have killed me if I'd let you, and there was no other way to get the sack on your head."

Through the mesh, Bill saw the deep concern and pain in Greg's eyes. "Don't worry about that," he said, "I understand."

He looked around, wonderfully free of the controlling force that had guided his thoughts ever since he came to Paradise.

Paradise! He laughed bitterly...and then he remembered Letha. He whirled, eyes scanning the cavern through the mesh. "Where did she go?" he asked.

"The girl?" Greg replied. "Princess Letha? I don't know. She ran up the stairway as soon as you fell. I should have killed her. I think she is responsible for this whole mess. That's why I tried to warn you to throw her in a pool of lava, but I knew you wouldn't."

"Ridiculous!" Bill exploded.

"Yes? Then why do you suppose she was eager for you to kill me? When she returns with help, she will want your death as well, because you're now free of their control."

"I don't understand. I'll never believe there is evil in Letha."

His full senses seemed to be returning now and he saw once more the interior of the cavern. The boiling pits of lava, the moaning wretches chained to the burning sands—it was literally Hell.

And where once they had cheered his victory over the serpent-man, the bitter hate of those wretches seemed now turned upon Bill and Greg. They no longer chanted in unison, but the animal sounds from their throats were a continuous roar of hate, and the words, "Kill! Kill!" came through.

Greg said, "We've got to get out of here or those poor devils will be on us. Think you can move on that leg?"

Bill struggled up painfully. Even as he did so, the ministering girls moved among the chained ones and began releasing the bonds. A half dozen of the men were rising and lumbering forward as if in a stupor. Bill raised his flamer threateningly.

"Don't shoot any of the poor devils if you can help it," Greg said. "They're in the same fix you were."

"Then let's get out. Is there any way but up beside the stairway? I don't think I can make the climb."

"There's a long, dangerous passage that leads to the outside world from this cavern. I've made it twice, but cave-ins nearly got me both times."

"We'll risk it," Bill said. "Let's go."

HE TOOK a dozen steps on the leg wounded by the spear. Combined with the weakness imposed by his war wound, he felt it would be impossible for him to walk a hundred feet, but he took one step and then another—and kept on going.

"All right?" Greg asked. He picked up the spear with its bloody point.

"Come on."

The howls of fury increased. Crazed women screamed and tore their hair and shrieked epithets. Bill increased his labored pace. The bedlam was driving him close to madness.

But those who were free of the chains came on, leaping between the lava pools, arms swinging and hoarse shouts bursting from their throats.

Greg retreated slowly, holding the spear leveled. Sweat streamed blindingly into his eyes.

"Get back!" he warned. "I'll spear the first man that comes any nearer."

Their crazed expressions gave no sign that they had heard, and they bore onward. Greg was near the edge of one of the pools as the nearest man leaped. He raised the spear instinctively. The man hurled himself upon it, then dropped screaming into the molten rock.

The suddenness and utter futility of his death threw a hush over the madmen. Greg felt a sweeping nausea, then he whirled to Bill. "Into the opening!" he called to Bill. The latter had been forced to drop two of the wretches with the flamer.

"It can't be helped," Greg said sadly, "But we can seal the cavern so they can't follow."

The black tunnel was only a small opening in the side of the large cavern of the Flame Pits. It was narrow, not high enough to stand erect in.

When they had entered, Greg jabbed the spear into the side of the opening and the roof. After a dozen jabs a huge crack appeared. Greg leaped back, almost knocking Bill to the floor.

"Look out! It's coming down."

Falling debris plunged to the floor of the cave with an earthquaking roar and dust spumed into the narrow confines, blinding the two men, sending them into spasms of coughing.

"I hope we didn't catch any more of those poor devils in that cave-in," Greg said.

"Are we safe enough for the time being?"

"Yes—for the time being. I don't know how long. Maybe the tunnel can be flooded from the lake. They'll do it if they can. As a matter of fact, they could destroy the whole place, and probably will—if they can't get us any other way. We're a deadly menace to them now."

"Who are you talking about?"

"I say 'they' figuratively. All I know is that Princess Letha seems to be in control. Whether there is someone or something behind her, I don't know. I *do* know, however, that everyone here—except you and me—is under some kind of mental compulsion. Why, how, or what the nature of it is, I haven't the slightest idea. I accidentally stumbled upon the fact that the copper mesh shields the brain from that influence, and ever since then I've been a hunted man. You can see the results."

He indicated the wounds on his body.

BILL NODDED. "I know what you're talking about. I felt it when I first woke in our ship after landing here. It seemed that a blanket was placed about my brain so that I couldn't think the way I wanted to. Anytime a thought of doubt or criticism of this place came to mind, or a desire to leave, it was immediately smothered out. A moment later I couldn't recall the thought."

"Fortunately, I was never under its spell," Greg said: "When the *Empress* was taken over and driven into Derelict Sea, I was experimenting in the machine shop with these head sacks as a means of overcoming space sickness. I was just lucky enough to be wearing one at the time. When the mutiny occurred I felt as if someone or something were trying to scratch its way into my brain, but was being blocked by the mesh. I saw how funny everyone was acting and had enough sense to keep the sack on, since it seemed to protect me.

"The force, or whatever it is, appeared to give up after a while, as if the intelligence behind it supposed that I might take the sack off. When I didn't, however, everyone on board the ship tried to kill me. I managed to get one radio message out before going into hiding. When we landed I went exploring, but was forced to remain hidden—sometimes not too successfully; they're determined to kill me. The food I brought here with me is gone and I haven't found out anything definite yet."

"Have you made any plans?"

"Yes. My idea now is to get back to the landing field and try to get one of the small ships out of here and back to Earth. We can tell them what we know and perhaps a defense, built on the idea of these copper sacks, against this controlling force can be found. I don't know. I'm not an engineer. This can't be a matter of mass delusion; the mesh sacks wouldn't shield that. It's definitely a force outside our minds."

"But what conceivable purpose could it have?" Bill said. "All that happens is that people are brought here and given everything they want—except for these poor devils here. Or isn't that true? Does it look different to you than it did to me?"

"I don't know how it looked to you, I've not seen much but this hell hole down here. But it's the damndest thing—it seems these people are here because they *want* to be. Those chains can be removed any time they wish, but they literally sit and fry in hell voluntarily."

Bill nodded in the darkness of the tunnel. "It checks," he said slowly, "They would be the hypochondriacs—those who enjoy sickness and sympathy. And they get the attention and sympathy from the girls who, dressed like harlots, minister to them."

"I don't get that."

"I was told that this is Paradise because every person may have his deepest desires satisfied. The deepest desire of the hypochondriac is attention, sympathy. So to them this hell is Paradise."

Greg swore softly, "It's fiendish—and what is its purpose?"

"Your guess is as good as mine. It would seem that an intelligence providing this elaborate world in space would be getting something in return for it. But what? What are these men and women giving—or what is being taken from them in return for sharing this Paradise?"

"I don't know," Greg said slowly, "That's what scares me,"

THEY HAD been slowly inching their way forward in the darkness while they talked. The conversation helped keep Bill's mind off the pain surging through him. It seemed to him that they had traveled miles, but it was probably no more than a third of a mile, he supposed. At times they were forced to claw their way over fallen masses of debris, hardly daring to breathe lest they bring down new avalanches.

Finally Greg said. "We're near the opening. One more turn should end this."

There was a very faint warning of dawn lighting the opening as they rounded the corner. Nothing suspicious could be seen outside.

They came onto the beach by the lake, cautious and alert, but could see no sign of danger.

"It'll be a long way around the lake on that injured leg of yours," Greg said, "and we've got to attend to it as soon as we can to keep the infection down. I think our best bet would be to see if we can knock together a raft and float it across the lake. That would cut our distance by more than half."

"Sounds okay, but there's something else. Do you have any more of these sacks?"

"Two. Why?" Greg indicated a pair of them at his belt.

"Remember Doc Hodges?"

"Sure. What about him?"

"He's my partner in our express business and right now he's hibernating in a cottage across the lake. I wonder if we could nail him down and tie one of these sacks on his head."

"We can try."

While Bill stood guard with the flamer, Greg went out to look for material to make a raft. The spot where the tunnel opened on the beach was beneath the high crags that held the House of Flame. The storm had abated completely now and only the last ragged scraps of clouds sped across the sky as if in a hurry to be gone before the sunlight broke upon them.

Greg disappeared up the beach and Bill waited anxiously for his return. Presently he saw a slow movement in the water of the lake and brought up the flamer, eyes trying to pierce the half darkness. Then the moving thing reached the beach and Greg rose out of the water.

"Can't find a thing except this forked log," he said. "It'll at least be stable. You ride and I'll swim and push."

"You just about got your head blown off, too," Bill said. "Next time we'd better arrange a signal if we get separated."

Greg laughed. "If you can't shoot any better than you did back in the Flame Pits I won't need to worry."

"I've wondered about that," Bill said. "It seemed that this force just took me over completely and I didn't know how to manage my body well enough to shoot. It was as if it didn't trust me to do the job under compulsion but just took over the whole job and botched it."

"Which was fortunate for me. Let's go. I think we can make it this way."

Bill was reluctant to let Greg do all the work, but it seemed the only way he could ever make it back to the landing field with the wounded leg. It was swollen like a football now, and inflammation was creeping into view. He limped down to the edge of the lake and waded out into the cold water.

THE LOG WAS small and his own weight nearly submerged it when Greg shoved it out into the lake and began swimming. Bill held the spear in his lap and kept the flamer ready. Somehow the ease of their escape made him feel uneasy. He felt as if they were being watched and that the unseen enemy was only waiting until the right time to pounce upon them.

Bill estimated it was about two miles across to Doc's cottage. It seemed like an ocean, though Greg was a strong swimmer and was making good progress considering his burden. Satisfied that they were temporarily out of any obvious danger, Bill lay lengthwise—his legs along the forks of the log—and lent the strength of his arms to the swimming. Their speed increased perceptibly.

They were more than halfway across when they first noticed the darkening of the sky and the rise of the wind that sent little choppy waves biting across the surface of the water like cat's teeth.

Greg paused and glanced up, "Looks like another storm. Hope we make it—before it breaks like it did last night."

Bill looked at the storm and the rising waves, "Storm! That's it! That's how they hope to lick us. They'll try to keep us from reaching shore again."

He slipped into the water, lashing his weapons to the log with his shirt.

Greg exclaimed, "Don't Bill! That leg of yours is in a dangerous condition. This may make it impossible to save."

"Rather be without my leg than my life," Bill said, "And that's what we'll both be without if we don't make shore before they get this storm whipped up."

"You think it's possible for them to deliberately cause one?"

"I'm sure of it. Look at the way those clouds are forming

directly over the lake."

As Greg saw, the storm was centering directly over them. The wind rose with staggering fury and savage whitecaps snarled from the tops of the waves that beat upon them.

One man to each fork of the floating log, they kicked and churned the water with all the force of their bodies. Bill shut his mind against the pain in his leg.

But their progress was slow, "We'll never make it with this log," said Bill. "Let's let it go."

"We might need it to ride out the storm if it gets too bad."

"If we don't make shore the storm will never let up until we're dead. The log will do us no good."

Reluctantly Greg agreed. The log was only slowing them and if Bill could not make it to shore by swimming, he'd have to be towed.

They abandoned the raft, not even bothering to retrieve the weapons. Lashing spray filled the air and made breathing nearly impossible. Bill tried diving deep and swimming under water to save his energy from fighting the waves, but progress was slower that way. It seemed as if fierce currents were being created in the water to carry them back toward the center of the lake.

Not the least of their difficulties were the mesh sacks. Water filled the tiny openings and blinded and strangled them, but they dared not remove them.

The clouds above were black furies riding the sky. Lightning raced through the ebon masses and rain began to fall.

At last Bill knew that he would never make it. He could see that Greg was holding back to stay with him.

"Go on, Greg," he gasped. "You can make it. Never mind me."

"No— Here, let me give you a hand. Rest a little while and I'll tow. I'm to blame for that leg. I could have been more careful."

"And I would have killed you. Look, Greg, we're less than a quarter of a mile from Doc's place—the little white cottage over there. There's a good chance you'll find a boat on the place, maybe a motor boat. If there is you can use it to pick me up."

Greg looked from him to the still increasing fury of the storm and knew that Bill was right. "All right," he said. "I'll get a boat if I have to build one. I'll be back."

BILL WATCHED his long, powerful strokes with satisfaction. He would make it in spite of the storm's fury, even though he could never return in time to save his companion. But there was satisfaction in knowing that one person with knowledge of the mystery of Paradise would live to carry word to Earth.

Mere treading of water became more of a task than Bill felt equal to. It would be so easy simply to cease his motions and let the waves have him...forever.

And then he saw a sight that miraculously revived his strength. In the distance Greg was rising from the water and wading shoreward. He had made it. Now, regardless of what happened to Bill Scott, Greg would carry through the work of ending the threat of Paradise of Derelict Sea.

Suddenly Greg started running. Motivated perhaps by something he had seen, perhaps a boat in the little cove by the house. Abruptly, as he was almost out of Bill's sight around the corner of the building, he seemed to twist into midair and plunge to the ground out of Bill's line of vision.

Almost immediately, Doc Hodges ran out of the cottage toward Greg, a flamer in his hand. As near as Bill could tell he had shot Greg full in the face.

The mystery of Derelict Sea would never be revealed now—unless someone else should stumble on its secret.

It had to be made known, Bill thought grimly. He was now the only man alive who had the answers, so he must live on.

Once more he stroked out and faced the current, then realized there was no more need to go toward Doc's cottage. He could not hope to overpower Doc, nor did he have a mesh for Doc's use.

The current was actually carrying him toward shore at a point where the carriage road lay. He struggled on in that direction, following the path of least resistance as long as possible.

As if seeing its quarry on the verge of escape, the storm whipped new fury down on his head. The screaming of the wind and the roaring of the waves beat a maelstrom of sound about him. Weakness became sheer exhaustion, for he had lost a great deal of blood in the water.

Gradually the current ceased to aid him as he reached a point where it swirled back from shore. Gauging his progress by landmarks, he saw that his progress had almost stopped. He could never make it against that current. As long as he went along with it around the lake he had a faint chance of survival—until he grew too weary to remain afloat. But bucking that current was hopeless.

He turned for a last despairing look at the hateful sky. The faces of devils were in the black clouds, and their forked tongues of lightning lashed down at him from evil mouths filled with thunderous laughter.

He wished that he might have seen Letha once more. Princess Letha. He smiled dreamily. She was so lovely as a princess—like a child playing at a game of make-believe. Greg was wrong about her, Bill was sure.

He sank lower into the water and a wave washed a great weight of water over him. He struggled to the surface. One or two more like that—

CHAPTER EIGHT

HE IMAGINED someone was calling his name. *Delirious,* he told himself.

But it came again. "Bill! Bill—hang on!"

There was the putt putt of a motor and a bull-like voice roared over the waves: "Swim, damn you—!"

He struggled frantically and turned toward the sounds. A small motor boat sped toward him, rocking perilously on the lashing waves. Standing in it were Greg—and Doc!

Bill knew he was dreaming now, or this was some other bitter illusion of Paradise. But there was no dream about the sudden hands that reached down and dragged him aboard.

"Put him on the cushions," Greg said, "and head for shore. I'll take the flamers."

Doc nodded and took over the helm. Bill noted with flagging vision that both of them had the mesh sacks on their heads. And then he quit thinking about it—and everything else...

Rain lashed down like solid hail, but the entire fury of the storm could not prevail against the little boat as it neared the shore.

They drove it hard onto the sands and Doc lifted Bill to his shoulders and raced up the beach, Greg following with guarding flamers in each hand. Their goal now was the landing space three quarters of a mile away. As they left the lake area and raced through the gardens and lanes, the sun came out and the storm was gone.

Scores of people were in the gardens enjoying the morning sun. They looked at the running figures plowing recklessly through the flowers and across the gardens in the shortest possible path towards the landing field, but no one made comment or offered opposition.

Doc was puffing hard under his burden. "I—think—we're going to make—it."

"Put me down," Bill said. "I can manage."

"Quit your yammering," Doc said.

They neared the field. In a few minutes they were at the port of the *Mote* and Doc set Bill on his feet. "Just like we left her," said Doc, "Let's get inside where we can piece this thing together and figure out something to do about it."

Nothing had been disturbed, but another ship had landed close to the *Mote* so that its nose was across the prow of the tiny freighter. Doc went out to move the other ship while Greg sterilized and dressed Bill's wound with supplies from the ship's medical kit.

"What I want to know is what happened at the cottage," Bill said, "I thought Doc got you."

"Simple, I heard him coming and fell as he fired. I figure he was being controlled in the same incompetent a manner as you had been, and he probably wouldn't know it if he missed me. So I played possum until he came up where I could jump him. Once I had the sack on his head he was okay."

"You saved my life, Greg..."

"Yes, but I'm going to lose it for you if we don't get that leg taken care of. Let's get out the sulpha-light cabinet."

"But I can't sit in there for a half hour!" Bill protested. "We've got to get moving."

"We don't even know what we're going to do yet, so calm down. Doc's coming and we can talk things over while you're in the cabinet."

RELUCTANTLY, Bill submitted and assisted Greg in setting up the chamber. "What about this sack?" he said. "The light can't get at my head. The copper will shield it completely."

"That's right. I hadn't thought of that. But, look—you can go inside and then take the sack off. You will be entirely enclosed in metal and that should be a better protection than the sack against—well, whatever we're trying to protect ourselves against."

Bill was dubious. He hated to give up the protection of the sack while in this weird Paradise. He remembered only too well the struggle that had gone on in his brain before Greg had forced the sack over his head.

He stepped into the cabinet and turned on the lamps. The faint blue glow filled the tiny chamber with eerie radiance. Bill tried to switch on the normal light and gave a short growl of irritation.

"What's the matter?" Greg said.

"Light's burned out in here."

Only the blue glow, a thousand times as powerful in its germ destroying properties as the ancient sulpha drugs from which it took its name, illuminated him.

"Well, never mind. You can see by the light of the sulpha lamps. It won't be for long, anyway. Hey—Doc!"

Greg's sudden exclamation of despair rang out through the ship.

"What's the matter?" Bill shouted.

But there was only the sound of Greg's running feet as he leaped out of the *Mote*. Bill snatched up the sack again and fitted it over his head, then threw open the door of the chamber, grasping a towel for a loincloth. He raced to the port and saw Doc running in the distance, with Greg close behind and loping mightily to overtake him.

Doc's mesh sack was torn and flapping about his neck. With its protection gone, he was once more under the influence of the powers of Paradise.

It appeared hopeless that Greg would catch Doc before he was into the city. Doc was fleet in spite of his age, and Greg had been too late in taking up the chase.

Bill stepped to the controls of the *Mote*. He started the motors and they thundered out a welcome roar. He started the ship rolling gently forward, passed Greg and went on after Doc. It would be difficult to dislodge him should he get well into the garden area.

He passed Doc, seeing the madness once again in his eyes, then swung the *Mote* sharply in front of the old man and headed him off. Doc took up a new course, but it was one that enabled Greg to cut corners and shorten the distance between them.

Bill repeated the maneuver. Doc swerved, looking about like a hunted animal. Once more Bill repeated the trick, then Greg nailed Doc with a flying tackle.

He leaped on his back and threw him to the ground. Doc clawed and cursed wildly. But Greg's youth held greater strength and kept him pinned to the soil.

Bill hurried out with a length of rope from a locker. Swiftly they tied up the frantic man and carried him back to the ship.

"What happened?" Bill asked, "How did his sack get torn?"

"I don't know. All I know is that he suddenly started running over the field like the devil was after him. Then I saw his torn sack and knew why. Unless we can fix it, we'll have to keep him tied up until we get out of this."

DOC STRUGGLED with renewed frenzy as they lifted him into the port, but his body slid forward on the floor and came to rest near the open sulpha-light cabinet.

Greg helped Bill up the step and said, "Now get into that cabinet and stay there before I have to saw your leg off."

Bill wasn't listening, though. He was staring at the eyes of Doc. Doc was lying there sobbing—not with grief, but with joy, and the wild frenzy had gone out of his eyes.

"Thanks, fellows. You'll never know what it was like to have that feeling coming over me again. They were slow and quiet about it the first time, but this time I could feel them jumping into my brain and taking over. It was like they pushed me aside completely and sat down at the controls. It was awful—"

Then he was staring, as was Bill, "The mesh sack! You didn't fix it!" he cried. "I accidentally snagged it in coming out of the ship next door."

Doc's head was still free of the sack, but it lay directly in front of the opening in the sulpha-light cabinet.

"The sulpha-light!" Greg exclaimed. "That's what's doing it."

Bill stepped to the cabinet for an instant and slammed the door. Doc suddenly writhed like a madman. Bill reopened the door.

"Don't do that again!" Doc cried.

"This is it," Greg said, "We can take the sulpha-lights from the other ships around here. The *Empress of Titania* has a big battery of them in two rooms used for precautionary sulpha-light baths."

"We can mount those batteries of lights on the outside of the *Mote*," Bill said.

"The outside?"

"Yes. Then we'll move slowly along the streets of the city and get a large group in the light and lead them back to their own ships. We can't rob the ships of all the lights because they'll be needed for the crews while they pilot their way out of here. But with just a few more hand attacks and the big ones on the front of the *Mote*, we should eventually be able to get them all out."

"That just might do the trick."

Doc said, "How about untying me?"

There was a moment's argument about Bill going back into the cabinet, but Greg finally persuaded him and he let Doc take his mesh sack. While Bill treated his leg, he repaired Doc's torn sack. Meanwhile, Greg and Doc made a quick job of robbing the *Empress* of her supply of sulpha-lights, hooking them in the nose of the *Mote* so that a wide beam of light could be thrown ahead. Then they rigged small hand lights for use in overpowering single individuals.

They were through by the time Bill's session in the cabinet was over. "Let's head for the palace," he said. "We can probably find Letha somewhere there—probably Ma, too. As far as we know, they are the only ones free to come and go from Paradise as they please. I wish I knew what *that* was all about."

"It's obvious," Greg said. "It means they know the secret of this place."

"It *could* mean that," Bill admitted. "I hope it doesn't."

He tried to imagine again where Ma and Letha could fit in with the devilish business at hand, but it just didn't make any sense. Ma Jergens certainly didn't have the abilities needed to create or control the mental force that had been unleashed in Paradise. And likewise it seemed impossible that Letha, while an intelligent and skilled engineer, could be the mastermind behind the great power that had overwhelmed so many. Bill remembered the sweet girlishness of Letha as the Princess of Paradise. Was that only a role of fantastic innocence to hide a deeper purpose of equally fantastic evilness? Bill closed his mind and forced his thoughts away from that direction.

He would know soon enough, for the *Mote* was rolling swiftly down the avenue, far faster than the fairy carriage had traveled. But the *Mote* seemed to be attracting little attention from the people in the gardens. It would seem that space ships taxiing down the avenues of Paradise were a common sight.

THEY DIDN'T want to betray their possession of the sulpha-lights as a weapon, however, until they had made an assault on the palace. They rolled up the luxurious drive and halted before the glass and crystal magnificence of the palace of the Princesses of Paradise.

"Swing the ship so the beams cover the main entrance," said Bill, "Then I'm going in there without the sack on my head. I'll take it in my pocket for emergency use. I want you to come behind me, Greg, and cover me. Doc, you guard the ships with both the lights and the flamers. You can expect an attack. Let's go."

They switched on the main beams and stepped out into them. Bill removed his mesh sack and pocketed it. He felt no different.

He strode up the broad path between the quiet, shining pools and on into the great hall where the eternal feasting was going on.

THE SCENE was almost the same as when he had first witnessed it. The orchestra was playing soft music and the water players flashed through the indoor pool to the entertainment of the diners.

As he stood there, watching, at the far end of the table one of the princesses rose between her subject guests. Bill's heart bounded with relief as he recognized Letha.

She seemed equally glad to see him. She smiled and he thought her lips formed his name, but she was too far away to be sure. After a moment's hesitation she turned from the table to come toward him. Then she stopped and her expression slowly changed. From sweet innocence it went through all the shades of dark passion to a murderous fury.

"Kill him!" she screamed. A slender white arm pointed towards him in a gesture of murderous fury. "Kill him!"

FOR A MOMENT Bill stood there, stunned by the impact of her viciousness. He had not even contemplated anything as deadly as this reception.

The music stopped; the diners rose to meet him. On their faces slowly grew the same maniacal fury that filled Letha.

"Come on," he challenged suddenly.

The nearest came on—and walked in to the beam pouring through the entrance from the ship outside.

The sudden transformation of their faces was a pitiful thing to see. They stood transfixed while the hate and bitterness washed away, then their faces softened as they realized what had happened to them. Many broke into tears. The ones behind them didn't know what was happening apparently and they continued rising from the table and surging forward into the beam.

As if realizing what was happening, Letha stood out of reach of the beam. Suddenly she cried out, "Stay back! It's a trap!"

Those who had already walked into the beam reached back and began dragging their companions into its radiance. It was the beginning of a fantastic chain that moved slowly towards the *Mote*.

"Keep them in line!" Bill called to Greg. "I'm going after Letha."

With his flamer and the small sulfa-light in hand, Bill put the mesh sack on his head and approached Letha. He felt his appearance must be like that of some demon character out of mythology. He turned on the small light, but its potency at this distance was too weak.

Slowly and carefully, Letha picked up a long knife from the table and drew her arm back. Then, swift as light, she hurled the blade with all her might. Bill dropped to the floor. The knife hissed over him and clattered to the marble floor.

The girl turned and ran. Bill sped after her as swiftly as his leg would allow. As he ran he heard a tinkle within the hand light that he carried. He glanced at its face. When he dropped to the floor to dodge the knife he had broken the lamp. His only weapon was the flamer—and it was a weapon to kill.

He debated going back for another lamp, but if he left now he might never find Letha in the mazes of this palace. He kept on, racing after her up the narrow stairway beside the musicians' stage.

It turned out to be a long, winding spiral that led to the floor higher than the domed hall on the left wing of the palace.

The stairs seemed to wind endlessly. Bill ran recklessly, then halted with a lurch that sprawled him on the steps. He had almost run into the deadly glow of a flamer spewing death high on the stairway.

It was in Letha's hands as she waited for him at the head of the stairs. Carefully, Bill estimated the width of the beam and its intensity. He examined the fastenings in the impregnated space garb he had donned in the *Mote*. If it were tight, he could endure a leap through the beam, provided it didn't touch his head.

He decided to gamble it. If he were quick enough he could be at the top of the stairs before Letha could change her aim. Backing down a few steps, he threw all the force of his body into a lunge that carried him upward, leaping as high as possible to keep his head out of range of the lethal beam.

His momentum carried him on to the head of the stairs. Letha was there, crouching on the floor, her eyes burning with hate as he leaped through the beam. He flung his weight against her. It knocked her aside and the flamer spun to the floor, but she scrambled away as nimbly as a cat and raced headlong down the hall.

BILL CURSED his clumsiness. It seemed she literally had slipped between his fingers. One of his hands had closed about her wrist and another about an ankle, but she had broken his grip as easily as if his fingers were threads.

He rose and spotted the doorway into which she had vanished. Both flamers were in his hands now, but they were useless. He could not fire upon her. It would be sure death because ordinary, unprotected clothing was no barrier, and her thin garb was as penetrable as air.

The door burst open at the touch of his shoulder and he plunged into a bedroom.

Luxurious hangings covered the walls of the spacious room. Thick, soft carpeting covered the floor and his feet sank into its depths.

A huge bed that would dwarf anyone as small as Letha stood against the far wall—and Letha was standing beside it.

Twin flamers were in her hands, pointed towards Bill, "The closer you get the quicker you die!" she said grimly.

"Princess Letha," he said softly. "I'm Bill Scott, cavalier of the Princess. You love me, Letha, just as I love you. That's why you can't kill me."

He hoped his words might bring back remembrance of the way she had felt, the things her eyes had revealed when he held her for a moment in the Flame Pits before Greg came upon them. It was in vain. The bitter hate did not leave her face.

"You came to steal my kingdom. For that you must die. The Princess Letha demands loyalty."

"Love includes loyalty and overshadows all else."

"I know nothing of love. A Princess belongs to her subjects."

Slowly Bill's steps carried him forward. His flamers were trained upon her as were hers upon him. But he knew that he would never fire even if it cost his own life. What he had said was true. He did love her. The part of her that was sweet and innocent—that was wholly alien to the mad harpy threatening him now.

He saw it in her eyes then. She was going to fire. In an instant those twin beams would be spraying over his unprotected skull, burning the life out of him, and Letha, the beautiful, the incredibly evil Princess of Paradise would rule unchallenged.

Then his eyes leaped upward and he jerked the flamers in his hands. Simultaneously he flung himself to the floor. Letha had anticipated this move. The weapons in her hands came down, bathing his torso in flame.

Abruptly the flame was cut off. The tremendous weight of the hangings on the wall behind Letha dropped upon her as the fastenings were burned through by Bill's weapons. The massive folds fell, smothering her under their folds.

Bill gathered her struggling form tight within the folds, binding her arms, and then his hands reached through the thick fabric to wrest the flamers from her.

Both of her weapons were still blazing, burning holes in the drapery. Bill feared she would injure herself in the frenzy of her struggles. He picked up a heavy ornamental statue from the table by the bed and brought it down on her skull.

Letha's struggles ceased instantly.

He gently uncovered her from the drapes. Even in unconsciousness her face held the look of fury and evil that had possessed her, and Bill's heart grew heavy within him. Was this the real Letha? Was the innocent Princess only an assumed character to deceive him?

He lifted her tenderly, passed through the doorway and on down the stairs. He entered the banquet hall, now emptied.

GREG SAW him coming. "Bill! I thought you'd got lost. We've got to get these people to their ships. We've rounded up more than we can keep in the beam now, and more are coming in!"

Then he saw the figure in Bill's arms. "She isn't——?"

"No, I had to hit her on the head. She'll be all right—I hope. It's just that I'm afraid she's—oh, hell, I don't know. Put her under the light and bring her to, will you? I'm afraid to watch."

"You think she's really behind this?"

"I don't know—I don't know what to think any more. Take her."

"You should be there. Perhaps your fears won't be realized. I saw you in nearly the same condition once, don't forget. You tried to kill me."

"All right," Bill said wearily. He carried her into the *Mote* and placed her on one of the narrow bunks. While Greg applied restoratives, Bill rigged a sulpha-light over her.

Almost instantly, the drawn tension in Letha's face began to disappear. The lines of hate that had been frozen about her eyes vanished. She became once again Princess Letha, the girl that Bill had fallen in love with.

He whispered her name softly, "Letha."

Her eyes opened. She looked about in a moment's wild fright, then she recognized him—and seemed to remember. Her arms came up and her hands clutched at him frantically, "Oh, Bill—Bill! Don't leave me. Don't let them get me again. It's horrible, Bill. Don't leave me!"

"I'm not leaving—ever," he said softly, "Rest now and you can tell me about it later."

"No! There's mother. You've got to get her."

"We will. Don't worry."

"Right," Greg said. "Look who's coming."

Bill turned. Through the open port he could see Doc Hodges marching towards the ship. In front of him was an immense form with short massive legs that were like wobbling tops moving towards the *Mote*. It was Ma Jergens, dressed mannishly in a slack suit of some coarse weave.

She whirled on Doc as she came to the opening. "Give me a hand at least, you—"

Doc hoisted her with a shove that sent her sprawling. She got up and turned on him. "Why, you—!"

"Keep moving. It's about time you learned who's in charge around here. I don't want any more of your lip."

Ma's eyes lit up as she saw her daughter on the bunk, "Letha—you're safe. You got away from them, too." Then suddenly her eyes misted and she turned to Doc. Her arms went around him and she was sobbing on his shoulder. "Take me home," was all she said.

Doc's arms slowly came up in an attempt to enfold her, "Sure, Ma….sure…I'll take you home."

CHAPTER NINE

GREG PASSED a hand over his brow. "Well, I'll be damned. Now I've seen everything!"

Letha rose to a sitting position and took Bill's hand. She smiled happily. "This is the best day of my life! How I've hoped they would get together someday."

"I don't understand," Bill said.

"Didn't Doc ever tell you?"

Bill shook his head. "Tell me what?" There was a long pause before Letha responded…

"He's my father."

"What?" Bill gasped with surprise. "You've got to be kidding…"

"It's true," Letha continued, a wistful smile creeping across her face. "He left us long ago because he and Ma kept butting heads. Ma insisted on running things her own way and wanted a life of adventure, while Doc thought he was the one that ought to be having the adventures." Letha paused and threw a knowing smile in the older couple's direction. "But I think they've both had enough adventure for a lifetime now. They'll probably be willing to settle for a little chicken farm."

Doc disentangled himself. "Not on your life, daughter! I thought I'd go nuts that one day I spent sitting on a porch by the lake doing nothing. The best part of the whole deal was when Greg came along and tricked me into thinking I'd shot him. I knew then that it was action that I wanted and that's what I'm going to get. I'm going to get to the bottom of this phony Paradise of yours if it takes the rest of my life."

"It won't take that long," Ma said, "It's all my fault—you've got to do for the rest of these people what you did for us."

"How is it your fault?" Bill demanded. "What is the power that controls the people here?"

Ma stared in dejection out over the golden city. "They came and took me up on a hill and showed me all the gold and lands in the universe and said it could all be mine if I would follow them. I did—and this horrible place is the result."

"Who are you talking about? Who made such a bargain with you?"

"*They*. What shall I call them? Parasites? I guess that's what they are. For eons they have lived in space, semi-dormant in its cold vacuum. At times some of them have found haven on the planets, but they have always been driven off.

"These life forms," Ma continued, "can exist in space, but require a human being or similar high life form in order to make themselves active—physically active. They are just like the parasite worms in animals on Earth. They are about as big as a golf ball, small white things like garden slugs. When they find a human being or equally high form of life, they fasten themselves to the back of the skull. They flatten out and dig into the nerve roots of the brain. There they live, gaining sustenance from their host and eventually causing death.

"In order to have a society of their own they construct artificial societies for humans to live in. They constructed this Paradise so that every person could have their most fundamental desires fulfilled without effort, so that those who came would live here in satisfaction and happiness and have no desire of ever departing. Few ever desire to leave and when such thoughts arise, the parasites quickly crush them through their powers of mind control."

"I'll say they do!" said Bill grimly, "But why can't we see them?"

"I'm not sure. It may be actual invisibility or it may be due to their powers of mind control. One thing I *have* learned is that when they lose mind control over their host, they detach themselves and become semi-dormant again. Anyway, I saw one of them just once—it showed itself to me. But they normally don't allow us to see them on the back of the neck. Again, this is probably accomplished through some invisibility power, perhaps even forced illusion.

"Their mind control is exerted in varying degrees. Total control is practiced only in emergencies, and generally is not necessary. They get better nourishment from us when we are more or less 'free.' Once attached, they are able to completely read the mental makeup and complete personal history of their host. But the host rarely knows of this intrusion. There are exceptions, though. Take me, for instance. I'm one of the few they had direct communications with. The parasites learned everything they needed to know about me by delving into my brain. They knew I was a money grabbing, evil old woman who would sell her soul to the devil for a gold coin."

"Mother—!" Letha cried.

"It's true. You and Doc know it is, and so does everyone else that ever had anything to do with me. But that doesn't mean I'm always going to be that way. I've seen the suffering I've caused and I mean to make up for it."

THERE were tears of genuine grief in Ma Jergens' eyes and Bill believed her. "But what did the parasites require of you?" he asked.

"Well, they had to have a few people to start with. They made themselves known to me on one of my space runs. Several of them had attached themselves to the side of my ship. They talked to me telepathically. What a surprise that was at first! We communicated...negotiated. They gave me their promise. I brought a few people out here and that enabled more of the parasites to be activated. This in turn enabled them to begin the construction of this Paradise out here, which is real—yet only an illusion. The people I first brought were older. I thought I was doing them a favor. I knew they'd be receiving the kind of life most folks only dream about."

"What is it? How is it built?" asked Greg.

"Out of the essence of our minds and the forces and energies that lay wasting away in space. I can't begin to understand it myself. All of it is basically unreal, yet it's real enough to somehow be able to sustain life in the emptiness of space. It's all nothing but the gathering of intangible forces that are held together by the mental power of the parasites. If they should cease to hold it together, it would collapse like a bubble.

"Anyway, I had to bring a few people here so the parasites could get started. It snowballed after that. They eventually gained enough power to capture spaceships themselves. At that point my real value was ended, but I made a few more trips, the last one just recently. They gave me the job of bossing the place—as long as I didn't interfere with their plans. That was my deal. That was *my* Paradise. That—and all the wealth I wanted. But, like Doc, I've had enough. From now on, I'm taking orders instead of giving them."

"So the parasites gave you permission to keep going back after more recruits?" Bill asked.

"Yes they did. They provided me with the means of getting money-promising people to come here. A new life…a life in Utopia with fair maidens or handsome man-servants to wait on them. There were plenty of customers, too. Actually, the parasites could give the appearance of halting age, but that was an illusion, too. Death is eventually brought on by them in about half the remaining life span of the host. I knew about this. I knew about it but never told any of my customers." Ma wiped a tear from her eye. "I think that's why the parasites came so far out into space. They had actually set up the same Paradise on Earth and other planets, but were forced out when it was discovered that a premature death was the final 'benefit' of a life in Paradise."

"I should think there would be some evidence if they had ever been on Earth," Bill said.

"Don't you think there is? Where do all the legends of Paradise and Heaven and Hell come from? This scenery is so old it's about worn out. They've used exactly the same thing since the beginning. The Flame Pit you saw was the Inferno Dante saw and wrote about. How he got out, I don't know, but others have apparently slipped from the their clutches in times past.

"Take the legend of Orpheus who went down to the pits of Hell to rescue his wife, Euridyce. You just reenacted that old story yourself, with modifications. The modification being that Letha wasn't your wife, but I hope she will be. That wench of mine needs to be tamed before she grows into a wicked old harpy like her mother."

"No danger," Doc said.

"That business in the Flame Pits puzzles me," Bill said. "What were you doing down there, Letha. Didn't you have the power to escape?"

"Of course. It was all part of the great illusion. But it was part of my Paradise, too." She blushed suddenly. "You see, the parasites read in my mind a deep desire to be a beautiful princess and be rescued from a horrible fate by my Prince Charming. In your mind they read a desire to be a Prince Charming and rescue fair maidens. So—they killed two birds with one stone."

Bill nodded sheepishly. "Those devils certainly know how to get a man's number. But how about when I tried to kill Bill, and you tried to kill me?"

"The parasites took full control then," Ma said. "But they were clumsy and, as you saw, they failed to control your body very well."

"Well that sums it up," Bill said. "The problem now is to get all these people back to their own ships and find a way to kill off the parasites."

Ma Jergens shook her head. "I think there is nothing that will kill them. Once the last human is freed from their clutches, however, they will all go back to a semi-dormant limbo. Perhaps in the interim, before they find another means of gaining power, we can find some way to block their resurgence. The ancients apparently succeeded in doing it because the parasites abandoned numerous paradises on Earth. Maybe the secret lies in the ancient conflict between white and black magic, I don't know."

THEY GAVE up the discussion then. Bill directed the ship to be turned about so that the group outside could be led back to their own vessel while staying in range of the sulpha-lights that had power to drive away the parasites, just as the copper mesh sacks had power to drive them from their place at the base of a person's skull.

The crew of the *Mote* disposed of the rescued group and returned to round up another. A third and fourth time this was repeated. Then the crews of other ships were able to help by rigging sulpha-lights on their own vessels.

Gradually, the city's inhabitants thinned. Then, as the *Mote* was driving down the avenue in a search for stragglers, there was a sudden, high, deafening note that rang out and knifed through the city. Ahead of the *Mote* the great, golden towers of the city shattered with a sound like the collapse of a great bell.

"Paradise is collapsing!" Ma Jergens cried. "We've driven enough of the parasites back to dormancy so that the remaining ones are too few to be able to support the city. In a moment there will be nothing here."

"There are still hundreds of people we haven't found," Bill said. "We've got to step it up! Come on."

He drove the *Mote* into the dying city. Those who came within range of the beam he shouted out instructions to flee to the safety of the ship.

It appeared the parasites were admitting defeat now and deliberately releasing the humans and destroying the city to cause their deaths.

"The Princesses—can't we make one more trip to the palace?" begged Letha.

"We can try," Bill said. They were not far from the magnificent structure. Already they could see huge cracks in its mighty walls. The *Mote* drove up the path to the main entrance and crashed its way into the main hall. Even as they did so, the crew saw a score of the lovely princesses huddled together in terror at the far end.

"This way!" Letha stepped to the port and called to them.

The girls raced toward the ship. The great dome of the hall gave an ominous crack of thunder. Pieces of the shattered structure crashed, narrowly missing the girls.

Bill jumped out, followed by Greg. Doc kept the hand lamp trained on the girls, but it seemed unnecessary. The parasites had abandoned them.

They reached the *Mote* and Bill and Greg shoved them roughly into the port. Inside, Letha and Ma helped them more gently, until the last of them was in.

"Are there others?" Letha asked. One of the sobbing girls nodded. "About a dozen of them went to the roof garden when the city began to fall."

Bill surveyed the scene of destruction. "We might have a chance—"

Greg shoved him off balance into the *Mote* and closed the opening. "It's hell to have to leave any of them," he said. "But we've done all that's humanly possible. Can't you tell the air is vanishing out there?"

Saddened, Bill realized this was the truth. Even as he protested, a great chunk of the dome crashed upon the *Mote*, and the distant wall at the end of the banquet hall slowly caved in with a crash of thunder.

Suddenly below them great black caverns appeared, opening to infinity in the floor of the palace hall. It was interstellar blackness into which they were gazing.

"It's gone," said Ma Jergens.

The occupants rushed to the ports for a look at the death of the golden city. The great black patches were eating through it like a monstrous disease. Then the golden light outside vanished. In the sudden starlight a few drifting fragments of Paradise floated for an instant then melted like colored ice in a glass of liquid.

The *Mote* floated in the emptiness of space.

About them were the scores of other ships that had found their way into Derelict Sea. Lights came on in those hulls, and as if by common consent, they turned for Earth, led by the mighty *Empress of Titania.*

In every ship was sorrow for those who had died in the holocaust, but there was gladness, too, for their own deliverance from the menace of the parasites. And there was a fearful task burdening those who knew the secret of Derelict Sea. Somehow, space would have to be permanently freed of the menace of the parasites.

Clad now in more decorous garments, Letha sat beside Bill in the pilot's seat. It was crowded, but he didn't mind a bit.

"I'm glad I found out what your innermost desires are," she said.

"Why?"

"I'll take care that you have excitement and adventure for the rest of your life. Marriage with me won't be tame, I promise."

"What do I have to do? Rescue my fairy princess from some predicament once a week?"

"Twice."

"There's only one thing I want you to keep in mind," he said.

"What's that?"

He glanced back where Ma Jergens was shaking a finger in Doc's face. Doc was sputtering so fast his plates were slipping.

"Don't forget who's boss," Bill said.

THE END

THE CURSE OF ETERNAL YOUTH...

Something had happened in their past lives that had turned them into immortals, leaving them completely invulnerable to the ravages of age and time.

Was it chance...or had it been planned that way?

Come and discover the astonishing answer in this nail-biting story, penned by one of the best and most prolific authors of science fiction's golden age, Rog Phillips.

CAST OF CHARACTERS

HELEN HANOVER
She didn't know she wasn't the only immortal, nor did she know of the amazing adventure she was about to undertake.

AGNES
She hated her mother for looking younger than herself and outliving her father—and for that she vowed revenge…

HARVEY TRENT
He introduced Helen to the world of the Immortals…and soon fell in love with her.

CHARLIE HAINES
This seedy detective was hired on by Agnes. All she wanted him to do was make Helen's life miserable.

GEORGE GRANVILLE
He helped newly discovered Immortals understand their way of life, and helped them discover the cause of their immortality.

PHIL COOGER
He was the top crime boss in all Chicago—and he wanted the secret of immortality for himself.

ALEX POTOCKI
Head researcher on the hunt for Immortality for all. How noble were his intentions?

THE
INVOLUNTARY
IMMORTALS

By
ROG PHILLIPS

ARMCHAIR FICTION & MUSIC
PO Box 4369, Medford, Oregon 97504

CHAPTER ONE

"WHEN I first met him he was alive and young. Now on his deathbed he's sixty and looks a hundred, while I am still the same, the twenty I was so long, long ago."

Helen Ranston smiled sadly to herself while she sat waiting for her husband to die. Without turning her head she was aware of the presence of her daughter, Agnes, at her shoulder—hating, hating the mother who had borne her, who remained a vibrant, youthful twenty in every respect except years, while she was growing old at forty.

"You're still young because in some secret vampirish way you suck the life of those around you—mother." That thought, in Agnes' hate-filled voice, spoke in Helen's mind as it had spoken in actuality so many times these past few years. So much vitriol in that one word, "mother." A word that should mean so much, and with all the meaning curdled into hate and jealousy. The jealousy of a woman growing old for a woman who never seemed to grow old at all.

Carl opened his faded eyes and looked up at Helen, loving her even now while the pains of death tore at his heart and mind. He was speaking. She bent close to hear his almost inaudible words.

"I've been a very lucky man," he was saying, his lips trembling with effort. "The bloom of youth has never left you, Helen. I pray God it never will."

"It's your love for me that has kept it so," she soothed him. "And something strange that makes me afraid."

"I know," he said. "I've often wondered about it myself. But I say now that you should not fear it whatever it may be. Nothing but good can ever come of it. Some day you will know what it is."

His strong face contorted in a spasm of pain. He dropped back on the pillow. Helen touched his forehead gently, with the palm of her hand, and knew he was gone. She bit her lip and turned away, feeling something depart from her heart that left it vacant.

"He's gone!" Agnes' shuddering whisper held disbelief. "He's GONE!" Conviction turned her voice into a shrill scream.

"It was *you*, mother," Agnes accused. "YOU killed him by drawing his life into your own body just as you are doing to mine and all those around you!"

The words, full of hatred, pelted Helen's ears like hail and echoed painfully in her now lonely heart, mocking its emptiness. There was nothing she could say to comfort her deluded daughter. Nothing she could do.

She didn't KNOW. Agnes could be right. Maybe she did drain the life from those around her in some unknown way to preserve her youth.

"Maybe I did!" It was her own despairing thoughts accusing her now. "Maybe I do!"

SHE MOVED into the outer room. As she stepped through the door, waiting relatives drew away from her. A wide-eyed youth hid behind his mother's skirt, peeking at her with an owlish stare. He was Carl's nephew, and he believed her to be a witch or vampire because she was still twenty after forty years as Carl's wife.

"If they knew how old you REALLY are!" Her thoughts were torturing her again. She had lied when she married Carl. How could she tell him she was over a hundred even then?

She had told him once and he hadn't believed her, had laughed as if it were an absurd joke. She had finally joined in with his laughter and silently resolved to keep her secret. On the marriage certificate she had placed her age as twenty. Each year she had added another year to that twenty while her body, her face, her eyes, and her spirit had remained the same.

"If I only knew why!" She had said this to herself so often. She didn't know why. She had never been any different than her own sisters and brothers, except that they had grown up, grown old and died long ago, while she had just grown up and stopped changing.

She didn't know why, and she would have to move on now, on into a lonely world and change her name again and say she was twenty—and look lovingly into the admiring eyes of some male whose great grandfather was in diapers when she was already mature.

It would all have to be done over again. There was nothing else in life for her except to love and marry and raise children who would all too soon look older and feel older than she.

What had the poet said? "If you can see your life work broken, and stoop and build it up again with worn out tools..."

She smiled tremulously at the nephew. Timidly he smiled back, then buried his tear-stained face in his mother's skirt. Wordlessly she continued across the room past the silent statues of mourning people and climbed the stairs that led to the second floor of what had been her home for so long.

The carpeted hall muffled her footsteps. The hoarse crying of her nephew downstairs followed her to her room. The bitter, angry sobbing of her daughter Agnes seeped through the hall faintly, depressingly, like a damp dark fog.

She began taking down pictures and removing them from their frames. Hours later she had accumulated a trunkful of trinkets, pictures, and keepsakes. She couldn't take them with her but she could store them. They were all that was left of forty wonderful years. Someday in the far distant future she would get the trunk out of storage and open it, and live over again those happy years with Carl.

But now—she dropped the lid with a bang. In her mind that action symbolized the closing of the door to the past. She could not close the door to the future, as Carl had done. Nor could she guess how long or how short that future might extend. Another century? A thousand years? A million? Would she be another legendary figure moving through time, unable to die?

She slipped the trunk key in the lock and turned it. The click of the lock brought the first sign of emotion to her smooth, beautiful face. She almost gave way to the grief she had been holding in. Almost.

In the back of the closet she unearthed three traveling cases. Opening them so they lay flat on the bed, she took her dresses from the closet and folded them in carefully. Her toilet articles followed.

BELOW, the sounds indicated that most of the relatives were departing. Sharp sounds of footsteps on the front porch, the grinding of starting motors, the snorting of motors as they caught, and the smooth purr they made as they settled down to idling speed.

Agnes would be coming up soon. Helen didn't want that. She couldn't stand much more of the accusing look in her daughter's eyes, the mad thoughts and hatred in her heart.

She was afraid of Agnes. She knew that. She had sensed thoughts in Agnes' baleful eyes. Thoughts of murder and cruelty. She didn't want to be alone with her in the same house.

Her fingers were nervous as she locked the last suitcase and slipped the keys in her handbag. She wished fervently that the halls weren't carpeted so that she could hear approaching footsteps. Agnes might this very minute be standing outside her door, waiting. Waiting for her to come out, or perhaps waiting for the courage to open the door and face her mother with the gun Carl always kept in his desk.

There was the window. She could climb through the window and step to the branch of the tree just outside. She could be down and away without running any risk.

The thought of slipping away from her own home in such a fashion made her smile to herself. She couldn't. She did what she had known she would do all the time, squared her pretty shoulders, held her head up bravely, and opened the door.

The hallway was empty.

She looked down its full length, at its wide ribbon of rich carpet, its high walls so close together, to the space where the stairway led downwards. It was empty. As empty as her life.

Agnes wasn't there! The relief was overwhelming. She had SO wanted to be left alone, to suffer her grief in hallowed silence, have this last night alone with Carl. Carl!

Like a giant Sequoia falling majestically in a quiet forest; like the surface of a deep stream rippling from currents below; she bowed her head and wept. The soft sounds of her weeping drifted in the empty hall like the sad-sweet cry of the mourning dove at daybreak when all other sounds are still.

Her smoothly rounded shoulders shook under the loose white blouse she wore. Her soft hands, with their long, skilled fingers hid her face. Alone she mourned for her husband and let the salt tears of her grief dampen her cheeks and her hands.

Gradually peace came. She dried her eyes with a wisp of lace handkerchief and stole softly down the hall down the stairs, across the darkened living room to Carl's room.

For a long time she stood beside Carl's bed and looked down at him. Then she left, closing the door softly behind her.

As the door closed, one of the heavy drapes at the window stirred. A hidden hand pulled it aside. Agnes stepped out. Her face was etched with lines of suffering. Her fingers clenched and unclenched slowly.

She approached the bedside of her dead father. There she dropped to her knees and buried her head in her arms.

"Dad," she sobbed. "Dad. I solemnly swear, by all I hold sacred, I will live to make a year of her life miserable for every year of your life and mine she has stolen. I'll follow her wherever she goes. In the end I will see her dead. I'll make her pay. I swear it, dad."

Her voice dropped to a hoarse whisper

"I swear it."

CHAPTER TWO

MAY I help you?" The masculine voice was strangely attractive.

Helen had not looked at her seat companion yet. She paused in the act of lifting her light overnight bag into the rack above the seats to look down at him.

He was rising hastily. His general appearance told her he was young—no more than twenty-five. His smile caused her thoughts to whisper, "Nice."

She was angry at that thought, coming so soon after Carl's death.

"No thank you," she replied curtly.

Immediately she felt ashamed. To cover up, she resumed her efforts to lift the bag into the rack. Just as she was on the point of confessing failure and asking the young man's assistance she felt his hand take the handle from her with firm insistence and saw the bag raised the extra half inch necessary to slide it on the rack.

A contrite smile on her face, she turned to thank him. He had already resumed his seat, his face turned toward the window. She sat down feeling ashamed.

Her eyes analyzed the profile of this man who had managed to put her in her place so effectively. His nose was a trifle large. His chin and jaw had a smooth line, which, coupled with something about his cheekbone, gave the impression of westernness. His loosely combed hair accentuated this with its soft brown color.

Only the tailoring of the blue pinstripe suit he wore indicated that he was a city product. He carried it too naturally, and it fitted him too well.

His head began to turn toward her.

She hastily buried her eyes in her vanity case, pretending to search for something. She could feel his gaze as he looked at her.

She hadn't felt so flustered in a century. The near truth of that brought back the realization that she was old. Too old to be flustered by the glance of a young man.

She closed her purse and looked up. His head was turned toward the window again.

His hands lay loosely in his lap. They were well formed with long straight fingers. Even in repose they seemed alive and intelligent—those of a musician or some other craft that required trained hands. They were like hers except that they were wider and the fingers larger around.

A small gold pin on his lapel caught her eye. It had a design that was unfamiliar to her.

Outside, the station started to recede as the train moved.

The pin had an emblem on it. It was a small leaf of some sort, shaped like a Maple leaf. A drawn out figure eight laying on its side passed through the center of the leaf. It looked something like the infinity sign in algebra with the left hand half partly hidden by the leaf.

A sudden suspicion made her look up. The young man's eyes were looking at her. She smiled guiltily.

"I must apologize for being curt with you," she said.

"Quite all right," he answered. "Your home town?" He moved his head backward in the direction from which they had come.

"Yes." Carl rose before her eyes. Carl as he had been when they were first married. This young man was like him in some ways. The same age, but a little more mature. A little more—grown up.

"I'm Harvey Trent," he was saying. She jerked her thoughts back to the present.

"Glad to know you, Harvey Trent," she said. "My name is Helen, Helen Hanover."

SHE WONDERED why she had chosen that name. Hanover was her maiden name, the name she had been born under. She had never even told Carl that name, yet she was using it now.

She glanced down at the lapel pin again. Harvey raised his hand and rubbed the pin with his fingers.

"A sort of a lodge pin," he explained. A very exclusive lodge."

"In what way?" Helen asked. "You don't look like the sort of person to join exclusive organizations."

"I'm not, really," Harvey answered. "And its members aren't snooty or anything like that. As a matter of fact it's the most democratic group in the world. Only, you almost have to be born into it."

"Oh," Helen remarked. "Are there any women in it?"

"A few, I suppose," Harvey said in a tone of dismissing the subject. "Are you going to Chicago for a visit?"

"No," Helen replied, smiling to herself at the adroit way he had changed the subject. "To live there. Perhaps just to visit and then go on to some other place. My father just died and there isn't anything to hold me in Dubuque any more."

"I see," Harvey said. "Sorry to hear it."

"That pin," Helen said. "What does the symbol mean? It must mean something."

"Lodge secret," Harvey winked slyly. "We have to solemnly swear never to tell."

Helen found herself laughing gayly, feeling as young as she looked. She wanted to know more about this young man named

Harvey Trent. He was enough older than she looked for her to recapture the feeling of being young.

"Do you live in Chicago, Mr. Trent?" she asked.

"In a way you might say I do," was the reply. "With me all roads lead to Chicago; so you might call it home, though I average less than two months a year there. The rest of the time I'm following my work."

"What is your work?" Helen asked.

"Something you've never heard of, I'll bet," Harvey answered. "I just travel around, eating in cafes, living in hotels, going to churches, libraries, parks, and wherever my nose leads me. I'm national pulse feeler for a concern that thinks it's worth money to have an expert constantly feeling the national pulse."

"Sort of a Gallup poll on the hoof," Helen joked.

"Right." Harvey grinned. "They have an advantage over the mail order type. There you just find out the opinions of a cross section of the public. With the galloping poll we can be Paul Reveres when the occasion warrants it, and sort of shape public opinion in certain directions."

"Then you aren't the only one doing this?" Helen asked.

"Oh no," Harvey said. "Right now there are thirty of us."

"Do they—" Helen hesitated. "Do they all wear that button you are wearing?"

"Why do you keep coming back to that?" Harvey asked, looking at her queerly. "Are you just curious?"

"Not exactly curious," Helen answered slowly. "But let's skip it. What I'm thinking would be too utterly fantastic to be true. If you'll excuse me—?"

She rose and walked down the aisle to the powder lounge. She had to escape and have time to think. That algebra symbol meant infinity—or eternity, if you applied it to time; and the leaf symbolized life. The two together, the sign of eternity piercing the symbol of life—could there be others like her?

But of course not. And if she were foolish as to give away her secret, this young man, Harvey Trent, would either think it a big joke as Carl had done, or he would think her insane.

HELEN looked at herself in the mirror. Reasoned with herself. Her powder puff shook in her hand. And for the first time in her life she felt apart from other people.

She was suffering the hopes of a sparrow in a land of robins who for a moment thinks she sees one of her own kind. It had never occurred to her that there might be others like her.

She looked into the eyes of her reflection in the mirror and was amazed that in her century and a half of knowing she was different she had never once thought of others, somewhere, being the same.

That possibility, thrust at her so forcibly as an almost actuality, had the force of a physical blow. The practical side of her nature told her that it was most likely not true that there were others, leaving her with a deeper loneliness than she had ever felt before.

It was torturing. She had gone out into the world in search of someone to be happy with and enjoy for a time this life of hers that stretched into an endless future. That was all she had hoped for, all she had dreamed of finding.

Now, for the first time in her life, it had dawned on her that there might be others like her, and as she appraised herself in the mirror she knew that never again could she go through what she had gone through with Carl. Seeing another man she loved grow old, and die, watching another child she bore grow up, and then grow older than its mother—it would be too much to take over again.

She could remember when her daughter Agnes had begun to change toward her. At first Agnes had been proud when someone remarked, "Why Agnes...you are as grownup as your mother already."

Agnes had been twenty then. The two of them had looked more like sisters than mother and daughter.

Carl, always the lover, had taken them together when his business permitted an evening of relaxation. They had worn the same clothes. They had laughed at the confusion of young men when Agnes introduced her mother. It had been heavenly—for a year or two.

Inevitably someone had remarked that Agnes was beginning to look a little older than her mother. Occasionally Helen had discovered Agnes looking at her strangely analytically.

She had sensed the bewilderment in Agnes' mind. She had watched it change to something else that was an ever-changing mixture of jealousy, fear, suspicion, and finally hate.

She had watched the progress of the mental cancer, unable to do anything about it. The carefree parties had ended. Agnes had taken to avoiding her mother as much as possible.

Eventually she had married. Helen never saw Agnes' husband. Carl had met him. Helen understood and sympathized with Agnes on that. She understood all too clearly that Agnes, a beautiful woman of twenty-eight when she married, could not introduce her husband to a vibrant young lady who seemed no more than twenty and say, "This is my mother."

It might have been all right after that, but Agnes kept torturing herself by coming home. Each time she came she looked at her mother closely, looking for some sign of age, some line or wrinkle that hadn't been there before.

Then her husband had left her. For a year Agnes stayed away from home. Carl, gentle loving Carl who understood so little about women, insisted she come back home to live.

That had been seven years before; and during those seven years Agnes had remained at home, tortured by irrational fears of her ever youthful mother, fears that were all the more horrible because they MIGHT be true.

HELEN snapped back to the present and found that she had been sitting for some time, her powder puff resting against her cheek, her eyes far away. Putting it back in the compact with a tired sigh she took one more look to make sure she was presentable and returned to her seat in the coach.

Harvey looked up from a magazine with a bright smile as she dropped beside him.

"Another hour," he said softly.

"Yes, another hour," Helen echoed, her voice sounding queer to her. She looked past him, out the window at the moving scenery.

He looked at the bitter lines on her lips, opened his mouth as if to speak, then shrugged his shoulders and returned to his magazine.

A few minutes later, without looking up, he spoke.

"Don't you think it might help if you told me about it?" he asked softly.

He didn't look up. Helen appreciated that. If he had he would have seen the motions expressed on her face. The hopelessness, loneliness, bitterness, sadness.

"There's nothing I could tell," she said, her voice muffled. "Nothing. Nothing that would make any sense to you."

"This is certainly a strange story I'm reading," Harvey's voice changed to polite conversation. "Quite unusual. It makes for emotional drama, in a way, but is so impossible. It's the story of a man who never grows old. He always stays about twenty-five while his beautiful wife grows older and older until people are mistaking him for her son."

Helen glanced at him sharply. His eyes were still turned away, resting on the pages of the magazine. She followed them. The title of the story was at the top of the page. It was THE STOCTON MURDERS.

Now she was trembling again, so violently that she had to grip her hands together until the knuckles were white and bloodless.

Harvey was looking at her hands. His face was expressionless.

"Perhaps I could tell YOU the meaning of the emblem on your button," Helen said breathlessly. She bit her lip. There was no turning back now. She would make a fool of herself, a complete fool. When the train stopped at the depot in Chicago she would run and run, until she had escaped from this—escaped into the comfortable world she was looking for. But first she had to make a fool of herself. She had to, or spend eternity wondering.

Harvey didn't answer. His eyes watched her tense hands.

For some reason Helen couldn't speak. She wanted to cry. She wanted to laugh hysterically. She wanted to get up and run down the aisle, through car after car.

Her hands were fumbling with the clasp of her purse.

Harvey laid a strong, warm hand over hers, squeezed them together until they hurt. For the first time he looked directly into her eyes.

She let him look. She could feel him probe, feel the pity and gentleness of his soul. And a growing wonder possessed her.

These were not the eyes of a twenty-five year old child. They were the eyes of a man. They were the eyes of one who had seen—the things SHE had seen.

"You know?" she asked faintly. The trembling was coming again while she waited for him to speak.

"You never thought there would be others." Harvey's eyes widened in surprise. "You thought you were all alone!"

"Did I?" She laughed giddily at her silly question. The last bit of uncertainty left her mind. Harvey was as old as she herself. There was a club of people all as old as she was. There were dozens of them. Hundreds. Thousands.

She pulled her hands from under his.

"I'm all right now, Harvey," she said, settling back. "I feel like I had just been born."

Gloom and noise exploded outside the window accompanied by the feeling of braking. The train was coming into the station.

"Have your bags ready please." It was the conductor's practical voice as he passed through the car. Harvey got the bags down from the rack.

"Have your bags ready please. Have your bags ready please." Station sounds, steam engines steaming in lazy motionlessness on other tracks. Baggage trucks being pulled noisily in long strings by small trucks. People scurrying on the concrete outside the window, and people moving down the aisle inside.

And Harvey moving beside her, protectively, as they edged their way along between the seats. Chicago!

CHAPTER THREE

"SHE PICKED up with some guy on the train."

The speaker, a man in his early forties, held the phone against his ear with a hunched shoulder while he carefully rolled a cigarette.

"That's what I said," he went on in a sad voice. "They got off together. I tailed them to the Palmer House where she rented a room. No, he didn't register. He lives someplace, I guess.

"Yeah. I managed to see what name she signed. It's Helen Hanover. The guy's name is Harvey Trent. Nice looking fellow."

The speaker grinned, creasing the side of his face with two deep wrinkles. It gave him a hawkish appearance. His eyes, even in good-natured repose, were cold, unemotional.

"Yeah, sure, Agnes," be said after listening a full minute. "Yeah. I'll do that. You want to stay in the background. I understand. How much did you say you were getting from your father's estate?"

He blinked his eyes and whistled softly.

"O.K., Agnes," he said. "I'm your faithful servant. I'd suggest you go to the bank and borrow a few thousand until the estate is settled though. It may be a couple months, and I only run on cash, not promises.

"O.K., I'll mail you a report every day. Unless something comes up I'll meet you at the station next week. Meanwhile see about getting more money...I don't want to run short. O.K. G'by."

He pulled the phone booth door open and stepped out. There was a look of satisfaction on his thin face. His price of twenty-five a day and expenses was based on getting only short time detective jobs. This one seemed likely to run into some dough. The expenses—Charlie Hains was already cooking up angles to pad the account. He hoped Helen wouldn't go any place expensive. Then he could report that she had and add maybe twenty or thirty dollars a day onto his bill.

He stopped at the cigar counter in the lobby and indulged in a fifty-cent cigar, casting his eyes possessively over the expanse of quiet richness around him.

"I don't know what the score is," he said to himself. "But as long as it adds up to at least twenty-five bucks a day and life in places like this..." He beamed at the girl behind the counter and walked over to the desk to register.

He turned in time to see Harvey and Helen crossing the lobby from the elevator to the street doors.

"Have a boy take my bags to my room," he said hastily. He reached the sidewalk in time to see Harvey slam the door of the taxi. Another taxi was waiting.

He climbed in, flashed his badge, and ordered the driver to

follow the taxi ahead.

"Sorry, bub," the driver said. "That's an out of town badge. No can do."

Charlie sighed and let go of a ten-dollar bill. The driver hesitated, then took it.

His sigh changed to an audible groan when the taxi ahead stopped after going three blocks and let Harvey and Helen out at the marquee of a restaurant.

"Thanks, sucker," the cabby said dryly as Charlie stepped out.

"You're taking part of my heart with you, dear," Charlie replied.

"No doubt," the driver said, easing away into the traffic.

"THERE are over seven hundred of us so far," Harvey was saying as Charlie seated himself at the table a few feet away. "There must be many others, like you, who never suspected, thought they were alone. We hope someday to have them all together. Then maybe we can find the cause. There MUST be something that happened to all of us to produce it. It's too much to believe that through some quirk of evolution a few hundred or thousand people suddenly became immortal. We are all old enough now to rule out simple longevity."

"But how can you find it just by getting us all together?" Helen asked.

"It might not take all of us to do it," Harvey explained. "What we have to do is keep on comparing our lives from the very start. In that way we'll find the common denominators, the experiences that we have in common. Among them will lie the single incident that began it all."

"What could it possibly be?" Helen asked.

"Who knows?" Harvey said. "Were we all in the same section of the country at some time? That's been ruled out already. What is the time factor? We've narrowed that down considerably. Whatever happened, it took place in eighteen forty-eight. We feel sure of that. There's one man who was quite old at the time. He began growing younger. There was a forty-five year old woman with cancer. In that year it unaccountably began to shrivel up. The youngest of us was a seven year old boy in eighteen forty-eight, and the oldest was that man, seventy-three years of age."

"I was born in eighteen thirty-one," Helen said quietly. It felt strange to say it. A few hours ago she had almost forgotten it entirely. It was in the past she had kept hidden.

"I'm nine years older than you are, thank God," Harvey remarked.

The waiter came with their food and they started talking about other things.

Charlie Hains, on the other side of the post, had heard every word. There was a dazed look in his eyes.

"They *must* be crazy," he tried to assure himself. "They *must* be!" The sick realization remained that they were not. But if they weren't crazy, maybe it was some sort of a joke he didn't see the point to. It COULDN'T be that—that... His mind refused to formulate the statement.

The waiter was standing over him patiently. He ordered half-heartedly, feeling that he wouldn't be able to eat. How could he eat, he asked himself, when there were two people so close to him that should be dead?

His meal came and he found he was hungry after all. He kept his ears cocked on the casual conversation around the post. After a few bites his mind began to churn with thoughts. When he took the job of following Helen on the train he had thought it was another divorce buildup. When Harvey entered the picture he felt sure of it.

Even when Agnes had talked as if his job might last for as long as a year he had still thought it a routine job of gathering evidence of infidelity. But now...

He gave a short laugh. All his life he had wanted to latch onto something big. His ideas of big had never gone farther than blackmail. He had become a detective with that in mind.

With Agnes providing the money, and something like the secret of immortality within reach, it was a different story.

SUDDENLY he began to tremble. He was afraid. For the first time in his life he was afraid. It wasn't a fear of physical danger. It was a fear born of the conviction that there were people alive who were going to live forever, and that if he failed he might die. He was over forty and seventy would come so quickly. People being born would just have time to become men and women before he tottered into his grave.

A feeling of resentment grew in him against Helen and Harvey, talking so casually about visiting the zoo and the museum tomorrow, so smug and secure in their deathlessness. He could understand Agnes' feelings toward Helen now. Agnes didn't know about Harvey; but she evidently knew all about Helen.

"I have a daughter," Helen's voice caused Charlie to prick up his ears again. "Her name is Agnes. She's forty now and has grown to hate me with a consuming hatred."

A satisfied gleam came into Charlie's close set eyes. So that was the setup. He relaxed and pulled out another fifty cent cigar. He had nothing to worry about. With what he could tell Agnes now he could be sure of a continual and inexhaustible source of money. Maybe he might even go for Agnes when he saw her again. He had only seen her the once, the day before, when she had called and then come to his office and given him the picture of Helen, two hundred dollars, and instructions to catch the noon train and follow Helen. Then she had been merely a slightly excited client with some cash in her hand—too rich for him to get careless with. He frowned and wished he had taken a better look at her.

Helen and Harvey were getting up. Charlie made no move to follow. From their conversation he knew that Helen was going straight to the hotel, and that Harvey would meet her in the morning at ten thirty.

He watched them weave through the tables toward the front and blew some cigar smoke after them in farewell.

"G'by, grandma," he said softly. "Me, I've got to get some boys together. Good thing I have references from the right places."

HARVEY settled in the cab beside Helen with a disarming smile on his lips.

"I hope you don't mind, Helen," he said. "But I ordered the cab to drive us to a friend of mine. I was going to tell you about it inside but decided not to. There was a man sitting behind the post at your back in the restaurant. I'd noticed him in the lobby at the hotel. Of course, it might just have been coincidence, and he couldn't possibly have heard enough of our conversation to know what we were talking about unless he had unusually keen hearing. Just the same I felt alarmed about him."

"That's quite all right, Harvey." Helen said.

He reached over and took her hand.

"I guess I was alarmed over nothing though," he went on. "When we reached the front I looked back and the man was still sitting at his table, smoking a cigar as if he didn't intend to leave for half an hour yet."

"Even if he knew our secret what good would it do him to follow us?" Helen asked.

"I don't know," Harvey shrugged. "If he's after the secret of immortality, so are we. And if he knows our secret it won't do him any good to tell it to the world. The world would just laugh at him."

The taxi slid smoothly to a stop in front of a brownstone mansion.

Harvey pressed a bell under a metal plate with the name, George Granville, engraved on it. There was a two-minute wait before the loud buzzing indicated the inner door had unlocked.

Harvey held the door open for Helen to pass. The gloomy stairs led upward steeply, twisting until they ended at the third floor.

George Granville was standing in the open doorway waiting for them. His eyebrows lifted in curiosity as he saw Helen.

"Helen Hanover, may I present George Granville," Harvey said. "George, she is a new recruit."

George was a full head taller than Harvey, blond, the classical picture of a Viking. He shook hands solemnly with Helen.

"Welcome into our circle," he said. "I hope you plan on being with us a long time."

He backed into the room and stood to one side so that Helen and Harvey could enter, and closed the door carefully while they began taking off their coats.

"So you're one of the immortals," he said, "I must say you carry your age well. Even so, I would say you are about—a hundred-and-forty-one?"

"Three," Helen smiled.

"You don't look it," George said solemnly. "May I ask how you found Harvey?"

"I didn't," Helen said with a twinkle in her eye. "He was my seat companion on the train. I saw his lapel pin and put the symbol for life and the symbol for infinity together and got four."

"That's why we adopted that lapel emblem," George said. "To the common man it might be interpreted that way also, but to him it would have no special significance. To you it did."

"Yes," Helen said. "Until I saw it I had never dreamed there might be others who were as old as I."

"That's part of Harvey's job," George explained. "He is a pulse feeler, but along with that he, and several others, just circulate so that people can see that emblem and wonder about it, and if they are into their second century of life they will get the right meaning."

"George is a sort of personnel chief," Harvey explained. "His job is to interview the newly found persons and find out how they have been living and help them adjust themselves to the rest of us. You'd be surprised how many of us hadn't done much in the way of planning our future before we came here."

"I'm afraid I haven't done that either," Helen said ruefully. "When you met me, Harvey, I was on my way to creating a new identity and a new life, with marriage, children, and the same ending as the other time, with me still young while those around me grew old."

"How many times have you done that?" George asked.

HELEN didn't reply for a long time. Finally she said faintly, "Three times."

"We won't require you to go any further into that," George said hastily. "The joys, the love, and the heartbreaks of the past are your own personal property and are classed by us as your apprenticeship in life. We facetiously call them the initiation into the ancient and honorable order of ancients and honorables. You're now the ancient and honorable Helen Hanover, if that is your original maiden name. Is it?"

"Yes," Helen said, turning her eyes to Harvey. "For some reason I gave you my real name right at the start. I didn't mean to, but it came out."

"Yes," George said dryly. "I can see that you two are that way about each other. It reminds me of a joke. Oh, well, I'll skip the joke. How about a little refreshment? Would you like some tea and sandwiches?"

"The tea would be nice," Helen replied. "But we just had an enormous dinner."

She liked the jovial giant. His living room was filled with luxurious antiques. It was a room such as one she had seen in her childhood, and which was called modern then. She wondered briefly what the rest of the apartment contained. George seemed to sense her thoughts.

"One thing you must learn now," he said, preparing the pot of tea on an all purpose bar of rich walnut, "is to be self-sufficient and continually pursuing intellectual subjects. One way to get into it is to see how the rest of us do it. Later I'll show you through my apartment and you can see my library, laboratory, and workshop. Unfortunately I am more interested in culture than science. Some of us, however, spend most of our time being scientific. It's really necessary for them to be that way. They have a definite job, to find out what made us immortal so that we may give everyone the same blessing."

"Oh, but I'm afraid that to some people it might be a curse, mightn't it?" Helen asked.

George and Harvey looked knowingly at each other.

"Definitely not," Harvey took up the conversation. "We've proven that after a hundred years or so of life even the most hardened criminals get tired of it and settle down. Especially do they get over their bad traits when their physical health remains perfect year after year."

George poured the steaming tea.

"Of course," he said quietly, sitting down, "we can't know how many of the immortals found life increasingly intolerable and committed suicide. We can't know how many become insane and were placed in asylums where doctors eventually gave them mercy death to end the expense of keeping a patient who seemed destined to live forever. Those were automatically eliminated, and all of us we can find are those who found life at least tolerable. Among those we have one man who started out in life as a murderer. By the year eighteen-fifty he had killed ten people and amassed quite a fortune in business. But, as he confesses, from eighteen forty-eight on, his heart wasn't exactly in it. He finally gave it up. Sanity took two years to make a complete conquest of his mind. There is a woman who started out as a halfwit. In eighteen forty-eight she was twenty-seven years old and had the mind of a child. Her parents died and she was placed in an institution. She escaped and lived as a wanton for almost fifty years. During that half century she traveled, finally learned to read and write, and is today a professional author who has gained fame under three different names successively. It took her a century to arrive at intelligence and sanity and capability.

"So you see, Helen, eternal life is the great leveler. It leads us all to the same goal."

"But you couldn't just make everyone on Earth immortal if the way is found," Helen objected. "What of the dictators and those whose driving urge is power? Immortality would enable them to achieve their ambitions."

"For a time, perhaps," George said. "Eventually they would grow tired of power, and of people stupidly debasing themselves to the idol of one man's self esteem. Their sense of values would change just as it did with the murderer for money."

"You may be right," Helen said slowly. "You see, I haven't thought of these things before. It's too big for me to grasp it all on the first day I learn about it."

"You mean that yesterday—?" George exclaimed.

"Yesterday," Helen said. "I attended the funeral of my husband, Carl, who died of old age. I was surrounded by his relatives who believe me to be some sort of a witch. My daughter, Agnes, who hates me with all the hate one woman can have for another, stood in back of me, wishing with all her heart that she could push me into the grave and fill it over with dirt."

"But that was yesterday," Harvey said softly, reaching over and putting his arm around her affectionately.

"Ahem. Suppose we look at the rest of my domicile," George said hastily.

CHAPTER FOUR

CHARLIE HAINS hopped lightly to the safety island from the steps of the surface car and walked rapidly to the sidewalk. Half way down the block was a modest neon sign announcing the "CLUB Rouell." A block further on, and on the other side of the street, was a similar sign announcing the "LOUNGE Rouell."

Charlie did not think this strange. He liked the rouell drinks himself. In 1964, after the end of World War III, alcoholic drinks had become practically nonexistent. Grain shortages all over the world were the cause of that.

Providentially, or perhaps not so providentially, depending on the point of view, some obscure chemist had discovered a drug which, in very minute quantities, had all the effects of alcohol. Carbonated water, artificial flavorings, and less than a pinch of this drug produced a beer indistinguishable from the finest of natural brews.

This drug had a name that only a trained chemist could pronounce in full. In some way, the name "rouell" had been tagged to it and stuck in the public mind. The ersatz beer made a fortune overnight for the chemist. Within a year he had concocted other drinks with a rouell base instead of an alcoholic base. They sold for prices comparing with those of the alcohol drinks, and with alcohol unobtainable, had no competition.

It wasn't until the harvest of 1966, which passed all records, and grains were again available for producing alcoholic beverages, that it was discovered that a person who had been drinking rouell for several months developed an intolerance for alcohol, so that even one glass of beer with alcohol in it made that person violently ill.

There was a mild flurry of excitement and worry over this. A move was even under way to prohibit the sale of rouell when tests proved that this intolerance for alcohol of the rouell addict wore off completely if both alcohol and rouell were left strictly alone for six weeks. It had already been proven that rouell had no harmful effect on the body. Scientific assurance that anyone who had the will power to leave drinking alone for six weeks could switch back to alcohol, pulled the fangs on the anti-rouell movement.

It also took the profit out of the alcoholic beverage industry.

Rouell champagne, superior to the real thing, could be turned out at the rate of thousands of gallons a day for a few cents a gallon. Ersatz whiskeys identical in every way with the real stuff except in specific gravity could actually be sold for twenty-five cents a fifth in a price war.

The distillers, not suspecting the allergy to alcohol built up by rouell, had not prepared for competition by forcing through special taxes such as those that had existed once on imitation butters. The government, not dreaming that the grain shortage would last so long, had neglected to put any tax on the rouell products.

And who wanted to layoff liquor for six weeks anyway? Rouell stayed and elaborate distilleries went bankrupt.

Charlie entered the CLUB Rouell casually and went up to the bar. The place was dimly lit.

He ordered a beer from the bartender and took his time surveying the place while he drank it. A piano player was lazily making some cultured noise. Charlie listened and couldn't detect an identifiable tune to the music.

Mildly intoxicated people danced on the small square reserved for that. Others sat sophisticatedly and watched the television screen, which at the moment was showing a newsreel in Technicolor.

DARK CURTAINS hung over a wide entryway in the rear. Over this space a sign on the wall announced rest rooms. Charlie finished his beer and moved toward the curtains. Other people were doing the same. Still others were parting the curtains and coming out.

On the other side of the curtains was a wide hall. At the end of this hall double doors were just closing. Charlie pushed one of them open and walked through. He was in a large room with dice tables and card tables occupying most of the floor space.

He ignored these and continued walking until he came to a door that had "OFFICE" painted in gold letters on it. He rapped politely on the door and waited.

A man Charlie had seen fighting in the ring a few years before tapped him lightly on the shoulder and told him if he had any complaints to tell him about it.

"No complaints," Charlie smiled. "I want to see Phil Cooger. Blacky Arbuster told me to see him."

"Blacky?" the bouncer said with respect. "You a friend of his? It's O.K. then." He gave two short raps, waited, then rapped once more. A loud click sounded. The door opened.

Phil Cooger was a man who had risen to power in Chicago almost overnight, ten years before. He was short, five feet six and three-quarters inches. His shoulders were broad and powerful. His once jet-black hair was streaked with gray. His face, aside from a trace of age under the eyes, was youthful appearing and strong.

He was encased in a citadel of rumor built up by word of mouth and by repeated newspaper crusades against him. He held the rouell industry in Chicago in his clenched fist. Those who tried to muscle in either dropped out of sight or settled down to become owners of clubs or bars or lounges with Mr. Cooger getting most of the profits.

The newspapers claimed that no one committed a crime within a hundred-mile radius of Chicago without first receiving permission from Phil Cooger. They also claimed that the police couldn't make an arrest without an O.K. from Phil Cooger.

The CLUB Rouell was his headquarters. His office was the most unpretentious one Charlie Hains had ever seen. In contrast to the luxury of the gambling room and the air of richness of the dance floor and barroom, there was a bare wooden floor, a cheap desk, several wooden chairs, and five phones.

The phones were silent when Charlie entered. They were no different than other phones except that each had a different number and each number was unlisted.

Phil himself sat at his desk, his hand still curved over the edge where the push button that opened the door was located.

"This guy says that Blacky Arbuster sent him to see you, Mr. Cooger," the bouncer said respectfully.

Phil Cooger glanced swiftly over Charlie's features, nodded imperceptibly, and sat back in his chair.

Charlie showed his badge and credentials. Phil Cooger took them and examined them with seeming carefulness.

"Seem all right," he finally said. "What can I do for you?"

"I'm on a job," Charlie explained. He shrugged his shoulders and added. "Nothing much. Just to follow a woman and a man and try to get evidence against them for a divorce. I need a couple of good boys to spell me off on it—the kind that do what they're told and don't get too nosey."

"What's the names of this man and women?" Phil asked.

"I suppose you'd find out anyway from your boys, so there's no harm in telling you," Charlie said. "The woman is going by the name of Helen Hanover. The man she's running around with is named Harvey Trent."

"Tell me more," Phil said.

"Hanover is a fake name. I can't tell you her real name. Lives in Dubuque. Caught the train this noon. Picked up with this guy Trent or he was on the train by pre-arrangement, I don't know which. They went to the Palmer House where she registered. After that they went to a nightspot. I figured they wouldn't do much this evening, and decided to get a couple of boys to help me on this."

"I guess I can help you out," Phil Cooger said carefully. "What's your address here in town? I'll have the boys over there in a couple of hours."

"Fine!" Charlie said, relieved. "I'm at the Palmer House too. Don't remember the room number. Just had time to register before I had to follow them to the night spot."

"In case they aren't satisfactory or you want more help," Phil said, rising, "Call BEN 5550 and register it on the recording. I'll get it. Want to do a little gambling while you're here?"

"Not tonight, Phil," Charlie said expansively.

"Mr. Cooger," Phil Cooger said frigidly. "And don't ever forget it." His eyes were ice as they lashed at Charlie.

"Sure, Mr. Cooger," he stammered. "Sure. Sorry I forgot my place."

"O. K.," Phil Cooger said, shutting off the ice and smiling warmly.

Charlie left his office feeling that he had been far from being in command of the situation.

AS THE DOOR closed on Charlie Hains, Phil Cooger walked

across the room and bent over, holding a signet ring on his finger an eighth of an inch from a small dirt spot on the wall close to the base board. Behind him a section of the floor started to rise. Rising with it was a compact group of filing cabinets and card indices.

Quickly he took out a file card and wrote the name, Helen Hanover, on it. After that he placed it in its alphabetical place in one of the card files.

Next he took a letter folio and typed her name on the filing tab. This he placed with others in a filing cabinet drawer. His fingers paused over the name Harvey Trent in the file, lifting out the folio. From it he extracted a picture of Harvey and inspected it briefly.

"So you've found another recruit, Mr. Trent," he said softly. Replacing the picture he closed the drawer and pressed a button. The entire section dropped back into the floor, leaving no sign of its existence.

Back at his desk he lifted one of the phones and spoke briefly. A few moments later he pressed the button that unlocked the door and two young men walked in.

In looks and dress these two young men seemed to belong on some college campus. The habitual innocent cheerfulness of their features was never ruffled by circumstances. A few months previous, a high government man had felt hot lead pouring into his body while he watched those unchanging, innocent faces above the spitting guns. He had died convinced that his eyes deceived him.

"I have a little job for you boys," Phil Cooger said. "A Dubuque detective, friend of Blacky Arbuster, is in Chicago on a divorce case. He needs a little assistance so he can knock off and sleep and play once in awhile. You'll find him at the Palmer House. His name's Charlie Hains. Ask for him at the desk. And whatever he pays you is O.K., get it?"

The two young men looked at each other in amazement.

"I don't get it, Moe," one of them said. "Do you?"

"I don't get it either, Schmoe," Moe answered. "Do you suppose we'll have to sweep out after the customers leave pretty soon?"

"We don't get it, Mr. Cooger," Moe pleaded, an anxious look on his face.

"It's just what I said," Phil Cooger smiled, enjoying their puzzlement. "Your job is to do what this Charlie tells you to, and incidentally report everything to me every day."

"I think I'm beginning to get something, Schmoe," Moe said.

"Me too, Moe," Schmoe agreed. "When do we start, Mr. Cooger?"

"An hour or two from now will do," Phil Cooger said. "Be careful."

"I see a little more, Moe," Schmoe said with a worried frown. "When Mr. Cooger says that to US it means he's afraid he might have to find two more boys to take our place in the near future."

"We'll be careful, Mr. Cooger," Moe smiled. "We know things wouldn't be the same for you without us around."

CHAPTER FIVE

HELEN HANOVER drove her iridescent yellow coupe onto the receiving platform of the automat garage. As she stepped out a sign lit up, saying, "Be sure to get your parking ticket. Pay 50 cents."

She had the half-dollar ready. When it dropped in the coin slot under the lighted sign a card dropped out.

The coin also started the parking mechanism to functioning. The coupe moved slowly into the garage, where automatic machinery would carry it to the spot denoted by the number on the card. Later, when she returned, she would have to place the card under an electric eye which would read it and then bring the automobile back out again.

If she had cared to she could have placed half a dollar in the service slot and had her car washed on the way to its cubicle. Two more half-dollars would have also given it a gloss coat after the wash.

It had been two months since she first met Harvey Trent on the train. Those two months had been fun of experiences and revelations that were rapidly changing her whole outlook on life and her place in existence.

Harvey had had to leave on another of his continual trips.

George Granville had been the genial host, guide, and understanding companion during the first week.

After seeing Harvey off at the depot, she had been rushed through offices, laboratories, libraries, studios, and even machine shops, being introduced to dozens of people who were as old as she, or older, and who all looked no older than she did. The appearance of the women was that of twenty years of age, and that of the men was twenty-five.

She had remarked about this difference in the appearance of the men and the women. George had explained that IF, the immortality factor, seemed to arrest development at the same stage in both men and women, that a woman of twenty was at maximum development, while it took twenty-five years for a man to arrive at the same degree of physical maturity.

"IF was never a bigger word to anyone than it is to us," he had remarked smilingly. "Someday we may be able to put an equality sign after it and write a series of chemical symbols and numbers."

Helen found after the first few days that she was gaining a comprehensive picture of the group and its activities and purposes. The search for IF was divided into two distinct approaches. In the first, everyone spent occasional moments or hours on their memory books in which they jotted down whatever rose from the depths of their memories of the incidents of their lives during the years from 1845 to 1850.

She read several of these. Reading them, she began to recall her own life during those years, and to realize what a difficult task it would be to recall every uninteresting incident.

"In all probability," George had remarked gravely, "The incident that set up IF was something so insignificant that no one will recall it at all. It may have taken only a second or two. It may have been something of which no one was consciously aware, such as a strange virus from outer space that settled into our atmosphere and found foothold in a few hundred people before being killed by an unfavorable environment. If that's so, then there will be no chance of solving IF in this way. Still, since we don't know, it is our best bet."

THE SECOND approach to the answer to IF would, as

George put it, "Ensure success eventually, even if it took a thousand years."

She visited huge laboratories where men studied individual cells isolated from the human organism and living in nutrient fluids that were carefully controlled.

These laboratories occupied the top ten floors of a fifty-story, one-square-block building a short distance from the lake in the heart of Chicago.

When they first went there, George introduced her to a short man, broad-shouldered, with the blackest hair she had ever seen. His name was Alex Potocki.

"We're all old enough so that we don't need a boss over us," George had said jokingly. "Alex is the nearest thing to a boss we have. He's the chief coordinator of research. In these ten block square floors of laboratories are three hundred of us engaged on research that grows increasingly complex. All this research is devoted to one thing, the human body as a cell complex. The data must be continually coordinated. One man must hold this coordinated pattern in his mind, not because he is smarter than the others, but because that's the only way it can be done intelligently."

"Do you think you'd like to go into this work?" Alex Potocki had asked her.

"I don't know," she had replied. "You see, I've never been anything but a housewife. I don't know the first thing about science."

"I see you aren't quite used to your immortality yet," Alex laughed. "With all the future ahead of you it is a mere trifle to spend twenty or thirty years thoroughly mastering some complex subject. The normal human barely has time to do that before he is too old to make any real use of his learning. He rushes through college, getting a doctor's degree in six years. After that he spends thirty or forty years teaching or working for some company for a living, devoting his spare time to research. We, here, consider this merely a temporary task to be done and put behind us, not a life's work to engross us for all the future centuries."

"Would you like to spend a few weeks going over this?" George had asked eagerly. "After all, you will never be a housewife again, even if you marry. You must go into intellectual pursuits or become bored with life. Maybe this is it for the time being."

Helen had thought it would be interesting to really study something so vast as this research. She had agreed.

After George left, Alex took her to what he called the Induction Office. There he had taken her picture and fingerprints for the files. She was assigned an office next to his where she could retire whenever she chose. There was a small bedroom and private bath connected with her office; but she had remained on at the Palmer House, waiting until she "found herself" before making permanent plans on where to live.

During the two months since that day she had learned much. She was beginning to get an understanding of the work. Typed reports and explanations had helped. Alex's continual answering of her questions had helped fill in the picture.

She knew now that the human body was a complex mass of cells that had developed from one single cell. Through the successive divisions of the parent cell all the various types found in the adult body were produced.

The various types of cells fell into two distinct types. The first was the true types. These, by analogy, were as different as a horse and a fish. Of common parentage they might be, but they were totally dissimilar.

THE SECOND classification took in the cells that were different only as an electrician and a pianist might be different. In the body they might look entirely different and have different functions, but isolated and placed in controlled baths they became identical. Their differences in the body arose entirely from their specialized environments. Their differences in function arose from the differences in food intake from their surrounding medium.

This type of cell was found in a geranium stalk, for a well-known example. A cell that ordinarily developed into a leaf would instead develop into a root if immersed in wet sand.

Cell genealogy was an intermixture of the effects of environment and of a fixed pattern. A V type cell (one whose appearance and function changed for different environments) might produce one T type (true type) in one environment on division, and a distinctly different T type in another. Or it might produce the same T type regardless of environment. So cell genealogy was a very complex thing. Most of the research work at present was on cell genealogy, inextricably linked with the study of the effects of specialized environments, artificially created in the thousands of small tanks that filled the laboratory shelves everywhere.

These specialized environments not only duplicated those found in the body, but also took in chemicals and fluids never found normally in the human body.

A work arising from this first phase was that of reciprocal environments. Any cell in any environment took certain things from that environment and replaced them with other things. The things it took were its food. The things it put back were its waste products. Part of the food of one cell might be waste products of some other cell, and part of its waste products might in turn become the food of still another cell.

Each cell, due to inherent properties, selected only the food it liked from any environment, leaving the rest of the environment intact, except for throwing out its waste products. This interchanging of the roll of food and waste in any aggregate of cells was extremely complex.

Every phase of this complexity was being patiently isolated and studied in the thousands of experiments going on all the time by the scientists. The results were sent to the coordinating department.

This whole work, cell genealogy and environment analysis, was lumped under the heading of middle stage research, or body chemistry. There were, in addition, two other stages of research; nuclear research which probed into the physical and chemical structure of the cell itself, and organ research, which used the techniques of middle stage research on body organs intact.

The organ research labs contained tanks with hearts, glands, stomachs, and every other type of organ, living in controlled environments, with their waste products subject to continued analysis. The various organs of the living body were not only subjected to environments normally found in the body itself, but also to environments never found in the living body.

THOUSANDS of various chemicals were introduced into the environment of every isolated organ, one at a time, and their effects on that organ studied.

"Anyone of these chemicals might be the IF factor," Alex had explained. "We have the research as a whole far enough along now so that, say, on Monday we can start research on some particular chemical compound, and by the following Monday have its detailed effects on every organ and cell in the body tabulated. We can know, for example, that the chemical retards production of some hormone produced by some gland by a certain amount, the effects of this retardation on the body as a whole, and what becomes of the chemical during this action. We can know that it changes the cell genealogy in certain respects, and know those changes in detail. We have, for example, seventy-eight different chemicals that we call M substances. We call them that because they produce cell types not ordinarily developed in the body. These new cell types are nearly all of the type known as cancer. That is, they develop by rapid division into cancerous tissue. With all of them, once the M substance had produced them, they become a true mutation and develop in the normal body environment into malignant tissue without needing any more of the M substance to help them along."

Now, after two months, Helen was beginning to see how this stupendous research project might eventually find the IF factor. By systematically introducing every known substance into the research and tabulating its effects, eventually the substance that was the IF factor would be used. The study of its function in the body would reveal it for what it really was.

She had gotten acquainted with different workers and listened to them talk about their work. Each one practically lived and breathed his own isolated part. One, for example, studied only type E-40 cells. For ten years he had spent eight hours a day on the one type of cell. He had developed an intuitive attunement with that type, so that he could sense its reactions to new substances, feel it withdraw in fear, or advance hungrily, or squat indifferently as the strange, ionic fields of an intruder touched its sensitive skin. To him it was not a cell but a living thing complete in itself, just as surely as the tiger in the jungle or the trout in the swift mountain stream. In its function and structure, it was beautiful beyond the beauty of a painted scene or the strains from an orchestra or the rhythm of a dancer.

And now, though her understanding could comprehend all this and stand breathless before its magnitude, there had grown within her a realization that it was not for her. It was not that it was too complex, and too full of microscopic details for her to find a place in it. She knew that in ten years she could become one of these scientists. It was no feeling of incapability in her that had brought her to the decision to turn away from this. It was something different, a feeling that such a life was inadequate for her.

The study of this research project had opened her eyes at last to the true magnitude of the meaning of being immortal: with endless years ahead to grow mentally, with all the inexhaustible possibilities open to mankind through teamwork over the ages, with the unlimited possibilities for perfection and attainment that were denied those who withered and died at the moment of their greatest promise.

With her eyes opened she remembered her years of blindness and groping in the darkness of mortal surroundings. She felt again the heartaches, the despair, the hopeless quest. If it were not for the chance meeting with Harvey she would be once again embarking on a course that would lead to a lonely turning away from a fresh grave that all too soon had claimed the aged corpse of one who, in his prime, had held her in his arms and stood with her at the altar, and whispered, "Until death do us part."

SHE REMEMBERED, and wondered how many others there were that were doomed to continue on the path she had escaped by chance. If she could find even one of these she would feel better. She owed a debt to some one of these unfortunates. Until he or she had been found and lifted up into this little world of immortality within the world of mortality as she had been, she couldn't feel free to enjoy it herself.

Part of that feeling, she knew, was due to her love for Harvey, and her womanlike feeling that the work of the man she loved was better than other vocations. Yet she also knew that it lay deeper than that. Perhaps someplace there was someone who, like her, had stood beside the grave of a loved one and looked into a hopelessly repetitive future, and was about to cut off that future with deliberate intent, not knowing what promise and what potentialities for fulfillment of life existed here.

If she entered the work of the research project that unknown person might do that which could never be undone. True, if she entered the project it might be she who would accomplish the last crucial bit of work that would open up the promise of immortality to ALL mankind. That was a remote possibility compared to the more easily understood one of finding one of the lost immortals, and bringing one more into the fold.

So she had made up her mind, and now she was going to break the news to Alex Potocki. After that she would go back to George Granville and ask for a roving commission like Harvey's.

Engrossed in these thoughts, she did not look up when someone blocked her way into the building. She stepped to one side in an attempt to pass. The vague figure in front of her moved with her. Annoyed, she glanced up. Cold shock struck her with an almost physical violence.

Agnes stood there, blocking her way into the building; and on her aging face was a smile of malicious triumph.

Numbly Helen looked at her daughter. It had been only a few months, but it seemed like something in the long forgotten past. She stepped back. Alarm, revulsion, and fear of the flame of hatred in Agnes' eyes, sent icy fingers into her mind.

"Hello, Agnes," she said, feeling her heart pounding painfully against her ribs.

"Hello, *mother.*" Agnes gritted. "I thought it was about time you and I have a little talk. Do you mind?"

"Why, no," Helen replied, her frantic thoughts searching for some way to escape. "There's a restaurant on the tenth floor of this building. Should we talk there over a cup of coffee?"

"If you think you can drink it," Agnes mocked politely. The flame in her eyes veiled. "After you, mother dear," she said.

Feeling the dreams and hopes, she had found so recently, tumbling into depths of oblivion and despair, Helen pushed through the swinging doors into the building.

"Please, Agnes," she said, turning around and putting a pleading hand on her daughter's arm. "Can't we just drop all this? Surely there can be nothing you want of me. Carl left you over a million dollars. I've been through so much with you, and to no avail. I can't take any more."

The sneering, taunting, mocking smile of hate remained unmoved. Agnes shook her head slowly.

"But what good can it do?" Helen asked. "What do you want of me?" She looked into her daughter's eyes and shuddered at what she saw there. Turning away, she went toward the elevators.

CHAPTER SIX

THE TENTH floor restaurant of the Science Building was a thing of strange beauty. Occupying the full square block of floor space, it was a garden of flowers, lawns, shrubs, and dwarf trees.

The waiter led Helen and Agnes to a small table next to a dwarf fruit tree. Apples and pears glistened in ripe invitation from its low branches. A bright yellow canary perched saucily on a weak branch, singing as if it thought it could drown out all other sounds.

The smell of freshly mown grass mingled with the scent of a thousand flowers. Almost circling their table was a winding brook, its rocky bed stirring the crystal clear, swiftly moving stream into tortuous swirlings. A large trout flirted its tail playfully on the surface as they sat down.

From a distance came the sound of an organ playing. The ceiling, though only ten feet overhead, was so skillfully constructed of translucent plastic of sky blue that it seemed almost to be a summer sky far above.

No other table was visible. When the waiter took their order and departed they seemed alone in a fairyland far from the heart of the largest city in the world.

Neither Helen nor Agnes seemed to be aware of all this. The canary, frightened by the tense atmosphere that clothed these two visitors, took wing with a flash of gold. The trout disappeared underneath the grassy overhang of the brook. And the two were alone.

"Are you surprised that I knew where to find you?" Agnes asked derisively.

"I hadn't thought about it," Helen answered in surprise. "I

assumed it was a chance meeting. Wasn't it?"

"No," Agnes gloated. "I know all about you. I'm going to continue knowing all about you. Wherever you go, whatever you do, you're going to find me just around the corner waiting for you."

"What do you mean?" Helen asked, her heart filled with a nameless dread.

"Here's what I mean," Agnes said. "Right now your new boy friend is getting a letter from me telling him how old you are, and warning him that you will steal his youth as you did father's and mine."

"Yes?" Helen said, amused.

"I don't think he will call me mad," Agnes said confidently. "I enclosed a society clipping from a 1935 newspaper that showed you and father. That will prove it to him."

"Perhaps it would interest you to learn that he knows how old I am," Helen said.

"I don't believe that," Agnes retorted.

"It's the truth," Helen murmured. "Look here, Agnes. If you'll listen to me I want to tell you a few things I didn't know when I left Dubuque. Will you listen?"

There was no reply, so Helen went on.

"You think my seemingly eternal youth is due to some vampirish principle I use," she said. "Since I didn't know why I never grow old, I couldn't deny it. But I've learned that there are others like me. My boyfriend, as you call him, is the same as I. There are hundreds of others. And our youth is due to something we haven't learned the secret of yet, but are going to learn before long. When that secret is found you'll be able to use it and so will everyone else in the world. Believe me, if I knew how, I would give you the same eternal life I have."

"I don't believe it," Agnes reiterated.

"You MUST believe it," Helen said. "You're my daughter. In spite of your hatred of me, your mother, I would give you what I have if it were possible. It's something perfectly natural. We just don't know what it is yet."

"Words!" Agnes exclaimed. "Do you expect me to believe you? If there's such a group you've been to them before. You KNOW the secret. You'll never give it to me."

She stood up, quivering with rage.

"So Harvey Trent is the same as you," she said. "Well, I swore on father's deathbed that I would make you pay a hundred fold for all the misery you've caused me. And I will. I'll find other ways to torment you. I'll follow you wherever you go. I have a million dollars. Yes. I'll spend every cent of it to make you suffer."

SHE TURNED her back and walked hurriedly along the path until she was out of sight. Helen watched her go without moving. There was a look of intense pity in her eyes.

"She must have hired a detective to follow me," she thought. Her decision to turn down research and travel in search of other immortals came back to her. Now there was all the more reason. If she stayed here, Agnes would haunt her. If she traveled, it would be possible to elude the detective and see to it that her daughter didn't know where to find her.

Suddenly a longing rose up in her to see Harvey and talk about it to him. She decided to call George Granville and find out where Harvey was now, and join him.

At the elevator bank she hesitated. She should go up and tell Alex Potocki about her decision first.

She let two elevators go while she remained undecided.

"I can call George from upstairs," she argued. "But also I can call Alex from George's. I should tell Alex what my decision is before seeing George; but maybe I'd better talk it over with George before definitely telling Alex that I'm not going into research."

In the last analysis, it was human values that carried the decision. George Granville, the towering giant with his genial, understanding smile won over Alex Potocki, the short broad-shouldered scientist with his jet black hair and preciseness of action. She took an elevator going down.

She called George from a pay phone on the first floor, telling him she was coming over. On the way to the automat garage, and on the drive to George's place, she tried to spot whoever might be following her. There seemed to be no one at all. The faces behind her changed continually. The cars in back of her that looked suspicious always turned at the next corner and never came back.

George met her at the door to his flat. He listened while she told him of her meeting with Agnes, of her decision that had already been made to go on the road, and how Agnes' madness had made that decision all the more imperative.

"Alex will be very disappointed," George said. "He's been taking a great personal interest in you. He told me only yesterday that he's been preparing a special lab room as a surprise for you, to be all yours as soon as you tell him you're ready to go ahead on research."

"That's too bad," Helen said, an expression of mental pain clouding her face. "I like Alex."

"But you love Harvey," George said with a smile.

"Yes," Helen said frankly. "Strange, that after so many lifetimes I can still fall in love. Sometimes I marvel at myself, that I could love Carl so devotedly for forty years, and with his last words of devotion and worship still ringing in my ears I could lay that love aside like a discarded cloak and put on another."

"There's nothing so amazing about it," George said. "It was a completed picture. If it hadn't been completed, final, you couldn't have done it. A week before, you wouldn't have looked twice at Harvey. You wouldn't have noticed his lapel emblem. You would have passed him by without seeing him."

"Where is Harvey?" Helen asked.

"On his way here," George said. "He's bringing a new recruit."

"He'll be here? Today?" Helen asked, a glad note in her voice.

George nodded. "Should be here any minute," he said, glancing at the clock. "Your daughter, Agnes, seems a trifle unbalanced on your eternal youth doesn't she?"

"It seems so," Helen replied. "It worries me, her making a solemn oath on Carl's deathbed to see that I suffer."

"That's why I'm wondering," George said slowly. "It's possible, now that she knows there are several of us, that she might make trouble for us."

"But how can she?" Helen exclaimed in surprise.

"Did it ever occur to you," George asked quietly, "why we don't simply come out and announce our existence and ask all immortals to come forward?"

HELEN caught her breath sharply. That question had been in her subconscious without ever rising to the surface.

"There are many reasons why we don't," George went on. "For one, the whole economy of the nation is based on the assumption that everyone dies. The only exception to that is the corporation, which theoretically can live forever. The corporation, however, is not an individual and cannot think. What do you think would happen if the information got out that there were over seven hundred people in Chicago and spread over the country who were each a century and a half old and from all signs would live forever? First of all, there would be an investigation that would disclose we possess accumulated assets of over four hundred million dollars, and that we own the patents to a great many of the key inventions of our modern industry. It would be found out that we have an area of ten square city blocks of research laboratories devoted exclusively to the study of the human body.

"About that time Congress would get high handed and seize our research records. Then there would be a big blowup. It would be discovered that we had the cure for cancer and that we hadn't seen fit to give it to the world yet, so that the millions of dollars spent on cancer research each year could be spent buying rouell drinks instead of going into research. This, and many other important things we have discovered but have not made available to the public, would lead Congress and the American people to conclude that we were hoarding our discoveries and planning to take over the United States and perhaps the world with them."

George stood up and went over to the bar to pour a drink.

"The resentment your daughter has against you is just one example of the universal resentment that would grow against us. We would be forced to disband and spread and lose our unity and our potentiality for eventual good. No doubt many of us would be killed by mob violence. Stories would grow. I rather imagine the research "machine" would become in the public eye a huge, horrible monster where we dissect living humans and prey on the innocent public to preserve our immortality. The thousands of people that disappear every year would automatically be pictured as winding up in our ghoulish laboratories, brought in through secret underground entrances to be tortured and cut up. The living hearts pumping away in glass tanks for all to see, the lungs in their tanks, breathing in monstrous isolation, all would add to the fuel.

"That's why we have been so secretive. I more or less assumed you would know all that without being told. That's why I didn't swear you to secrecy. After all, you kept your own secret all these years."

"I'm sorry. Terribly sorry," Helen said. "I didn't think. I thought I saw a way to give Agnes hope, and perhaps help her. She is my daughter."

"Well, don't let it bother you," George said, handing her a glass of wine. "I doubt if any of those things will happen. I think we'd better see what can be done about your daughter before she has a chance to carry on her mad schemes."

The door chimes interrupted them.

"That must be Harvey!" Helen exclaimed.

GEORGE pressed the button that unlocked the downstairs entrance and then opened the front door. He and Helen stood there waiting for Harvey.

The sound of footsteps came up from below, growing louder with each turn in the winding stairs.

A young lady came into sight first, followed by the familiar face of Harvey. An arrow of jealousy shot into Helen's heart. The new recruit was a woman.

The next hour saw a repetition of her own first visit to this place. The new recruit was named Alice Heeb. She seemed to radiate health and beauty to Helen's jealous eyes.

When Alice turned to Harvey she had a habit of laying her hand on his arm possessively. Her life, it developed, had not been the prosaic one of a housewife who had just buried her husband. It had been the more glamorous one of travel over the world, careers, and adventure.

Harvey's eyes, as they occasionally looked at Helen, were warm with unspoken feeling, yet Helen seemed to see the same warmth as he looked at Alice.

"May I go in the other room and lay down for awhile?" she finally asked George. She felt she had to be alone or give way to open despair.

"Why yes." George said, giving her a worried look.

Helen excused herself and went into another room. When she tried to close the door behind her Harvey was there. He closed the door and stood with his back to it, looking at her.

"Aren't you going to welcome me?" he asked softly.

"That woman?" Helen asked helplessly.

"Is just another recruit," Harvey laughed. "I believe you're jealous."

"Not jealous," Helen said, tears that she had held back now forcing their way out. "It's just that everything seemed the same as it was when I first came here. I—I've—Agnes met me today and told me she had sworn to follow me and torment me for the rest of her life. I told her about the immortals because I thought it might give her hope. Now I find that I've endangered the whole group. I—I feel pretty low, I guess."

"Forget it," Harvey said, putting his arms around her and lifting her face so that he could look in her eyes. "For your information I've told Alice Heeb all about us."

"You have?" Helen asked weakly.

Harvey kissed her on the lips.

"Now come back in the other room and be the hostess," he said softly.

GEORGE WAS explaining to Alice about the attempts to find the immortality factor by cross checking memory.

"First," he was saying. "You must try to recall the exact dates of your various movements. That gives you a sort of skeleton outline of your life during the period that it happened. For example, you moved into a certain house on a certain date. You moved away on another date. That's the skeleton. We cross check it with the others. After you get that outline more or less accurate and complete you have to start filling it in. You try to remember incidents—every little incident of the first day when you moved there. One by one the little things you've completely forgotten will come back. You write them down. Fill in what you recall later. And all the time we keep comparing with other records.

"Also, you will get a chance to read some of these other post mortem diaries. Reading them will help you recall other things you'd forgotten. Someday we'll uncover the one thing we all did without exception. That thing will contain the answer to IF."

"Tell us about yourself," Helen interrupted. "It was only a short time ago that I was here for the first time."

"Then you can understand what a relief it is to be able to speak freely," Alice Heeb said with an understanding glance from Helen to Harvey. "I know about you already, Helen. That's about all Harvey would talk about. I met him on a street corner in New York, day before yesterday. Noticed his lapel emblem and put two and two together. Quite a pleasant shock!

"I was born in Boston in 1827, married when I was eighteen, and later moved to Philadelphia. Born and raised a Catholic, I never married again after my husband died. Instead I turned to the stage and carved out quite a career for myself during the fifteen years I followed that.

"All the time I was studying, trying to find out if anything was actually known about people who were immortal. All I could get out of the Church was an occasional pokerfaced admission that it was known there were others like me."

"You mean the Catholic Church knows you were born in 1827?" George asked.

"That's right," Alice replied, smiling. "Not only do they know, but every priest in the country knows me by sight. I know that because I have gone to strange towns and to priests I've never seen before, and they greet me by name and seem to know my entire history."

"Well I'll be damned!" George exclaimed.

"About the turn of the century," Alice went on. "I wrote for eight or ten years. Even now I occasionally write a book under some pen name or other. It gives me a steady income. Since the war I've been living in New York. I enjoy living. Got used to always staying twenty long ago. The only thing I hate is having to pull up stakes and move when my friends start to get old. If I didn't they'd begin to wonder. It hasn't been so bad though. Since the thirties, beauty parlors have been given the credit for my eternally youthful appearance. The alibi of a good beautician has made it possible for me to stay in one place twenty years at a stretch."

She turned impulsively to George.

"What about you, George?" she asked. "I've heard Helen's and Harvey's stories already. "What's yours?"

"Mine is a sad tale," George said with a shy smile. "Harvey and Helen saw their loved ones die time after time. You moved about and managed to enjoy your own life without any entanglements after one experience with loved ones. I don't know where I was born or how old I am."

"You what?" Helen and Alice exclaimed in unison.

"The earliest I can remember," George said quietly, "I was something of an enigma to those around me. A sort of a village idiot in a small town in New Hampshire. I can still recall my earliest memory. I was standing in front of the local store. Some small boys were running down the street like the devil was after them. There was a dull throb on the side of my head. I was looking at things with absolutely no memory at all. I learned by patient inquiry that I was the village idiot, harmless, and fed whenever I asked for food, by whatever housewife I asked. There seemed to be a village superstition that anyone who refused to feed me when I was hungry would meet with calamity, and those who fed me would have good luck."

HE PAUSED for a moment. The room was without sound.

"That was in 1905," he went on. "I had wandered into the village one day in 1891, according to the local barber, when I asked him. No one knew where I had come from. With my questioning, the people began to realize that I had 'good sense' again. They were so happy about it that they chipped in and bought me some clothes and gave me a bath and bought me a railroad ticket out of town. I never went back." There was a wistful note to his voice.

"Then what happened?" Alice asked breathlessly.

"Nothing much," George said. "I seemed to have left town with the name George Granville tagged to me. I've kept it through force of habit. My mind cleared rapidly, but I could never recall my life as the village idiot, nor anything before that. My ticket took me to a town where there was a smelter. I started working in the smelter, learned to read in the evenings from my landlady, an elderly woman who liked to mother me. She gave me a liking for good books and philosophy.

"After ten years of that, my landlady died. Rather than find another one I bought another railroad ticket and moved on. In 1920 I decided to go to college. After graduating from college I went into business. I opened a wholesale hardware supply and built it up to a large concern. In 1935 I discovered that one of my employees was using dyes to make himself look middle aged. We made our mutual confession and got to thinking maybe there were others in the world that were deathless. I had the happy thought of combining the Maple leaf with the infinity sign. From 1935 to 1941 we uncovered fifty-two others. They were all men. When the Second World War broke out, we of course went into the army. Twenty of us lived through it.

"We pooled our resources and bought a site not far from Chicago to use as our headquarters. That was when we found Harvey. A little later we found Alex Potocki who was a born organizer. It was Alex who built up the research machine after we built the Science Building when a large Loop building was condemned and ordered torn down."

"So you are the founder of the Society of Immortals." Alice breathed.

"Yes," George smiled. "From village idiot to riches; a success story."

"It must have been that those kids hit you on the head with a rock or something," Alice said, her face full of sympathy.

"That's right," George agreed. "The luckiest thing that ever happened to me, no doubt. If I hadn't had that blow on the head I might still be a village idiot, or more likely, they would have burned me at the stake someday for not growing old."

Harvey looked slyly at Helen and winked knowingly. It was obvious that Alice had at last fallen. She was examining George's head as if it had just been hurt. And George seemed to be enjoying it!

CHAPTER SEVEN

HELEN STOOD alone on the floor of the lab, endless rows of tanks stretching away into the distance. She recognized it as organ research.   Several eyes watched her from a nearby tank—unblinking, egg-like orbs that seemed to see and to be aware.

She was dreaming. She wanted to awaken. Yet she clung to the dream with horrible fascination.

Somewhere Agnes was looking for her. Agnes was in the lab looking for her. She had a branding iron that she planned on using. She was going to press it against her forehead and brand her with the symbol of eternal life.

There was a sound of stealthy footsteps. Helen ran in panic, ran between rows of tanks with staring eyes. The footsteps were gaining on her. She turned to look and it was two young men with innocent grins on their faces. She sighed with relief and stopped running. They ran past her without seeming to know she was there.

They were in a dark sedan. It turned and disappeared between two rows of tanks.

Alice Heeb was in a tank, swimming underwater and looking out at Helen. She wondered why Alice didn't get out of the tank, and then saw that Alice's heart was fastened in the tank. George, in the white of the lab technician, was connecting tubes to it through the glass. There was blood on his head. He had been hurt.

Alex appeared suddenly in front of her and asked her what she was doing.

"I'm not going into research," she said firmly.

"Come with me," Alex said. He took her hand and led her into another room. "This is to be your own private research lab," he explained.

"But I'm not going into research!" she objected.

Alex turned to look at her, and it was Agnes, firmly gripping her hand. She pulled back. Agnes dragged her into the room. She had a branding iron in her other hand and was trying to swing it around so she could brand Helen on the forehead.

Helen broke away and ran. She tried to remember which aisle to run down to reach George. She had to reach him and find out where Harvey was.

Agnes was right behind her. She could feel the heat of the glowing branding iron at her back. Just ahead was a dwarf fruit tree with apples and pears on it. She reached it and stopped.

Agnes sneered at her, and turned and went away.

A sedan appeared and drove by slowly. The two young men were in it. They didn't look at her. Alex was riding in the back seat of the sedan. He looked right at her and didn't seem to know her.

There was a brook running at her feet. She looked into it and saw hearts beating slowly, with tubes running from them and going out of sight under the grassy bank of the stream.

She had to do something. She couldn't remember what it was she had to do. Suddenly she remembered. She had told Agnes about the lab. She had to find Alex and warn him.

She was on the elevator, but it was going down and she wanted to go up. Alex was up! The crowd pushed her out of the elevator. She tried to get back in but the crowd kept pushing her out.

Suddenly she was in the research labs again. She passed George and Alice. She noticed that George had Alice's heart in another tank now. He had her stomach out and was trying to cut it loose.

Alice saw her and waved cheerily. She waved back and kept moving between the rows of tanks.

The sedan appeared ahead and drove toward her. When it passed she saw the two young men in it. One of them was chewing gum. They didn't look at her.

She looked after the car wondering why Alex wasn't in it.

HARVEY appeared up ahead. He saw her and waved for her to hurry. She ran toward him, panic nipping at her heels. Each tank she passed there was a young man standing in the shadows, chewing gum and not looking at her.

Alex appeared suddenly between her and Harvey. He held his arms as if to stop her. His face was filled with rage. His eyes were deep black pits of anger. She heard a crash of glass breaking. A policeman had an ax and was breaking a tank.

Water was running through jagged holes in the tank. Hearts were flopping around on the bottom like fish.

The place was full of policemen, all with axes.

"You're responsible for this," Alex shouted.

Agnes appeared, a look of triumph on her face. People were coming in and looking at the floundering hearts in the empty tanks.

Agnes was laughing insanely, her eyes wild.

The people were pointing at her. Some of them started after her.

"No!" she said, holding her hand up as if to stop them. "No...You don't know what you're doing!"

"Hurry!" It was Harvey's voice.

She turned. He was still there, closer now. George and Alice were with him.

She broke into a run. The police and the people were swarming in front of her, blocking off her escape. Agnes' face appeared in front of her, screaming at her.

For a moment she couldn't see Harvey. Then she saw him and he was farther away than ever. She called to him, her voice nothing more than a sob of despair.

Everything around her was falling and crumbling. She knew that Agnes had managed to undermine the Science Building in some way.

Alice was standing beside a piano, singing. George was sitting at the piano, playing the accompaniment. Both of them and the piano were sliding rapidly down the steeply slanting lab floor, unaware that the building was falling.

Harvey was putting on his topcoat.

"Run!" she shouted hoarsely. He looked up at her and smiled, then went on putting on his coat. With a horrible grinding roar everything fell on her.

She opened her eyes. Alice was standing over her, pinning her to the bed. There was a worried look on her face. Her silky white nightgown revealed her firm, lovely body. A flash of lightning lit up the hotel room briefly. A crash of thunder followed the flash a second after.

"For gosh sakes," Alice said. "Do you always have nightmares when there's a storm?"

Recollection flooded Helen's mind, but with it came no relief.

"Let's go, Alice," she commanded. "I've got to use the phone."

Alice stepped back. Helen sat up and placed her feet over the edge of the bed, trying to find her slippers. She gave up and crossed the room barefooted to the desk phone.

Alice followed her anxiously and turned on the light for her so she could see to dial.

"What's the matter?" Alice demanded.

Helen dialed George's number with shaking fingers without answering Alice's question. The phone at the other end began ringing. No one answered.

Alice repeated her question.

"That nightmare made me remember something," Helen said, gnawing her fingernails nervously.

She tried Harvey's number. The phone rang without an answer.

"Get dressed, Alice," she ordered. "We've got to get out of here before it's too late!"

"But where'll we go in a storm like this?" Alice objected.

Helen dropped the receiver on its cradle and started to dress. Alice followed her example, obviously not liking it.

The two girls hid their uncombed hair under their hats on the way down the hall to the elevator.

"We're going to George's," Helen volunteered suddenly.

"Well," Alice said, relieved. "At least I got ONE sensible statement out of you." She squeezed Helen's arm reassuringly.

IN THE hotel garage Helen asked the night attendant if there were some other car she could take than her own. She gave her name. The attendant brought out a sleek sedan of 1968 vintage.

"Runs all right, anyway," he apologized.

Helen got behind the wheel and Alice climbed in on the other side. The attendant closed the switch that opened the outer doors.

The rain pelted in, the wind hurling it across the dry concrete floor.

As the attendant waved violently for Helen to hurry out she pressed down on the gas. The car moved out into the storm, the windshield swipes automatically starting with the first sign of moisture.

The headlights had also gone on automatically as the darkness affected the selenium control. They sent twin shafts of brightness into the falling torrents as Helen turned the car into the lane that led up to the street.

Water formed pools and rushing streams in the street. The black sky was shattered continually by jagged cracks of incandescence. The wild roar of thunder cowed the very Earth.

Helen hunched over the wheel, her face pale and drawn. Alice watched her silently, resigned to waiting for events to explain this mad ride.

The streets were deserted. Far ahead the dim lights of an oncoming car turned off to the left. Wind dashed sheets of rain against the overworked swipes, distorting the view dangerously.

Once the car skidded sickeningly for a moment before the wheels gripped the road again. To the north and west fire sirens sounded faintly through the din of thunder.

Alice's eyes lighted up with interest as she recognized landmarks that told they were only a block or two away from George's apartment. Ahead there seemed to be cars blocking the street. Large red spotlights peered at them drunkenly. Dark shadows moved in the street.

Helen slowed the car to a crawl. Her eyes were almost against the windshield as she peered ahead.

Without warning the whole sky exploded into a sheet of electric fire that lit up the surroundings with the brightness of day. Revealed were fire trucks and men in glistening raincoats. Some of these men were dragging hoses. Others were carrying stretchers to waiting ambulances.

This whole activity was centered on a mass of wrecked and grotesquely piled masonry from which hungry flames darted, to be driven back by the driving rain.

This was all that was left of the brownstone mansion whose top floor had been George's home.

Helen found herself repeating, "I was right. I was right. I could have saved him if I'd remembered. It's my fault."

"If you'd remembered what?" Alice said, shaking her.

"Alex Potocki in the back seat," Helen said listlessly.

CHAPTER EIGHT

THE RAIN beat against the car with an unsteady roaring undertone while the continual shattering roll of thunder formed the main theme of the bacchanal orchestration. The play was a horror picture, a unique version of the old movie, with the scenes going on continually but lit up in flickering sequence by the continual jagged flashes of lightning in the sullen sky.

The spectators were two. They sat frozen to their seats, watching through the rain swept windshield of the car as the swipes futilely cleared away the rain.

Their eyes followed each tarpaulin-covered stretcher, trying by sheer force of will to see underneath the drab cover and discover if this one or that carried George Granville.

The large red warning lights of the fire trucks and ambulances waved back and forth drunkenly like batons of hellish directors who were themselves invisible.

Holding the center of the stage was the shapeless pile of stone and splintered wood that had been the three-story brownstone flat. Red tongues of fire licked out here and there like festering wounds. Dark figures moved here and there, pulling aside debris in search of more bodies.

"It must have been Q.P.," Alice said breathlessly. "You know, that explosive they used in World War III that explodes inwardly instead of outwardly, so that it doesn't throw things all over."

The full realization of what must have happened penetrated her bewildered senses. She began to weep.

"Don't cry, Alice," Helen said. "If you have any faith in destiny you know that neither George nor Harvey COULD have been killed."

Her eyes were caught by a moving figure that stumbled away to the side, coming toward the car. Her hand clutched Alice's arm. Alice looked up and followed her gaze. A lightning flash lit up the man briefly.

"George!" the two girls exclaimed in unison.

They were out of the car into the rain. Unmindful of it they stumbled through puddles to the staggering figure and held it up between them. Alice was crying and laughing at the same time.

"Was Harvey in there?" Helen asked.

George seemed to shake his tousled blond head in the negative. Alice opened the rear door of the sedan and climbed in, pulling on George while Helen pushed.

Other figures were coming toward the car, glistening, raincoat clad figures. Helen slammed the rear door and climbed behind the wheel. The motor was still running.

Slipping the car into reverse she backed with roaring motor until a side street appeared. The men outside were running after the car now.

With a clash of gears Helen slipped into low and twisted the wheel, heading the car down the side street. A disjointed report from the back seat, consisting of words from Alice and groans and mutterings from George, told that he would live. No bones were broken.

On hearing that, Helen slowed the car to a crawl. She had to wait until George told her where Harvey was. Harvey didn't have a place of his own in Chicago. When he brought in a recruit he either stayed at a hotel or at George's.

The wailing of sirens came from all directions now. To the north the sky was red from a fire someplace. Just ahead a lonely red light indicated an arterial stop. Some of the sirens suddenly became louder. Fire trucks and ambulances shot past the intersection headed toward the Chicago loop, their motors roaring.

IT WAS AS insane as had been her nightmare, Helen thought. And it seemed too much like a nightmare to be real. It was real, though. No thunder could be so nerve shattering in a dream. No lightning could be so bright.

Other fire trucks hurried by as she reached the corner and stopped. She sat there, waiting and watching. In the rear view mirror she could see Alice holding a scarf out the window to get it wet, and wiping away blood to see the extent of damage to George. His head had been a bloody mess.

She brushed away the sickening thought that he might have received another blow on the head that would leave him the village idiot again. She brushed the thought away, and it returned with reinforcements. Why didn't George speak up and tell her where to find Harvey? Why didn't he say something intelligible? Why didn't he say even ONE WORD?

The only words were those of Alice. Soft mothering words of tenderness and love.

And outside the whole world was mad, caught in a battle of raw elements, the Universe destroyed except for this one small island of insane forces about her.

As if to accentuate the madness of what was left she turned her head in time to see a car dart in from a side street a block away and pause in front of an oncoming fire truck that picked it up and tossed it neatly over on its back.

Flames leaped out of the back of the overturned passenger car. Two ambulances stopped. Other ambulances and other fire trucks circled the smashup with barely a pause and continued on toward the loop.

She pulled her eyes away from the strangely unreal scene a block away. She had to know now. With slow deliberation she turned around and faced the back of the car.

"George," she said loudly above the noises of the storm. "George, where's Harvey?"

As she looked she saw what she had known all along she would see. George's eyes carried no light of calm intelligence such as they always had before. They were dull and stupid and uncomprehending, the bewildered eyes of an idiot who finds himself transported from a village scene in 1905 to the interior of a sedan in 1974.

Alice took George's unresisting head in her arms and rocked back and forth, moaning softly. And still the mad sky flashed, and thunder roared with brittle sound, and rain came down to swell the torrents in the street.

"There's only one thing to do," Helen said suddenly in a voice that sounded shrill and strange to her. When she said it everything seemed to fall into place. It was the only answer.

It meant not looking for Harvey. It meant not going back to the hotel. But first... She fumbled through her purse. There was nearly five hundred dollars and her gas credit card. She kissed the credit card before slipping it back in her purse.

Then she turned into the arterial and headed north. In

Evanston she turned west. The blackness of night was being replaced by a sickly gray as the sun tried to get through. As she left Evanston and entered the farm area she could see the clouds turning white on the horizon.

The downpour slacked off until it was a summer freshet, a sprinkle, and finally ceased altogether. In the fields there were still rushing streams that tore jagged rips in the fertile land and undermined stalks of green corn.

AT ELGIN she stopped at a service station and slipped her credit card under the electric eye, filling her tank with gas. When the bell rang, indicating the tank was full, she hung the hose back where it belonged. The eye released her credit card. She was thankful that there were no humans around to see her and remember her later. She had enough gas in the tank to take them out of Illinois. That was all that mattered.

There was a lump in her throat as she climbed back behind the wheel. Alice was trying to explain to George what had happened. She was trying so hard to keep smiling as if there were nothing wrong.

Helen quickly turned her face away. Alice had been a skilled actress. She could smile and coax and act as if things were all right; but she couldn't.

She shut her ears to the horrible sound of childlike, uncomprehending questions George asked. She shut her mind to the future. She held her eyes on the road and thought only of getting out of Illinois.

In the rear view mirror she caught a puzzled glance from Alice occasionally. She knew Alice wanted to know more of where they were going. She didn't know herself.

All she knew was that in a nightmare she had seen Alex in the back of a car with two young men in the front seat, and that Alex should not have been there. What that meant, whether it had any meaning or not, she didn't know. Yet, because of it she had rushed madly to George's place only to find it in ruins and George badly hurt, his mind switched back to the forgotten past. From a scientific standpoint that lent probability to her unformulated feeling being grounded in facts. She had gone strictly on feeling.

Now, as she drove, she tried to place it on a more rational basis.

"The whole nightmare," she said to herself, "was created out of a combination of things already in my mind. It was probably an end product of several problems. The problems were, first, who has Agnes had following me and spying on me? The two young men who were always there but never obvious. I noticed them subconsciously but not consciously, so they appeared in my dream.

"George pointed out to me the danger of letting Agnes know about the immortals. My mind dramatized this into a thriller raid on Research. Perhaps the storm was the cause of this aspect of the dream.

"George's working on Alice's heart was obviously a distorted picturization of the fact that he had won her heart that afternoon. Their being at the piano together while it slid into space across the tilted floor of the lab was a picturization of the fact that they were oblivious to the danger, whatever it was.

"But Alex had changed into Agnes! And Alex had sat in the back seat of the car the two young men had been in. This associated Alex with the danger, made him a source of danger *equal* to that of Agnes. His changing into Agnes was symbolic; but was it symbolism or actual memory that pictured him riding in that car?"

Helen had no way of knowing. Something was there, in her subconscious, which was causing her to flee rather than go to any of the immortals for help. She was running away. She felt that every minute she stayed in Illinois increased the danger, and she didn't have the slightest idea what the danger was.

Could it be some danger from Alex Potocki? That was utterly absurd. Alex was an immortal. Not only that, he was the founder and prime mover of Research.

Helen scowled in concentration. She hadn't exactly liked Alex. She certainly hadn't disliked him, but there was a wide gap between like and dislike. She had respected him and perhaps held him in awe. He was more of the type conventionality would picture an immortal to be—a scientist in charge of Research, directing the detailed study of something terrifically complex.

Perhaps underneath there had been something approaching dislike or, more accurately, fear and awe. It might be that this had entered the dream a little mixed up and caused an association of

Agnes, whom she feared and dreaded, with Alex, whom she feared and respected.

This conclusion didn't satisfy though. It didn't have the right mental flavor.

Of only one thing was she sure. She would be as wary as a wild animal and trust no one but Harvey. So the immediate problem was to find someplace where she and Alice and George would be safe, yet where Harvey could find them.

As if in answer to her posing of the problem a road sign approached. It said, "Dubuque, 43 miles."

Agnes would never think of Dubuque. It was out of the state of Illinois. Harvey would come to Dubuque to begin his search once he was sure she was missing and not dead. It all added up. She even knew where they would stay; a second story flat in an apartment house she owned in her own name. If she remembered correctly that flat was vacant!

She glanced in the rear view mirror. Alice and the idiot-George had become friends. George was grinning happily. He had found someone who really seemed to like him.

Helen blinked back a tear and sniffed loudly as she slowed down for the bridge across the river to Dubuque.

CHAPTER NINE

IT HAPPENED so quickly. Helen had stopped the car as the traffic light turned red. It had just changed back to green and she was pressing her foot on the gas when there was a blur of motion. The right hand door opened, there was a movement of someone sliding into the seat beside her, and there was Harvey!

She was stunned. She had reconciled herself to settling down to a long, almost hopeless wait, cooped up in a room where she would have to keep watch on the street in the hopes that he might eventually appear on the sidewalk below where she could see him and run down and get him.

She wanted to laugh and cry and hug him. His nervous smile and quiet order to get going sobered her. Cars in back started to honk for her to move as she pressed down on the foot throttle and got the car in motion.

"Turn right at the next corner," Harvey said. "This car is too hot to go far in. There's a ten state alarm out for it."

As soon as he was sure she understood what he had said he turned around and looked in the back seat. Out of the corner of her eye Helen could see the color of his face change from a ruddy tan to a lead grey as he realized what had happened to George.

He turned back. Helen reached over with one hand and found his. They drove that way, with him directing her where to go. They were in the used car district after a while. Harvey had her slow down while he looked over the cars in the lots.

Finally he had her draw up to the curb. Half an hour later he came back in a 1970 Rummery Transcon sedan.

George laughed delightedly as he found the Earth apparently so unstable under his feet after the long drive. He seemed to have adopted the attitude that anything was perfectly all right so long as his new friend Alice was leading him by the hand.

Alice laughed with him, and Helen could detect no sign of the heartbreak underneath. She waited until Alice had led George into the back seat of the Rummery, then slipped into the front seat beside Harvey. She could relax now. Harvey was there.

She laid her head back and closed her eyes. Soon she knew by the sound of the tires that the heavy, noiseless car was in the country and speeding along the highway at a rate she had never had the courage to attain.

Just as she was going to sleep it occurred to her that perhaps she should be suspicious of Harvey too. Her last thought before sleep overcame her was that if Harvey were not to be trusted it would be better if she were dead.

She awoke when the car lurched off the highway into the gravel parking-strip in front of a highway cafe. George's petulant voice was saying he was hungry. Alice was assuring him that this was a place where they would give them food.

Harvey's face was an expressionless mask that put on a tight smile when he saw that she was awake.

"Sleep well?" he asked, his voice subdued. She nodded her head emphatically and gave him an encouraging smile.

Sometime later they were back on the highway again.

"Where are we going?" Helen asked.

"A place on the shore of the Pacific," Harvey said without turning. "It's one of the secret places we've saved up for a rainy day."

"A rainy day?" Helen echoed.

"There's a lot you haven't had time to learn yet about our organization," Harvey explained. "One is about our emergency setups. You see, in time you learn to think of every possibility. We more or less collected in the Chicago area. We took cognition of the possibility, not only of discovery and an attempt by the government or some other group to wipe us out, but also of treachery in our own group. We formed subgroups, each of which had a secret place it could escape to, where none of those outside that little group could find them.

"This place is the one I bought. Only twenty of us know where it is."

"Does—," Helen hesitated. "Does Alex know where it is?"

"No," Harvey replied. "You sound like you suspect him of what happened last night."

HELEN told him of her nightmare, and how they had found George. Harvey listened without interrupting. After she finished he explained.

"George and I had been out driving," he said. "When the storm came up we were just coming back into Chicago. I dropped George at his place and then took the car to the garage two blocks away. I just came out of the garage when I heard the explosion. I ran up the street to where I could see what had happened. Convinced that George couldn't possibly be alive after that, I didn't go any further. I knew it had been a deliberately planned job. The type of explosion was unmistakable. I went back and got my car. At the Palmer house I found you and Alice were gone. The hotel garage told me you two had borrowed an old Cadillac and gone out into the rain. I also found that the police were looking for you.

"I rushed back to the scene of the explosion and told a fireman I was a reporter. He gave me the story of the mysterious Cadillac that had picked up one of the victims of the explosion and escaped under fire. I knew then that you two had rescued George."

Harvey's face cramped with pain as mention of George made him remember what had happened.

"I sensed by then that you must have known something was going on. Why else would you ask to borrow a car when your own was in the hotel garage? Why would you go out into the storm? Why else, when you found George would you escape rather than assuming the police would help you?"

"There was no way of knowing where you would go. I had to make snap decisions. The only other place I knew of that was connected with you was Dubuque. I drove there as fast as I could."

"I drove north to Evanston and then to Elgin," Helen explained.

"That's why I didn't see you on the road," Harvey said. "I went straight west from Chicago. It was shorter."

The highway unfolded with smooth swiftness in front of them. The fluid drive turbine did its work with noiseless perfection.

"What really happened?" Helen asked finally. "Was my dream right? Is Alex Potocki really a traitor?"

"I don't know," Harvey said slowly. "Personally, I don't take too much stock in dream interpretation. It doesn't take into account the purely imaginative factors of a dream. It assumes that every incident of a dream is the result of unimaginatively put together elements. I would say that perhaps you didn't like Alex very much, and as a sort of revenge on him for your not liking him, you placed him in the roll of some sort of villain in the dream. I'm not discounting the possibility though. If he shows, up I'll be more suspicious of him than of anyone else until I'm sure of him."

ALICE HAD been listening to them. She asked a question now.

"Why would any immortal do something like that? From what you've been saying there must have been a deliberate attempt to kill some, if not all, of the immortals."

"All," Harvey said, his lips a grim line. "You evidently didn't have your radio on. A terrific explosion destroyed the upper part of the Science Building at four-thirty this morning. According to an elevator boy, all the workers had been called down for special duty during the storm. The latest reports before I found you were that everyone in the upper half of the building were killed.

"There were over a dozen explosions in various parts of the city. The addresses given were those where immortals lived. It looks as if a deliberate attempt was made to wipe us all out."

"But the police that were looking for us?" Helen asked, horrified.

"Probably had orders to kill you once they got you away from the hotel," Harvey said.

"But then—" Helen hesitated.

"Alex is either dead with the rest or the attempt to kill us all was his idea," Harvey said.

"But why?" Alice pleaded.

"Yes...why?" Helen echoed.

"I wish I knew the answer," Harvey said. "But it would be insane for him to destroy Research. He's the one that created it and nursed it into its full development."

He drove in silence, the miles slipping by rapidly on the broad transcontinental highway. City after city appeared in the distance and crept forward. At the outskirts the outer lanes continued straight while the center lanes dropped down to become an underground channel through the city. Above, the outer lanes came together to become a city street. On the other side of the city the outer lanes separated again while the center lanes came up between them.

"We'll get there sometime tonight," Harvey said.

George had gone to sleep, his damaged mind hidden behind his broad flawless brow, his tousled blond hair soft and fresh from the gentle administrations of Alice's loving hands as she dipped her scarf in the rain the night before and patiently wiped away the blood.

Finally she slept too, her head resting against his huge shoulder, pathetic and small.

"When we get to the coast," Harvey said softly, "We'll call in a brain specialist and see what can be done about him. I think there have been enough cases like him so that they will know just what to do."

"I hope so," Helen prayed, "Oh, God, I hope so."

THE SUN outdistanced them in the race toward the ever-retreating western horizon. George and Alice awoke while the car was crossing the Rockies. George was hungry and fretful so they stopped again to eat.

Helen dozed fitfully after that. Harvey had swallowed a Benzedrine tablet before leaving the cafe. He would be able to drive the rest of the way all right.

When she awoke, Harvey was shaking her shoulder gently. The car stopped. The headlights disclosed a house.

"We're here, Helen," Harvey said.

Alice and George were already climbing out from in back. Helen joined them.

She saw a sight she would never forget. The house at her back was on what seemed a high table land. Fifty feet in front of her the land ended abruptly. Stretching from there to the far horizon was the ocean. A giant moon poised just above the incredibly distant horizon, forming a carpet of gold across that great expanse right up to the place where the land dropped off.

A mile or two out, a toy sized freighter moved with slow dignity across the carpet of light. Millions of bright clean stars dotted the cloudless sky.

And from some invisible place down lower came the restful booming of salt waves dashing against a rocky abutment.

Helen turned to Harvey who had come up beside her.

"I think I could stay here forever," she said.

"I doubt it," Harvey said. "The tide's in right now, and the weather's perfect. But who knows? Lots of people are born inland and live most of their life there, only to discover that they were born in the wrong place and are really shore dwellers by nature."

He slipped his arm around her waist. She laid her head against his shoulder and closed her eyes, letting her nostrils sense the salt air, her ears reach for the distant sounds of sleepy shore birds, and for the silence which has a different quality on the edge of the vast Pacific than any other place in the world.

"Just twenty-fours ago I was waking up from a horrible dream!"

Helen said suddenly.

"Let's get some sleep," Harvey said, kissing her.

Helen nodded contritely. "You must be dead on your feet. Over two thousand miles of driving…"

"I am pretty tired," he admitted.

They turned and went into the house. As Harvey unlocked the front door lights went on in the back.

"Jerome must have seen us drive in," Harvey said. "He's the caretaker. Jerome Dolpin. I got acquainted with him and his wife Martha several years ago. Martha was sick. I helped them out and sent them out here to take care of the place."

Jerome came in from the kitchen as they entered the house. He had an automatic in his hand—which he lowered when he recognized Harvey.

THREE WEEKS passed slowly. They were heavenly weeks to Helen in many ways. She had a chance to be with Harvey continually and learn more about him.

The house turned out the next morning to be a long rambling lodge that had been built by a too ambitious yachting club. Concrete steps led down from it to the beach where a well-built dock jutted out two hundred feet. There was a beach to the north of the dock. To the south there was a beach only at low tide, the water coming into the twenty-foot embankment on which the clubhouse was built.

At the end of the dock was a boathouse. It contained two boats: a seventy-foot ocean-going speed cruiser, and a twenty-foot injector-jet racing boat.

Harvey took her out in the racing boat the first afternoon. After that they went nearly every day.

On the second day they saw the wreck of the Science Building in the local television news broadcast while Harvey recorded it on the television wire recorder for future playback.

The news commentator reported that it was believed to have been wrecked by an explosion of stores of chemicals being used in experiments, the explosion being set off in some unknown way by the unprecedented storm that had been raging at the time.

The list of dead had been appalling. Alex Potocki's name was among the missing.

There had been seventeen other explosions in Chicago that night. These had all, the news commentator blithely stated, been caused by lightning igniting escaping gas from leaky mains.

Aside from George Granville being listed as missing there was no mention of the four of them.

THE MORNING of the third day there, Harvey had driven from the coast to Olympia, and up to Seattle to find a brain specialist.

Three days later a truck had brought a portable X-ray, operating room equipment, and men to change a room over into a small hospital.

The four of them inspected it; three with hope in their eyes, and one with dull incomprehension.

After the workmen went away there was nothing to do but wait for the specialist to come.

They were days of heartache for Alice. George, the village idiot, was very likeable in his way. He didn't understand what had happened to him. He didn't try to understand. He liked Alice and enjoyed her constant mothering attention.

Helen and Harvey sat on the rambling front porch of the lodge while Alice would take George by the hand and go on long trips up the beach, teaching him how to dig for clams and teaching him over again when he forgot.

Whenever Helen tried to discuss the problems facing them in the near future Harvey avoided the subject.

"You must learn to think like an immortal," he chided her impatience. "You lived among mortals too long. You must learn that there are times when it's better to sit back and wait for days and days. In the coming centuries we will all, no doubt, reach the state of mind where we are content to come to a place like this and just relax and play for anywhere from ten years to a century and just call it a vacation."

With a women's intuition she guessed that Harvey was not as idle as he tried to appear. His only trip away from the lodge had been to see about medical attention for George. There were hours when he stayed in his room—and there was a phone in his room. There were times when he locked himself in a small brick building near the lodge that had an antenna tower above it.

When he appeared after one of these absences he was always calm and unconcerned, dismissing what he had been doing with a shrug and a casual remark.

So the three weeks passed. Three uneventful weeks during which Helen, in spite of herself, absorbed some of the philosophy of patience that was so dominant a part of Harvey's nature.

Then one morning she awakened to the sound of cars outside her window. Harvey's voice came reassuringly.

"Hello doctor," he said. "I see you're prepared for anything. An ambulance, assistants, nurses."

"That's right," a strange voice answered. "I don't want to make this trip again. I'm going to do it right the first time."

"Good," Harvey said. "Come in."

This was to be the day! The specialist was here to examine George, and operate if there was any hope of success. Helen's fingers shook as she dressed hurriedly. The clock on her dresser gave the time as five-thirty.

"What will George think of it all?" Helen wondered. "Will he be afraid?"

SHE PAUSED for a brief, hopeless look at her mussed hair in the mirror and then let it go and hurried downstairs.

There was a tense half-hour of being introduced to the doctor and his assistants, and of having breakfast with them. Alice— Helen could see—was even more tense than she.

When George appeared in the doorway of the breakfast room there was a split second of deep silence, George looked fearfully around, not sure whether to come in or turn and run. His eyes fell on Alice. He sidled over to her, his eyes warily on the newcomers.

Jerome brought in a plate of eggs and potatoes for George. He started eating. Helen could tell from the way Harvey and the doctor watched him eat that there was some drug in the food.

Her guess was right. A stretcher was brought in. The two interns expertly rolled George's inert body onto it and carried it out.

The doctor gave an audible sigh.

"Big lad," he said. "I'd hate to have had to give him a shot in the arm against his wishes."

The doctor then explained in a calm voice how it was necessary to inject an inert substance into the blood stream that would block the X-rays, so that the structure of the brain itself would show up in the pictures.

It was calm and cold like the advance descriptions of Research had been. Alice was crying.

One of the interns appeared in the doorway and nodded his head. The doctor stood up and went out.

"Like he was going out to take his turn at playing golf," Helen's thoughts whispered to her.

The nurses had disappeared without her seeing them go. There were only she and Alice and Harvey in the room. Harvey was smoking a cigarette. She had never seen him smoke before.

She had her arms around Alice. It was comforting to have something human to cling to for support. Alice had stopped crying. Harvey ground out the cigarette on a saucer and stood up. He looked at her briefly and turned away toward a window.

They waited. They had been waiting for three weeks. Helen realized that now. Nothing else had mattered, really; only that the doctor would come and take X-rays and decide whether he could operate or not, and whether it would do any good to operate.

Harvey, though she loved him, was not a genius or mastermind. His century and a half and more of life had brought him experience and good judgment not genius. She herself felt no wiser or stronger or more experienced than when she had really been twenty. She had a wealth of memories—nothing more.

The Society of Immortals belonged to George. It was his. Regardless of anything else, it was his. In every part of it, it had been first a dream that existed in his own mind, a dream that he had brought into reality.

If he died now, or didn't recover his old self, and remained the village idiot...

Helen felt cold. She wanted to go over to Harvey now and look into his calm eyes and tell him she finally understood. She didn't.

She didn't dare move. All she could do—all any of them could do, was wait.

The doctor appeared in the doorway with two dripping X-ray prints in his fingers. He went over to Harvey and held them up against the light.

Helen could see the dark spot from where she was sitting. The doctor's words meant little to her except that they were going to operate at once.

"His head is being shaved. We can start operating in twenty minutes."

Helen saw Harvey nod his head and turn back to the window. The doctor dropped his hand on Harvey's shoulder briefly, then left the room.

She wanted to scream "NO! he might DIE!" But it would be better for Alice if he were dead, if living meant an eternity of being an uncomprehending, good natured human pet, no better than a dog that wags its tail and does simple tricks.

CHAPTER TEN

"WELCOME INTO our circle. I hope you plan on being with us a long time." George was standing once more in the doorway to his flat, a twinkle in his eye.

"So you're one of the so-called immortals. I must say you carry your age very well—about a hundred and forty-one?"

"Three." Helen's lips formed the word soundlessly, then they drew into a smile.

"You don't look it." George stepped back into the room...

"But you love Harvey." George's kind, understanding smiled formed the words...

"I never went back." His smile was wistful. A pang of regret came.

"Maybe we should have taken him to visit his old home town before the operation," Helen thought to herself. She could see him, patiently docile, at the stoop of a back door in a small town, gratefully accepting a plate of food from some housewife. She could see him plodding down a small main street, little boys running after him and tormenting him.

"I learned to read and write from my landlady. She gave me a liking for

good books and philosophy. She died, and rather than find another landlady bought a railroad ticket and moved on."

A twisted smile on his kind, gentle face.

"From village idiot to riches—a success story."

Helen felt a soft hand on her shoulder. She looked up, startled out of memories. It was Jerome, holding a cup of steaming coffee. She started to shake her head and changed her mind.

Harvey was drinking a cup. Helen looked across the room and smiled tremulously.

The coffee was strong and bitter. It was real. It brought her mind back to reality. Alice was drinking some too. Helen looked at her watch. Four hours had passed already.

Almost immediately the doctor came in. Jerome poured him a cup of the coffee. He gulped it down noisily and sighed loudly with satisfaction.

His eyes caught on the three tense faces turned on him.

"Relax," he said good-naturedly. "The worst is over."

"Will he be O.K.?" Harvey asked.

"Don't know yet," the doctor replied. "Can't tell until he regains consciousness."

"How soon can we see him?" Alice asked. Her voice was shrill.

"Well," the doctor looked at his watch. "He should be coming out of it in—"

Helen found herself holding her breath while she waited for him to say—

"About—twenty minutes or so," the doctor added. "But you can only see him for a minute. Don't hope for too much, and don't be alarmed if there doesn't seem to be any change. I removed the pressure spot, but I can't do more than that. Nature will decide the rest."

HARVEY was beside her now. His arm circled her shoulder. His other arm was around Alice's waist. He led them out of the breakfast room, across the expanse of the huge living room, and into the hospital room.

George's face looked pale and bloated. His head was encased in a turban of surgical gauze. A black thing was protruding from his mouth.

A nurse was standing over him, the two interns standing nearby. The other nurses were sterilizing strange, inhuman instruments and packing them into black cases.

The three moved softly across the room until they were a few feet from the hospital cot. Alice moaned in sympathy as the nurse took the black thing and twisted firmly, pulling it out of George's mouth.

"He'll be waking up in a minute or two," the doctor said just behind them.

Helen found herself holding her breath again. She let it out slowly. Her eyes looked up at Harvey. He was looking at George, expressionlessly. Suddenly his nostrils flared. Helen jerked her eyes back to the bed.

George's eyes were open. She felt them pause on her and moved on to Harvey. She saw them move on to Alice. Then they looked up at the ceiling. Nothing about him moved except his eyes.

They came back and settled on Harvey. They stayed there while an arm moved across the white cover and crept up to explore the bandaged head.

Everyone in the room was watching, waiting.

George suddenly seemed to become aware of the atmosphere of tenseness. His lips cracked into a weak smile.

Alice broke away from Harvey and dropped beside the bed, her body shaking with sobs as she buried her face in her arms.

"I must have been hurt pretty badly," George said. "You all act as if I didn't have a chance until now."

Helen found her head against Harvey's chest, tears of happiness flooding her eyes. George had spoken in his old, humorous tone. The idiot was gone. The poor, poor idiot. The lovable village idiot.

Helen took a grip on her emotions and turned to 100k at George again. His huge hand was stroking Alice's hair, his fingers idly tangling it and mussing it.

The doctor came to life and told them they would have to get out. They could come back tomorrow. He pushed them gently until he had them at the door. Then he went over and took Alice's shoulders and gently lifted her to her feet.

Her hand went out. George took it and let it slip through his fingers. Helen put her arm around Alice and led her from the room.

THERE followed days and weeks of slow recuperation. The doctor, despite his first determination not to come down again unless George had a setback, paid frequent visits. The trim nurses stayed on, working three eight-hour shifts. One of them was always near, her practiced eye watching for signs of fatigue or mental strain.

Alice was again taking George for walks on the beach while Helen and Harvey sat on the porch and watched them; but now it was George who did the leading, and George who taught Alice the finer points of digging for clams.

Now and then Helen caught Harvey's eyes on the nurses, restless. She sensed that he was impatiently waiting until the day they pronounced George completely on the road to recovery, and left.

That day eventually came. The four of them, Helen, Alice, Harvey, and George, stood side by side and waved a last farewell to the doctor and the nurses as their car moved down the driveway and into the country road.

It was George who turned and said, "And now, Harvey. Out with it. Where are we? What's happened?"

Briefly Harvey explained all that had happened. He gave a bare outline first. The explosion, the trip to the coast, the weeks of waiting for the doctor to come. He told of the destruction of Research and the killing of most of the immortals.

George listened. There was a light in his eyes that Helen hadn't seen there before. He was no longer the indolent, joking host at the third floor flat in the brownstone house. His questions were to the point. His mind was alert and quick to seize on a point.

He had Helen repeat her nightmare several times and patiently questioned her on parts of it, trying to help her remember unimportant things she might have forgotten. He questioned Alice on when she had first noticed Helen's disturbed sleep, when the storm had started, and how Helen behaved after she awakened.

It had been early noon when he began his questioning. The sun had set when he finally relaxed and became silent. He sat on one of the stone steps of the lodge, his eyes looking to the west across the flat expanse of the ocean.

"So," he said softly. "So."

"What do you mean, 'so'?" Harvey asked with a short laugh.

"I mean simply this," George said in a flat voice. "All that I've learned adds up to only one thing. Alex Potocki finally found the thing that causes immortality."

"But that's absurd." Helen found herself saying.

"No," George said firmly. "It HAS to be it. Otherwise the destruction of Research and all its scientists is an insane act—no matter WHO did it."

"But was it Alex?" Helen said weakly.

"I don't think so," George said.

"What!" It was Harvey's turn to be surprised. "But it has to be Alex! If it wasn't—if he was not planning to get rid of us all and be the only immortal on Earth, he would have come rushing to you the minute he was sure he had found it and told you."

GEORGE shook his head. "You forget all the times it seemed he had the right answer."

"That's right," Harvey said. "The first time was five years ago when he thought that anti-EC10 factor was it. It might have been, too, except that it set up a manic imbalance in the endocrines. I see what you mean. Alex would probably have waited to make sure before jumping to conclusions again. But how do you know he didn't make sure? The right substance might have been found months ago, and he might have just made certain of it before the 'accident'."

"The reason I don't think it was Alex is contained in Helen's nightmare," George answered. "One thing both of you missed in that nightmare is the roll the emotions play in such a dream. In a woman especially the emotions play a more important part than logic. A picture painted by the subconscious of a woman is still painted to her satisfaction. It may be a nightmare, but her protective instinct is working in it."

"What do you mean?" Helen asked. She felt her body unaccountably trembling.

"Well," George said. "Take the roll Agnes played, for example. She had a branding iron. She was trying to brand you, but never succeeded. Why the branding iron? Why not a dagger or a gun?"

"I—I don't know why," Helen said quietly.

"I think I know why," George said. "But let's skip that for the moment. Why did Alex, who was supposedly trying to help you, change into Agnes with the branding iron?"

"Because her mind was trying to tell her Alex was a threat equal to that from Agnes," Harvey spoke up.

"Not necessarily," George said. "Remember, Agnes was her daughter."

"You mean that Alex was my son?" Helen said incredulously. "That's absurd! I had a son by my second marriage. That's true. But he didn't look anything like Alex."

"Tell us about him," George said quietly.

Helen was silent for a while. Her eyes took on a faraway look. She began talking so softly it was difficult to hear her.

"I met Arthur McCalmont in Spokane Washington in 1914. He was a mining engineer. He didn't want to marry me because he was so much 'older' than I was. He was forty-five, and I had told him I was twenty-three. It took a year for him to make up his mind. In 1915 we were married. We had a daughter in 1916. Then when we went into the war against Germany he joined the army. He left before our son was born.

"Tom McCalmont, our son, was born in March, 1918. Two weeks after his birth the War Department informed me that Arthur had been killed. Our daughter died during the flu epidemic after the war. I raised Tom alone. When he reached the age of fifteen I sent him to a private school, gave up my home in Spokane, and came east, settling in Dubuque, where I met Carl. That was in 1934. After that I went west every year for a short visit with Tom until he finished school. The last two years before he graduated I began to notice that peculiar, analytical gaze that I learned to recognize meant that my children were wondering why I didn't grow old.

"After he graduated he dropped out of sight. Although I tried to find him, he left no forwarding address at the school."

"What was Tom like?" George said. "Tall? Dark? Smart?"

"He was short," Helen said. "About five feet six inches. His hair was jet black. Although his grades in school were only average he had the most inflexible will I've ever known. I never knew him to give up on anything. When he was about seven years old there was another boy in the neighborhood that licked him in a fight. He came home with a bruise on his face and a bloody nose. About once a week after that for several months he came home beaten up. He picked the fights himself. Then one day he came home even more bruised than any time before, but that time he wasn't crying. He had licked the other boy."

"I see," George said. "And you say he simply dropped out of sight?"

"YES," Helen said. "I had maintained a mailing address in Chicago where he wrote me. I never told him I had married again. There was no way he could have found me, and when I couldn't find him I still kept that mailing address in case he ever decided to write. I still have it."

"Let's see," Harvey said. "He would be fifty-six now; wouldn't he?"

"Yes," Helen answered.

"Five foot six," George mused. "Jet black hair that would be turning gray now. Bulldog character—except that he wondered what made his mother stay young and apparently didn't follow up."

"He could have changed his name," Alice suggested.

"Yes," George said. "And come to Chicago and discovered that the address where he wrote to his mother was just a mailing address. He could even have found out where she lived and gone to Dubuque and discovered she had married again. He could have looked up the marriage records and found she gave her age as twenty. He could have kept track of her all the time, and when Helen came into our society he could have been hiring detectives to follow her and found out about us."

"And since she associated him with Alex Potocki as a self deception in her dream in one instance she could have in the other," Harvey said.

"Yes," George took up the line of speculation. "She undoubtedly noticed the two young men of the dream following her quite often, without consciously being aware of it—or maybe they were just symbolism. At any rate, the Alex Potocki in the back seat of the car now reduces to her son, Tom McCalmont, being the man behind the two young men."

"Probably her son's disappearance bothered her," Alice spoke up. "It went into her subconscious as a problem to be solved. Her subconscious took all the factors of his character and worked out a solution something like the one we are getting now. Since her conscious mind refused to listen, it came out in the nightmare."

"It's beginning to look like all your troubles began the day you found me," Helen said, crestfallen. "My children seem to be at the root of everything."

"That's something we can't be sure of," George said. "Even if it's true it isn't your fault, and anyway the damage is already done. What we've got to do now is locate Tom and go on from there."

"Do you have a picture of Tom?" Harvey asked.

"Yes. In a trunk I have in storage in Dubuque," Helen answered. ·

"I don't think we'll need it," George said. "Tomorrow morning Harvey can run over to Olympia with me and we'll pick up a picture. Unless I'm very much mistaken it will be a picture of your son Tom."

"Then he's in Olympia?" Helen asked.

"No," George replied. "I'll get it in the newspaper office. I won't tell you any more about it now. It'll be a picture of him the way he looks now, but if he's your son you'll be able to recognize him at once."

George took Alice's hand and stood up. Soon they were walking down the beach.

"I can't get over it," Helen said after a long silence. "George looks at something we've all been looking at without getting anywhere, and somehow it all seems clear to him. I can see where he is right about the dream. Tom had little resemblance to Alex. No one would ever connect them in any way. Yet I can see why my mind used Alex as a disguise for Tom. They are both short.

They both have black hair. But, more important, they both have the same driving force that won't back down. Alex built up Research. Tom would never admit defeat at anything he set his mind to."

CHAPTER ELEVEN

HARVEY parked the car as close to the newspaper office as he could. They had a half block walk.

"Who're we going to look for," he asked as they walked toward the newspaper office.

"We want to get a picture of Cooger, the gang boss of Chicago," George said, lighting the pipe he had bought on their way into town.

"Cooger?" Harvey exclaimed. "I never thought of him."

"I did," George said. "His name popped into my mind from the start, when I came back to life and found out all that had happened. Wait a minute. Here's a newsboy. Maybe his picture is in today's paper. You never know."

He fished a quarter out of his pocket and exchanged it for the paper. He and Harvey kept walking while he opened the front page up so they could look at it.

They stopped dead in their tracks. Staring at them from the center of the front page were two large faces. They were George and Helen.

The account underneath the pictures stated that they were identified at the scene of the explosion of the three-story brownstone, and that new evidence linked them with other explosions and with an international spy ring. There was ten thousand dollars reward for information leading to their capture.

"You'd better get back in the car," Harvey said. "I'll get the picture of Cooger as quick as I can."

"Right," George said. He held the paper up to partly conceal his features and yet appear to be just reading it, and went back to the car. Twenty minutes later Harvey rejoined him.

They drove in silence back to the lodge house. When they arrived the girls ran out to meet them. George thrust the picture of

Cooger in front of Helen.

"Is that your son?" he asked tensely.

"He's Phil Cooger, the big boss in Illinois," George said bluntly. "Now look at this." He handed her the newspaper.

She read it with Alice looking over her shoulder. The two men stood silently until the girls had finished reading.

"Now we know what we're up against," George said bitterly. "Cooger is known to have the whole state of Illinois sewed up tight. A politician can't run for office without an O.K. from him. A pickpocket can't even steal a wallet without getting an O.K. from Phil Cooger. If we're found we'll be taken back to Illinois, and we wouldn't stand a chance."

"But we won't be found here, George," Alice said.

"Oh, no?" George gritted. "The doctor and nurses that were here are probably looking at those pictures right now and thinking of that reward. THEY know we're here."

"You mean we have to leave?" Alice asked plaintively.

"I don't know," George said. "We don't dare do much travelling. We'd be picked up in a hurry that way. We've got to plan carefully."

"Jerome and his wife are safe," Harvey said. "The reward wouldn't tempt them. In fact, there's always a lot more than ten thousand in cash here they could help themselves to if they wanted it. I built up a reserve fund just in case of trouble."

"Maybe we could figure out some sort of hiding place in case the police show up," George said thoughtfully. "Helen and I could hide then, and you could say we had gone on someplace."

"As far as that goes," Alice said. "We could all take a long trip in the big boat and Jerome could say we saw the newspapers and left."

George shook his head.

"Somehow I don't think any of those things would work," he said. "If the doctor notifies Illinois where we are, and it's really Cooger behind it, he'll send some very smart boys out here and see through all those things. If we hid, probably the first thing he would do is look up the ownership of this house and have his men camp here indefinitely. Sooner or later that would smoke us out of hiding. If we took the boat we'd be in the same fix. It can't carry enough fuel to go to Mexico or South America."

THE FOUR had drifted over to the front steps of the lodge while they were talking. George sat down on the lowest step.

"Anyway," he continued. "All those schemes can do if they succeed is just keep us from being caught and probably killed as soon as we're back in Illinois where Cooger can do as he pleases. We've got to do more than that or we'll have to keep hiding forever, which is an impossibility if he really wants us out of the way badly enough.

"What we have to do," he said slowly. "Is go after HIM. He has the secret of immortality and intends to keep it secret, or he wouldn't be going to so much trouble to kill all the immortals. We have to get him and get that secret out of him."

"That means going back to Chicago," Harvey said.

"Or laying a trap for him here," Alice added.

"I think you have something, Alice," George said. "If we could catch him here we would stand more of a chance."

"I want to ask something," Helen said. "Why, if you plan on giving the secret to all mankind, do you still insist on secrecy?"

"Huh?" George exclaimed in surprise.

"Why do you still insist on secrecy?" Helen demanded. "There was a good reason when Research was still going. Now that we are the only four immortals left, so far as we know; why can't we let the world know all about it?"

George stared at her, a peculiar expression on his face. Harvey was doing the same. Then they looked at each other and grinned sheepishly.

"Looks like we've been shown up," George said.

"You mean I've DONE it?" Helen exclaimed. "Glory be!"

"First we have to get a controlling interest in some large newspaper," Harvey said after the laughing quieted down.

"First we have to make sure we don't get caught," George countered. "We've got to do that now. If the doctor notifies the Seattle police they'll wire Chicago right away. Before the day's over the place might be swarming with police or Chicago gangsters!"

"We're right back where we started then," Alice said.

"Not quite," George said confidently. "The Quinalt Reservation is only twenty miles north of here. Harvey can go to Seattle or Portland and see about buying a newspaper. We three can take the car and drive up there for a vacation. We can take enough food along and while you two squaws keep camp I can write up the whole story and hit the world right between the eyes with it. Publicity will be the only thing to fight Cooger with."

"Alice can drive down to Moclips once a week," Harvey added. "As soon as I get a newspaper lined up I'll let you know by writing her there, general delivery."

"Good," George said. "Now let's get busy. We'd better take the car you bought in Dubuque so it isn't around. You can have Jerome drive you to Olympia and catch a train, and buy a car later."

"One more thing," Harvey said. "I believe in playing every angle. You may have to get out of the reservation. Besides writing a letter I'll put an ad in the papers. Let's see. I'll make it read like this: 'Joe, come home. All is forgiven.' Then I'll give the address with the street number as initials, implying a name. For example, 1342 would be M.D.B., I think. What'll I do about the name of the street though?"

"Just sign it M.D.B.," George suggested. "Put another ad in the same paper offering a saxophone for sale for six hundred dollars or some other outlandish figure so no one will want to buy it, and give your right address there. That way, when we see the other ad we can look the address up in musical instruments for sale."

"Good idea," Harvey said. "Let's call Jerome and let him in on it." He turned and ran up the steps.

TWO HOURS later the long sleek Rummery sedan was ready. Helen's lips trembled as she kissed Harvey good bye. He stood in the driveway waving at them until they were out of sight. Not until then did he turn back into the house.

"I've never told you, Jerome," he said. "This house is in your name. I want you to go to the bank in Olympia and borrow all you can get on it. I'll take all the cash we have here except five thousand. That will be enough to make sure you have everything you need for the next year."

"Yes, sir," Jerome said. "Are you sure you'll be all right?"

"I'll be all right," Harvey said, laying a hand affectionately on Jerome's shoulder. "I only hope you will be. You might be having some trouble before the day's over. But get this straight. If anyone comes, tell them you own the place. That's true, legally. They will check on it. Tell them we were just paying guests with plenty of money. You don't know who we are. We left in a hurry and didn't say where we were going."

"Where will I send the money I borrow?" Jerome asked.

"Have a cashier's check made out to Harvey Snelzer and send it to general delivery in Portland," Harvey replied. "And get it as soon as possible. We're going to have to work fast."

Less than an hour later Jerome and Harvey followed the path the Rummery had taken across the scab rock meadowland to the county road. They turned east toward Olympia.

They didn't see the sleek jet two-seater that dropped down from the stratosphere over the lodge and followed their dust trail until the pilot could make out their license number. It turned up into a vertical climb and in five seconds was out of sight.

CHAPTER TWELVE

"WELL, my boy," the majestic appearing old editor said condescendingly. "I admire your ambition to own a newspaper. But unfortunately the controlling stock in this one is owned by the Syndicate."

"But on your masthead it says this is the only locally owned newspaper in Portland." Harvey objected.

"I know, I know," the editor said, waving his cigar expansively. "The truth of the matter is that I DO own some stock in it—or I wouldn't be the editor. But I venture to say there isn't a privately owned paper in the United States or Canada. It isn't on the books, mind you, and if you repeat what I'm telling you I'll have to call you a downright liar. You can't buy a single share in this newspaper without the O.K. of the controlling interests. If I wanted to sell you MY shares, for example, which I don't, I would have to write in and get permission, and more than likely they would snap them up and not let them go to a stranger."

"Where could I contact the ones that have to O.K. it?" Harvey asked.

"You might try—no. You'd just get the runaround," the editor said. "I'll tell you what. I like you. You're a rich young man looking for some place to put his money to work. Try Phil Cooger in Chicago. I think he's president of the Syndicate that owns this paper. If he isn't he might as well be. If he likes you, you're in. Whether you have enough money or not he'll get you your paper and give you a chance to be an editor."

Harvey left the newspaper building feeling very dejected. In only three days he had learned that the press was not for sale at any price anywhere. He could probably buy a small town weekly, but what good would that do?

He dropped into a cafe and bought lunch and mulled over the angles to a small town weekly. The more he thought about it the more possible it seemed. He could print several million copies and mail them all over the country. In that way the public would learn of the immortals and of the hold Phil Cooger had gained on the press.

He left his lunch unfinished and went out to his car. An hour and a half later he drew up in front of the Kelso Sentinel in Kelso, Washington.

"Why yes," the stooped, bald headed owner said delightedly. "I'd be glad to sell out. We can go across the street to the bank and I'll sign the deed and turn the mortgage over to you right now."

"How much paper do you have on hand?" Harvey asked, casting a proprietary eye over the flatbed presses.

"Enough for the next two weeks issue," the old man said. "You don't need to worry about paper though. You see, the newsprint syndicate issues us our paper on a prorated basis so that we get enough to print ten percent over our current subscription figure. It comes up once a month from Portland. The next shipment will be here next week sometime."

"But suppose you want to expand and print a few thousand extra copies?" Harvey asked with a sinking feeling.

"Can't get paper for that," the old man said positively. "I tried it five years ago. Had a little ambition then and wanted to take in surrounding towns. The Syndicate turned me down flat. Yes, sir."

"What's your production now?" Harvey clutched at a last straw.

"Four hundred and thirty-three," was the reply.

HARVEY turned away and went out the door to his car. He had to admit defeat. The only other thing, radio, was out too. He hadn't tried that for the simple reason that he had known all about it ahead of time from a big fuss about it in the press a few years before.

He started to get in his car, then realized he hadn't finished his lunch. There was a small lunchroom across the street. As he looked he noticed a face staring out at him. When it saw him looking it turned away hastily. There were two men sitting together.

Was he being followed? The face had been completely unfamiliar, yet he knew that in a good job of following a person the faces changed often, to be replaced by others.

There was only one way to find out. He dropped behind the wheel and started the motor. Out of the corner of his eye he saw the two men in the lunchroom get up and walk casually to the door.

Harvey released the hand brake and stepped on the gas. In the rear view mirror he saw the two men run to a car and start after him.

He slowed down, ready to speed up if they seemed intent on catching him. Their car showed no indication of closing the gap. It was apparent that they had orders only to follow him, not capture him.

That could mean only one thing. They hoped that eventually he would lead them to George and Helen. Evidently they didn't know yet where the others were.

The highway had several turns ahead. He knew that from his trip down on the bus. Should he try taking a side road?

He lowered the door window and looked up. A small plane was cruising overhead. He pulled his head back in and looked in the rear view mirror. The other car was half a mile back.

The first bend in the road approached. He rounded it and, on the spur of the moment, pulled over to the side of the road and stopped. He waited five minutes. The other car didn't come.

That settled it. The plane and the car were both following him. The plane had signaled that he had stopped. Undoubtedly the other car had stopped also.

If he took a side road the plane could follow him and signal the car where to go. He started up again. So far he had done nothing that would positively indicate he knew he was being followed. It would be better that way.

As his car ate up mile after mile he pondered the problem. He couldn't go back to the lodge or, least of all, go to the Indian Reservation and find George and the girls. That was what they were holding back for. If they thought he wouldn't lead them to the others they would probably kill him instead of wasting so much energy following him.

And yet, he had to get to the others. Probably there was a systematic hunt going on. They probably wouldn't know about Alice. She had just arrived in Chicago the day of the flight. She would be safe enough going to the post office at Moclips.

He reached Olympia without coming to any decision. He passed the intersection with the coast road and kept on through the city toward Tacoma. At Tacoma he decided there was nothing to be done except drive on to Seattle.

The other car was no longer behind him. The plane that had followed him from Kelso was gone and there were now three other small ones cruising aimlessly overhead, anyone of which, or all, might be following him.

There might even be some sort of invisible mark on his car so they could follow it unerringly through traffic. It was hopeless.

THEY probably knew the purpose of his trip to Portland by now. They had probably reported back to Cooger and he knew they were planning on publicity to fight him. He would most certainly plug any holes left in that sector.

Publicity was already an impossibility. There would have to be some other way. There WAS no other way. Phil Cooger held all the cards. The Press, the Radio, law enforcement agencies—all were under his thumb. It would be impossible to even get to him and kill him.

Cooger had gained all this power in one short lifetime.

Immortal, he would eventually rule the world. Against him stood only four people, immortal, but only so long as they managed to evade the highly perfected police system that had been designed to track down more experienced prey than they.

Harvey slowed down as his car met the street traffic of Seattle. Around him people walked and rode, free to do as they chose—so long as they weren't a threat to Phil Cooger. They would think him insane if he stopped his car and started to tell them the truth. They would laugh at him if he told them he had been born a century and a half ago.

And still no plan had come to him. Around him, unseen, were new faces watching him. It would be no use to single them out. They would be replaced before he could be sure. If he did anything, it would have to be by some system dead reckoning to eliminate ALL pursuit, regardless of what it might be. When he made his move it would have to succeed the first time. Once they found out he was aware of being followed they would take him.

First, he decided, he would check in at a hotel. He turned up to Fourth Avenue to the New Seattle Hotel. He turned his car into the street level elevator and stepped out. The doorman recognized him.

"Hello, Mr. Trent," he said warmly. Harvey gave him a smile and walked through the door into the lobby. At the desk he signed his name to the card the clerk laid in front of him and followed the bellhop to the elevator. His eyes took in the three men who entered the lobby. When the elevator doors closed one of them was crossing toward the room clerk's desk. He had never seen any of them before.

His room overlooked the Sound. It was a nice one with a modern television-radio-phonograph and expensive furniture. He took off his coat and shirt and took his electric razor out of his bag.

There was a knock on the door.

He stopped the razor and looked at the door, and licked his dry lips. It was beginning to get him.

The knock was repeated. He went over and opened the door. A bellhop, a different one than had brought his bags, asked him if there was anything he wanted.

"No, I guess not," Harvey replied. He fished out a dime and gave it to the boy with a wry smile. "That's all the change I have on me."

HE CLOSED the door and started to shave again, knowing that the boy was probably telling some man what he had seen.

The phone rang. It was the desk clerk.

"Is everything satisfactory, Mr. Trent?" he asked.

"Quite all right, thank you," Harvey replied.

"Is there anything we can do for you?" the room clerk persisted. "Are you expecting any guests? Is anyone waiting for you perhaps? That we can page?"

"No. No one," Harvey said. "I'll tell you what, though." He had been about to hang up, when a thought struck him. He debated hastily.

"Yes?" the clerk's voice came politely.

Harvey knew there was probably someone standing beside the clerk listening over another phone.

"What time is it now?" he stalled.

"It's four-twenty-three," the clerk said precisely.

"Good," Harvey said. "What time is dinner served in the dining room?"

"At five-thirty, Mr. Trent," came the respectful answer.

Harvey grinned to himself.

"Good," Harvey repeated. "I'll just have time. Have my car brought back up at once. I'll just have time to run an errand before dinner." He dropped the phone back on its hook.

There was an expression of elation on his face now. An afterthought made him turn back to the phone.

"Give me the flower shop," he said to the switchboard operator. He ordered a dozen roses placed in his car.

"That should do it," he muttered as he hung up. "It was so obvious, so simple, that I never thought of it."

Ten minutes later with a clean shirt on after his shave he stepped out of the elevator and crossed the lobby to the car exit. His car was waiting and the box of roses was on the seat.

CHAPTER THIRTEEN

HARVEY glanced at the girl at the reception desk and a look of disappointment appeared on his face. She glanced up and then looked back at the book she was reading when she saw him continue on toward the elevator.

"Third floor," he said to the seventeen-year-old boy running the elevator. He turned and looked back toward the entrance in time to see a man coming through.

When the doors opened on the third floor he stepped into the hall. His eyes lit up with satisfaction. The nurse was just what he wanted. She wore a white sister's uniform. He smiled at her.

"Visiting hours are over until this evening," the sister said, returning his smile.

Harvey ignored this. He laid his box of roses on the desk so that they were in front of the nurse. She looked down. Her eyes fixed on some writing on the box. The writing was on a slip of paper held in place under the wrapping string.

"Do you," the paper read, "Know of, or have you ever heard of Alice Heeb?"

Out of the corner of his eye Harvey saw the door to the stairway open slightly. If the sister said the wrong thing now it would be the end.

"I hope you can make an exception to the rule this time," Harvey said hastily. "I may not have a chance to visit her again. I'm leaving town tonight."

The sister frowned over this apparently inconsistent behavior. Then she smiled.

"I think we can," she said. "But you can only stay a few minutes."

As she stood up she looked at the lapel emblem on Harvey's coat. When she started down the corridor ahead of him her elbow moved in a way that told Harvey she was crossing herself.

"She's heard of Alice Heeb," he said triumphantly to himself.

In the hotel room he had suddenly recalled what Alice had said about being a Catholic.

"Wherever I go," she had said, "they know of me."

The sister paused at a door.

"You wait here," she said clearly. "I'll see if she's awake."

She opened the door and went in, closing it behind her. Harvey waited outside. He heard the soft murmur of voices in the room.

The door opened and the sister came out.

"All right, you may go in now," she said. "Don't stay more than ten minutes though, and if you want me I'll be at my desk."

Harvey stepped through the door, not knowing what to expect. The sister closed it firmly from the other side.

Another sister stood beside a hospital cot. On the cot was an incredibly wrinkled face, the eyes closed.

"I'm Sister Lenora," the nurse said. "Sister Amelia said something about an emergency, and for me to listen to what you say very carefully. She said to tell you she will keep whoever is on the stairs from coming down the hall."

"Perfect," Harvey murmured. "I'd never hoped for such understanding cooperation. You've heard of Alice Heeb?"

Sister Lenora nodded without speaking.

HARVEY lifted his hand to his lapel and fingered his emblem.

"I've heard of that also," she smiled.

"Do you think it's good?" Harvey asked.

"Alice Heeb is good," Sister Lenora replied enigmatically. She took the box of roses from Harvey and laid them on a table, taking the slip of paper and hiding it in her robe.

"Mrs. O'Hara," she nodded toward the old woman on the cot, "is under an opiate."

"I have to trust you completely," Harvey said. "I haven't time to do anything else."

Quickly he told her of the men following him and of Alice, George, and Helen, hiding in the Indian Reservation. He outlined quickly the extent of organization controlled by Phil Cooger.

When he finished Sister Lenora remained silent for a minute.

"Where are you staying?" she asked suddenly. Harvey told her.

"You may go back to your hotel now," she said. "And I'd suggest that tomorrow you try to buy a newspaper here in Seattle."

"But, but," Harvey sputtered.

"Don't forget," Sister Lenora said with a humorous twinkle in her eyes. "You just visited Mrs. O'Hara, the widow of George O'Hara, who has no close relatives and is an old friend of yours who," she glanced pityingly at the aged form on the bed, "will probably not last out the night."

She led Harvey to the door and opened it for him.

"Thank you for being so thoughtful as to bring her the flowers," she said wistfully. "God bless you Mr. Trent."

Harvey drove back to the hotel feeling a little bewildered. The two sisters had acted with keen and swift understanding of the situation thrust in their faces without advance notice, Sister Amelia had noticed the eavesdropper at the stair door without giving any visible indication.

Sister Lenora had grasped the situation he had sketched so briefly and decided in her own mind on a course of action. She had told him nothing, except to make sure he knew whom he had been calling on, and to advise him to carryon his futile attempt to buy a newspaper. That, obviously, was to give the enemy the idea he hadn't given up yet. A good idea. They would be content to leave him alone for another day or two. In that time maybe these new allies could cook up something.

When he stepped out of his car at the hotel he looked at his watch. It was five-thirty on the dot. In the lobby he caught the room clerk's eye, glanced up at the clock and back to the clerk, nodded and smiled, and went into the dining room.

HE WAS on his dessert when he heard himself being paged. The boy saw his signal and came over to tell him he was wanted on the phone. He rose and followed the boy to a bank of phone booths in the lobby.

"This is Sister Anna," the voice at the other end announced. "Sister Lenora has told me that Mrs. O'Hara is not expected to live, and that you are the only friend she has in the world. I must ask you to forgive me for calling at this hour, but the sister also informed me you were planning on leaving the city immediately."

"Well, I was," Harvey said. "But I've changed my mind. I'll be here another two days, anyway."

"Fine," Sister Anna's voice came. "The reason I called is that Mrs. O'Hara is a charity case. If you would be interested in seeing her funeral arrangements taken care of I'm sure her prayers would be with you. Would you care to do that?"

"Why yes," Harvey said. "I guess so. Why, of course. I'd be glad to."

"Perhaps you could drop into the hospital tomorrow morning," the sister suggested. "We can make all arrangements for the burial then. Would that be suitable?"

"Yes," Harvey said. "Tomorrow morning."

He heard a click at the other end. He smiled to himself and added for the benefit of whoever was listening in, "Money grabbers." Then he went back to his table and ordered fresh coffee.

"SISTER ANNA?" Harvey asked the girl at the reception desk. The ancient wall clock behind her said five after nine.

"Straight down the hall, third door on the right," she said.

Harvey followed her directions, knocking softly at the door. It was opened by a sister wearing a black robe. Inside were sisters Lenora and Amelia, an older sister who was obviously, by the process of elimination, Sister Anna, and three priests. They introduced themselves gravely. The three priests were Fathers Blent, Harris, and Reed.

"It will probably surprise you," Father Blent said. "But by now your friends are on their way to a place of refuge. We've been working all night. But we're stumped when we try to think what to do with you."

"That's stumped me too," Harvey said wryly. "It's impossible to shake free of those men who follow me all over, and I can't even know who they are. They change so often."

"Every minute endangers your life," Father Blent said. "If you go back to your car now it might be that they would get orders to kill you before you reached the hotel. Therefore there is no course for us but to spirit you off now, and hope that Mr. Cooger won't dare to attack us."

"He wouldn't dare," Harvey said. "After all, there's public opinion."

"Not for the last ten years," Father Blent said. "This entire hospital could be blown out of existence and it wouldn't get in the local papers unless Mr. Cooger's organization permitted it. So we're running considerable risk in helping you."

"I see," Harvey said slowly. "In that case, forget about me. If George and the two girls are safe...I've lived long enough anyway—and thanks."

He turned to go.

"Just a minute," Sister Lenora spoke up. "You don't understand. We can't let you go to your death."

Harvey turned back.

"If there were only some way you could vanish without them connecting it with us." Sister Lenora continued.

"Every step I take is watched," Harvey said. "And I'm afraid to look in the trunk compartment of my car."

"Could you hire a taxi and slip out in the thick of traffic?" Father Blent asked. "Or would the taxi driver be one of them?"

"He'd probably be one of them," Harvey said. "But even if he weren't, before I'd go a block they would discover I wasn't in the cab. The police radio would broadcast an alarm. Every police call box would start ringing. I don't stand a chance."

"Maybe we could follow and pick you up," Father Blent suggested.

"If I got away I might just as well have stayed here," Harvey replied. "The minute they're sure I'm definitely gone they'll backtrack to this place and it'll amount to the same thing as if I'd stayed."

"I was afraid it would add up that way," Sister Anna sighed. "Well, let's go ahead with our original plan then. It may mean trouble but we'll have to face it."

THE SISTERS turned their backs. The priest that had been introduced as Father Reed started to take off his habit.

"You're to change clothes with Father Reed," Father Blent said.

With a glance at the backs of the nuns Harvey took off his suit, shirt, and tie. He slipped into the priest's clothes. Father Reed looked surprisingly like him when he had finished.

"Now what?" Harvey asked.

"Come here," Sister Anna ordered. She pointed to a chair. Harvey sat down obediently. Thin aluminum forms were slipped into his nostrils. Hands rubbed a white cream over his face and hands.

At the same time Father Reed, in his clothes, was rubbing a dark face powder over the exposed parts of his skin.

"Now for an ugly wart," Sister Anna said with a satisfied grunt. "There's nothing like an ugly wart to hide a person's face."

She stepped back to inspect her handiwork.

Sister Lenora handed him a small mirror. He looked in it and whistled. He could see not the slightest resemblance to his own features in the mirror.

"You know what to do?" Sister Anna said to Father Reed.

"Yes," he replied. "There's a man waiting just outside the front door where he can look down the hall. I'm to step out as if I were planning on leaving. Then I'm to look alarmed and turn in the other direction. I run down the back stairs to the furnace room, taking off these clothes as quickly as possible. In the furnace room is another uniform I'm to put on. The powder washes off easily. If the reactions of the pursuers are right I should meet them on my way up the stairs again. I'm to say that I saw a man slip out the powerhouse door."

"Only if the engineer informs you no one is spying on the back door," Sister Anna said reprovingly. "If someone is, then you have seen nobody."

"What am I to do?" Harvey asked.

"You just stay here," Sister Anna said. "And keep you mouth shut." A nervous smile flashed momentarily on her plain but character molded face. "Be careful, Father Reed," she said softly to that man as he paused at the door and took a last look at those in the room.

He nodded briefly and opened the door. His eyes took in the man at the head of the hall in swift analysis, then turned in apparent hesitation. He had his act well in mind. Two slow, hesitating steps forward, then the swift glance at the man again, followed by a look of alarm, a swift turn, and a dash toward the rear of the building. He would have a hundred-foot start on the waiting man.

With a silent prayer he went through his act. As he turned and started walking swiftly he heard a shout behind him. He burst into a run as he heard the sounds of pounding heels behind him. He reached the door to the basement.

Something hot touched his shoulder blade. A sharp bark hit his eardrums immediately after. The door was open now. He plunged through onto the stairs. His feet should have taken the steps with ease. It felt strange to give the mental orders and feel that they went through, and then have his legs disobey him.

He saw the steps rushing toward his face and put up his hands to protect it. As he hit, he was conscious of the numb feeling from his chest down. It was as if his whole body had suddenly gone to sleep.

From some impersonal, logical well of the subconscious the knowledge emerged that a bullet had broken his spine and crushed all the nerves that controlled his body from the heart down.

Some will other than his own seemed to take control of his arms and force them to drag his body down the steps into the basement.

He heard a muffled roar and a whine of a bullet smashing the lock on the basement door. Footsteps sounded behind him, coming down the stairs toward him. He kept his face down, trying to hide his identity as long as possible. His arms kept reaching forward and grasping the edge of the next step and pulling his dead body downward.

The steps behind him stopped. The silence was ominous. He never heard the shot that entered the back of his neck and tore out a large part of his face.

"NOW DON'T be alarmed, lady," the man said to Sister Anna, closing the basement door and standing with his back to it to prevent her from going past him. "He was a very dangerous criminal we were after," I recognized him as he came in the hospital and waited for him. He tried to escape and I shot him in the line of duty."

He pulled out a billfold and showed her police credentials. Sister Anna looked at them numbly, nodding her head.

"That's better," he said sympathetically. "Now just go back in your office with me while I phone. O.K.?"

Sister Anna turned obediently and walked back to her office with bowed head. The officer followed her through the door.

"Well! Quite a gathering!" he exclaimed as he saw the others. His eyes rested briefly on each face. Harvey held his breath as they touched on him, and expelled it slowly as they passed on.

"One of you better go stand guard over the body of the man on the basement stairs while I phone," he said curtly. "The rest of you better stay here."

Harvey looked at the grief stricken faces around him and muttered. "I'll go." He left the room before anyone could object.

On the basement stairs he stopped beside the still form that wore his suit. A dark stain had spread over the back of the coat. There was a dark hole at the base of the skull.

He took the head carefully by the hair and lifted it until he could see the face. A high powered dum-dum must have been used. When Harvey saw what it had done a bitterness chilled him. He was safe now. But at a terrible price. The police would never be able to find out they had shot the wrong man.

Fifteen minutes later the body was lifted into a basket and carried out of the hospital to a waiting police ambulance to be hauled to the morgue. The look in the eyes of the priests and nuns tore at Harvey's heart.

Sister Anna, her eyes dull and lifeless, answered the officer's questions, answered his remarks, and served as spokesman for the rest of them.

When the police left she turned to Harvey.

"You had better go now," she said. "There's a car and driver waiting for you in the hospital garage that will take you to your friends."

The lids dropped to hide the grief in her eyes. She turned her back to him.

Sister Lenora looked at him pleadingly with bright eyes, brimming with tears.

"Goodbye," she formed the word soundlessly with her lips, her face a pale mash.

There was nothing he could say.

He turned and left.

"MIGHT as well relax, Father," the chauffeur said as the car crossed the floating bridge to Mercer Island. "It will take a good three hours to cover the four hundred and fifty miles to that spot where you're going."

Harvey closed his eyes. The sight of the face of the dead priest on the stairway rose before him. He opened his eyes quickly. He kept them open for the whole trip.

The car kept to the transcontinental highway through the states of Washington and Idaho. In Montana it turned off onto a state highway, and finally onto a dirt road. The dirt road passed through a small town after a few miles. There was only a store or two and a few houses, all badly in need of a visit from a paint salesman.

It passed through the town and wound in and out through densely wooded, rolling country. There were bad places in the road where spring rains had washed it away and summer winds had tried to fill it in again.

"About all this place is good for is a summer retreat of you fathers who need a vacation," the chauffeur spoke up politely. "Good fishing in the stream, they tell me. Too bad I have to get back to Seattle today. Wouldn't mind staying here a few days myself."

The car turned off the dirt road into a better preserved pair of worn ruts in the woods. This went back for half a mile and opened abruptly into a clearing.

A large log lodge nestled homily in the trees. Smoke rose in lazy spirals from a cobblestone chimney that spread out flat against the end of the lodge to form the back of what must be a fireplace inside.

The front door opened and George, Alice, and Helen came out on the porch.

Harvey opened the car door and climbed out hurriedly, rushing toward the trio. They stared at him politely as he took the steps two at a time.

The reason for this suddenly dawned on Harvey. He pulled the wart loose and threw it away. Their eyes widened in surprised recognition.

"Harvey!" Helen cried. She was in his arms in one swift movement. He was rustling her hair and grinning at George over her shoulder. Then he pulled her head away from him and held it between his hands as he feasted his eyes on every detail of her lovely face.

He suddenly remembered the chauffeur and turned to see what he was doing. The car had turned around and was going back the way it had come.

Alice and Helen began interrupting each other to tell him how much they had been worried about him, and how two priests had found them and brought them to this place.

Harvey told them haltingly what had happened.

Afterwards, the spell was broken by a large-hipped, florid-faced woman who radiated good-natured country personality as she opened the front door of the lodge and announced that dinner was ready.

Harvey realized suddenly that he was quite hungry. He glanced at his watch and saw that it was two o'clock, and he hadn't eaten since breakfast.

The massive construction of the log lodge house was restful. A faint murmur of cascading water filtered through the pine trees outside, and now and then the wind rustled the trees with a soughing, restful music.

Helen watched his features, strained and tense with what he had gone through, slowly relax into smooth lines. She saw his eyes become youthful again as the memory of the dead Father Reed retreated from consciousness under the soothing spell of her presence.

All too swiftly the shadows of dusk lengthened into the all pervading darkness of night and the housekeeper waddled down from upstairs to order them all to bed.

As she climbed into her bed she wondered why it was that in the country the beds seemed so much larger than in the city, and so much more comfortable. The window in her room rattled noisily with the wind, and the soughing of the trees had taken on a new, whining tone.

She reached over her head and turned out the bedlamp, and lay with her eyes wide open in the dark. Mysterious creakings came to her ears from other parts of the lodge. The rattling of the window became angry and scolding. The trees were alternately moaning and screaming as the wind gained in force...

THE SCREEN door slammed with a report like that of a gun. She suddenly became aware that she was bending over a pan of hot biscuits, sticking a straw from the broom in them to see if they were done. She straightened up and turned to see who had come in. It was Tom, her son. He was twelve years old. His black hair was tousled, one pant leg hanging down, the other neatly tucked up. There was a hole in the knee of one black stocking.

"He's skinned his knee again," she thought. She looked down at her own front and was surprised to see that she was wearing a skirt that went all the way to the floor.

Something strange about Tom made her look at him sharply. His face was unusually pale.

"Come here, darling," she ordered him.

He backed away from her defensively. She reached out a quick hand and seized his shirtsleeve.

"You can't get away from me that easily, youngster," she chided.

She felt of his forehead. It was hot and feverish.

"Ah ha!" she snorted. "Don't you know it's very foolish to try to hide it when you're ill? It's bed for you and some nice medicine."

"Ah," Tom wailed. "I'm not sick. I don't want to go to bed. I don't need any medicine..."

"Now this won't be bad at all," she coaxed. Tom pulled the covers over his face. She pulled them back down.

"You take some." Tom suggested cunningly.

"All right," Helen said. "I will."

The fluid in the bottle was a thick brownish syrup. The label covered one whole side of the flat bottle. Helen poured some of the fluid into a tablespoon very carefully so as not to spill it.

She put the spoon to her lips. The medicine tasted bitter, but the sugar in it gave it a rather pleasant taste, she thought.

"You may rest assured, madame," a smooth voice was saying, "That this medicine will do all I claim for it."

The word "madame" thrilled her. The peddler was so distinguished looking in his checkered suit, and she was only seventeen. She giggled nervously under the frankly admiring look in his eyes.

"I think I'll buy it," she said, trying to sound very mature. "How much is it Mr.—"

How did she know his name? Why, of course! It was on the bottle...

The face was only inches from her eyes. She tried to focus it, but it remained blurred. A dull ache throbbed in her head. She knew she was going to die.

The face came into focus for a brief instant. It was the doctor. Why was the doctor there? Was she sick? She must be, she thought.

"What's this?" she heard the doctor's voice speak sharply. "Huh! That patent medicine again. Darn funny. Henrietta had some of the same stuff on her stand. Just came from there. Same symptoms. I'd say they were both poisoned by this stuff. Throw it away. She'll be all right by morning. Somebody ought to catch up with that fellow and tar and feather him for selling poison like this."

"No please!" She sat up in bed, the movement sending waves of torture through her skull. "Don't throw it away," she added weakly. I won't take any more of it. I promise."

"Then why in tarnation do you want to keep it?" the doctor asked, exasperated.

The vision of the handsome stranger calling her madame... How could she tell the doctor that she wanted to keep it as a reminder of the first man who had looked at her as a woman?

"I—I," she hesitated. "I want to keep the bottle."

"Well, that's different," the doctor said. "But pour that stuff out. It's poison."

Poison...

It gurgled as it gulped out of the bottle and stained the dirt. A few drops splashed on her skirt. She giggled guiltily.

"I'd better wash the bottle out before I put it in my chest," she thought. Lifting her skirt with one hand so that it just cleared the weeds and grass along the path to the creek she hop-skipped happily.

The cool, swift water of the creek tugged at the bottle with kittenish playfulness. The surface eddies around her wrist distorted the label on the bottle so that it was difficult to make out the name on it.

She squinted her eyes, trying to puzzle it out. And there was a face looking out of the water at her. It was a reflection. A MAN was standing behind her, looking down at her!

She half turned and looked up without rising. She could feel her heart pounding painfully against her ribs. She KNEW it was the peddler, come back.

But when her eyes looked up, it wasn't the peddler. It was George Granville. It was the idiot George, and there was an ugly wound on the side of his head.

A single stream of blood dropped down to disappear under the collar of his shirt. His eyes had the soft surface look of something that had died. They looked at her without seeming to actually see her.

She rose slowly to a standing position. The bottle was still in her hand. The bottle was very important. She felt that strongly.

The idiot George held out his hand. He wanted it. He didn't say so, but she knew he wanted it.

She held it behind her and backed away from him. She felt her shoes fill with water. The swift current of the stream was pulling at her skirt. It was raining, and idiot George was bending toward her, blood all over his head.

It made her feel strange—as though she had been through it before in exactly the same way. But she had!

HER EYES opened. She was lying in bed. The screaming of the wind was trying to rise above the pounding of the rain on the roof. Memory came back in a flood.

She got out of bed and closed the window. Then she turned on the bed lamp. The rain had come in and formed a wet spot that went halfway across the room.

There was no thunder and lightning. She was thankful for that, at least. An ironic smile twisted her lips. It seemed that every time there was a storm she had a dream.

"And what a dream," she muttered aloud.

There was an electric clock on a small table on the other side of the room from the bed. Its hands pointed to ten after three. A worried frown appeared on her face. She glanced at the bed doubtfully.

The worried frown was replaced by a stubborn determination. She crossed the room and opened the door to the hall. The door to George's room was just across from hers. She knocked determinedly on it.

It seemed to her that everyone must have been wide-awake. Not only did George come to the door, but Alice appeared in her doorway, and a moment later Harvey stuck his head out of his, too.

She looked at them in triumphant silence while they stared at her sleepily. Then she made her announcement with the air of dropping a bombshell.

"I've had another dream," she said firmly.

There was a full minute of dead silence. It was broken by Alice who began to laugh.

"What are you laughing at?" Helen asked, a trifle angry.

"You!" Alice said between laughs. "At this time of the night we are awakened. You stand in the hall in your nightgown and solemnly announce that you've had another dream. I can't help it, Helen. Please don't be angry." She went off into another wave of laughter.

George and Harvey had been looking at her keenly.

"Let's go down to the kitchen and fix some coffee," George said seriously. "This I want to hear."

Alice stopped laughing abruptly. "What is it, Helen?" she asked with quiet seriousness. "Are we in danger?"

"No," Helen answered. "Did it ever occur to any of you that whoever made the stuff we all took way back in 1848 must have taken it too? That he is also an immortal?"

CHAPTER FOURTEEN

HELEN FELT strangely aloof from herself as she walked down the rough board stairs to the rambling front room of the lodge, and across its bearskin rugs and its oval shaped braid rugs to the swinging door that led to the kitchen.

She felt disembodied, as though she were a spirit keeping pace with her body, but apart from it. George led the way, his broad back bobbing in a way that advertised the tremendous strength of his shoulders. Alice and Harvey flanked her, each with a hand tucked protectively under one of her elbows.

Her dominant emotion was one of fatalism. At that moment her face would not have betrayed any other emotion if the whole world had suddenly gone mad.

In the kitchen she sat down woodenly and watched George make a pot of coffee. She concentrated every iota of her attention on his movements, forcing her thoughts to concern themselves with nothing else. She worried over the amount of grounds he put in, tried to estimate whether there was enough water for the amount of grounds, tried to estimate whether the grounds were drip, regular, or what.

She sniffed delicately, trying to catch the aroma, and decided the grounds were stale. She speculated on whether the water was soft or hard and decided it must be hard water in this part of Montana.

She watched the water as it began to have heat swirls in it. She watched it begin to shoot on its circuit in the coffee maker, watched the transparent water take on an uneven brown stain that quickly became a darker, more even color. She watched the slow pulsing of the ground glass heart valves of the coffee maker.

She watched the color of the water become the same shade as that of the glass where it indicated it was time to shutoff the heat. Her eyes watched George's large hands, so strong and steady, reach lazily to shutoff the butane flame.

She watched the coffee grow a deeper color than the shutoff color and approach the proper strength. She watched the heart valves slow their palpitation and finally lie still, while the coffee drained into the bottom, leaving the grounds wet and dripping.

She watched George pick up the coffee maker and tip it to fill the cups that Alice had set on the table from their place in a wall cupboard.

In her heart she felt that after this night the world would go on as it always had, ignorant of the gift of immortality that had almost been showered on its peoples.

She had always pitied Agnes, who grew old and hated her for remaining ever young. She had ached for the power to give Carl the gift of immortality so that he could always be with her. But now she envied them. She envied Agnes her aging. She envied Carl his well spent life and his passing when his allotted span was done. She envied his peaceful sleep that would never by interrupted by dreams bred of storms.

Then she felt their eyes on her as they waited for her to begin talking. She looked at George with his large, homely, kind face. She looked at Alice with her smooth beauty and spiritual eyes that were so expressive. She looked last at Harvey with his kind, sympathetic devotion.

A pain stabbed at her heart. She reached a hand out impulsively to Harvey and was grateful when he took it and squeezed it reassuringly.

After that she lifted her coffee cup, sipped the hot liquid, and told of her dream. Her voice was a clear emotionless tool as she listened to it recreate the dream in every vivid detail.

SHE FASTENED her eyes on a knot in the wooden surface of the table and kept them there. She did not lift them until she had reached the point where she awakened from her dream.

She didn't lift them then for awhile. She waited. The numb feeling had lifted while she was talking. She felt very much in her body now and a part of it. She could feel the tingle of her leg where it had gone to sleep. She could feel the hotness of the coffee in her throat when she swallowed it.

And she was aware once more of the sounds of wind and rain and the creakings of the building. She knew she was waiting for death to strike and she wanted it to strike swiftly—oh so swiftly. But she didn't want to see it come.

"You have a very remarkable mind." That was George's voice, subdued. "It seems to have a problem solving subconscious that hangs on with bulldog tenacity that never lets go, collecting all the elements of a problem and sorting them and re-sorting them until it finds an answer. When it does the answer seems to come out in a dream. Maybe it doesn't always come out that way; but when the answer contains something that you don't like, I think you must tell your subconscious to shut up. If it feels that it *must* talk it takes the Freudian way, a dream in symbolism that you can accept consciously because you don't understand it."

His strong hand came into the range of her eyes as he poured more coffee in her cup. She looked up at him and smiled timidly.

There was a bleak, almost hawkish look in his eyes. His lips smiled back at her slightly. She looked down at the table again.

"As in your other dream," he went on, "where you refused to identify things, your mind had to use subterfuge. The only truly logical interpretation of your dream is that I, who can't remember my life at the time we all took something that made us immortal, am the one who concocted it and sold it to the rest of us, and that if I could recall that first period of my life before I became a half-wit, I could remember the formula and consequently be able to make the stuff again."

"That's it!" Harvey exclaimed.

"Yes," George said calmly. "It's obvious that the one who made the stuff would remember most of the people he sold it to and put two and two together, if he weren't suffering from loss of memory. That is the only logical explanation. But there is one thing wrong with it."

"What's that?" Alice asked breathlessly.

"If that were the case," George went on. "Helen's subconscious mind would have no reason to resort to tricks to get the knowledge to her conscious mind. It would have come out as a simple thought and she would have told us at once."

"I don't get it," Harvey said.

Helen could feel her body trembling. She put the cup to her lips and let coffee seep slowly into her mouth. The bitter flavor helped her.

"Well look," George explained. "What is there in the dream? There's nothing to indicate that whoever sold Helen that bottle of medicine is now one of the immortals, if we assume that the peddler and myself were not one and the same person. Yet Helen's first remark to us after she said she had had another dream was that the person who sold all of us the bottle of medicine that made us immortal was also one of the immortals. I think I'm safe in saying that she got that idea from the dream. Is that right, Helen?"

"That's right," Helen replied with a quick smile, dropping her eyes again. Her fingers toyed with the handle of the cup as it rested on the table in front of her.

"So it couldn't have been me, when I lived in the days that are a blank in my mind," George said. "That leaves only one alternative.

That alternative is that the peddler came among us recognizing each of us as a customer back in 1848 when he was selling a patent medicine, and put two and two together, deducing that that medicine contained whatever it is that made us all immortal."

Alice gave a whistle of surprise.

"But that would mean—!" Harvey exclaimed.

"Exactly," George finished. "It would mean that since the former peddler didn't come right out and tell about it, it was he who planned how to kill off the rest of us immortals so that he alone would be left."

"But, then—*who?*" Harvey demanded.

"You," George said.

HIS EYES took on a cold, wary gleam as he said this. He still stood as he had before, with one foot on a chair and an elbow resting on the knee, but his casualness had disappeared.

"Me?" Harvey echoed. "Don't be silly."

"Look at Helen and try to deny it," George said curtly.

Harvey's eyes swung to Helen. So did those of Alice and George. For sixty torturing seconds Helen remained with her eyes fixed on the table. Then they lifted slowly, looking into Harvey's, mute and full of a dying, gentle spirit.

"But it isn't true!" Harvey's voice was a hoarse, unbelieving whisper.

"You drove me back to my flat and then took the car to the garage," George said.

"Yes, I did," Harvey said. "But how was I to know that there was a bomb planted?"

"The residences of all the immortals in Chicago were bombed, but no attempt was made to kill Helen," George continued, his voice dull.

"You said the police were watching my room at the hotel," Helen spoke up for the first time. "Why didn't they stop you when you showed up?"

"Why—why, I don't know. They just didn't," Harvey said.

"Where did the papers get the pictures of me and Helen?" George asked. "And why didn't they print yours too?"

"Wait a minute," Harvey said. "Helen. Who did the peddler in the dream look like?"

"You." Her lips formed the word, but no sound came out.

"And do you actually remember me as that peddler in real life?" Harvey demanded tensely.

Helen looked puzzled.

"That isn't important," George insisted. "How could she remember after over a century a face she saw for only a few minutes?"

"No, I can't," she had to admit.

"It is important," Harvey said. "Can you remember the bottle, Helen? Did you put it away in your chest?"

"I can't remember the bottle either," Helen confessed, her look of bewilderment increasing.

"What was it you said about dreams, George?" Harvey asked, a desperate grin on his face. "Wasn't it that a dream brings out in acceptable symbols that which the conscious mind would reject otherwise?"

George nodded grimly.

"Then we can say that the bottle is a symbol," Harvey said vehemently. "And I in the role of the peddler am a symbol too!"

"That sounds logical to me," Alice spoke up.

"Not to me," George said quietly. "It stands to reason that whatever we all took must have come in a bottle."

"Maybe it did," Harvey said coolly. "But there's one thing we've all taken for granted, which may not be so at all. We've taken it for granted that Helen's subconscious mind has actually solved the mystery of the substance we all took. Her subconscious may be mistaken. In that case her dream doesn't amount to anything."

"Maybe you're right," George said.

"No," Helen said firmly, her lip trembling slightly as her eyes looked at each of them. "The dream came from memories as well as subconscious logical processes. I feel sure of that."

"Well, anyway," Alice said, yawning. "It's four o'clock in the morning, and we're all running around in circles without getting anywhere. Suppose we go back to bed and sleep on it. Then we can study the problem with fresh minds in the morning."

"I think the original idea is the truth," Harvey said positively. "I think you were the one that started the whole thing, George, and if you could only remember the past it would all come out."

"We can go into that too in the morning," Alice said cheerfully, "Come on. Let's go to bed. Helen, you come in and sleep with me. The storm's still going strong and I want to be on hand if you have any more nightmares."

She put her arm around Helen's waist as Helen stood up, and the two women went ahead up the stairs with George and Harvey following.

THE GIRLS paused at the door to Alice's room. Harvey passed them and stopped at his door. George turned out the lights and came up last, pausing at his door. There was a feeble night light in the hall ceiling that cast enough light for them all to see.

"George," Harvey said. The way he said it caused the girls to turn and look at him queerly.

"Yes, Harvey," George answered wearily.

"Are you *sure* you can't remember anything of your life before those kids hit you on the head in that village? There is a possibility, you know, that you can, and have kept it secret. Then the murder of the immortals could be laid at *your* door, in the same way you tried to lay it at mine." Harvey opened his door. He smiled bleakly at Helen.

"I'd suggest," he said coldly, "that you barricade your door. It seems that one of us two is in all probability the most cold-blooded murderer in all history. And I would like to point out that if it were I, I certainly wouldn't have taken such trouble to have George's memory restored by an operation."

He watched the effect of his words for a silent moment.

"I might add," he went on quietly, "that you barricade your door. You see, that it was the only case of double amnesia he had ever heard of, and there was nothing in medical history to account for it."

With that he stepped into his room.

The click of the door latch, and the noise of the bolt sliding into place as he locked the door seemed unusually loud in the pregnant silence of the hall.

Helen and Alice looked at George with a light of dawning, horrible doubt. They backed into their room. George watched them without any change of expression. He watched the door after it closed. He heard the lock turn. He saw the knob wiggle and tilt slightly as a chair was wedged under it inside.

He stood there even then, shaking his head in a bewildered manner. Finally he took one step toward the girls' room, hesitated, and, seeming to make up his mind, went back downstairs.

Ten minutes later he came back up. Under his arm was an automatic rifle that had been stored away in a closet. In his hand was a box of shells.

He looked speculatively at Harvey's door, then entered his own room. He left his door slightly ajar.

The small light in the ceiling cast its feeble rays in the vacant hall. From the girls' room came the faint murmur of voices. A two-inch ribbon of black at George's door revealed nothing of what might be just inside. If George were waiting there, rifle ready, he could command the full length of the hall.

The sound of the wind outside had died down to an occasional whisper. The rain had stopped. The window at the far end of the hall was beginning to turn transparent with the first light of early dawn.

From a great distance came the crowing of a rooster, the sound seeming unusually sharp and clear in the washed atmosphere.

CHAPTER FIFTEEN

"WELL…" Alice said cheerily, "no doubt we've all thought of nothing but Helen's dream and what it might mean. Now suppose we relax and discuss it without any more accusations, and try to determine what it really means."

The sun was directly overhead. The four were standing on the bank of the swift mountain stream that passed near the lodge. They had by common consent refrained from bringing up the subject of the dream during breakfast while the cook was within earshot.

After breakfast Alice, who seemed to have taken the lead in things, suggested they all walk down to the stream where they could be alone.

The ground was wet from the rain of the night. The needle leaves of the pines and firs were glistening fresh. Large wood ferns shed drops of moisture, and here and there were a spot of blue, yellow, or indigo that came from the bloom of some wild flower.

"There are a few questions I'd like to ask you about your dream, Helen," George said. "The way I appeared to you when you turned around at the bank of that stream—was I dressed as I was when you and Alice found me after the apartment house blew up?"

"No," Helen answered slowly. "You were dressed like people used to dress back in the eighteen-fifties."

"Was I dressed like the peddler?" George persisted.

"I couldn't say as to that," Helen replied. "You were dressed much the same. I can't say what the differences were. For one thing, the peddler's clothes were very neat while yours were torn and mussed."

"Yet there was something about that particular part of the dream that made you wake up," George said.

"Yes," Helen agreed positively. "I've been trying to pin that down. It may be that it was so similar to when we rescued you in the storm that the resemblance is what made it seem familiar."

"There's another possibility," George said quietly. "It's possible that you met me or saw me during that period of my life that's blank."

"I thought of that, too," Helen said. "I've tried to recall. But I can't even vaguely remember seeing you before I met you in Chicago."

"Can you remember the peddler?" Harvey spoke up.

"I've tried all night to remember him," Helen said. "I can't. All I can remember of his face from the dream is impressions. When I don't try, I'm sure I could see his face just as clearly as in real life; but when I try, the features fade and I can't pin them down. A hat and a collar have a lot to do with a face. I feel sure the peddler wore a flat straw hat and a starched wing collar. Either of you two would look different with those on than you do without them. And even the haircuts in those days were different."

"That's true," Harvey said. "Maybe we could scrape up a straw hat and a starched wing collar someplace later on."

"There's one thing that strikes me," George said. "The doctor said that somebody ought to catch the peddler and tar and feather him. When I appear in the dream I have fresh blood on my head, trickling down under my collar. Before Helen turned to see me she thought I might be the peddler, but when she looked at me she felt sure I wasn't. She's known me as two people who are George, the idiot-George, and me. I was obviously the idiot-George in the dream, so it's possible that the dream in that respect is true memory. I might have been the peddler. I might have been caught up with and attacked. That might be what caused my first case of amnesia. Her distinct impression of my not being the peddler might simply indicate that she recognized I was changed, rather than that I was a distinctly different individual."

"CAN YOU remember the shape of the bottle or anything else about it?" Harvey asked. "That could be very significant. Bottles in those days were much different than the mass production bottles of the twentieth century."

"I can remember that the label on the bottle was pasted on a flat, sunken area," Helen said. "It had a lot of engraving on it, fine, curved lines like a bank note. At the top was a name in large black letters. The first part of the name was definitely a G, an R, an A, and an N. I'm quite sure there wasn't enough space left to spell out Granville, though."

"How sure are you that the first letter wasn't a T?" George asked quickly. "In those days a capital T was very ornate, with long heavy droopings from the cross bar."

"Yes," Harvey cut in. "And if the r, a, and n were not capitals the small a and the e in those days were easily confused. The name, Trent, could have fitted into a small space."

"Take it easy, Harvey," George said mildly. "We're just trying to consider every possibility and eliminate a few as we go along."

A startled look had come into Helen's eyes.

"Shut up you two," Alice said, holding up a hand for silence.

"I remember now," Helen said in an awed tone. "The name was all in capitals, and it was Grant! GRANT'S HOME REMEDY!"

A wistful smile flashed briefly on her tense face.

"Guaranteed to cure colds, coughs, rheumatism, and all kinds of fevers, besides drying up boils and carbuncles and softening up corns. When mixed with mustard it makes an excellent poultice. Spread on heavy paper it makes excellent flypaper after being allowed an hour to partially dry. I—I still have the bottle, too, It's in one of my trunks in storage in Dubuque."

"What!" Harvey said. "Then the bottle is real?"

Helen nodded.

"I can remember that stuff," Alice said. "It made me sick when I took some too." She frowned. "Unfortunately, my mother is the one who bought it, so I never saw the peddler."

"Grant." George whispered.

"Very much like Trent," Harvey said bitterly. "Why don't you ask me the obvious question, George?"

"It's also very much like Granville," George said, ignoring Harvey's remark. "You know, it's possible I got the name of the town and my name a little confused after I recovered my memory. It's all very vague now. I'd have to look at a map to even recall the name of the town where I was village idiot so long ago."

"Well, let's do that right now," Alice said excitedly. "We seem to be on the track of something definite."

Ten minutes later they were studying a map of New Hampshire in a much worn Atlas. In less than a minute Alice's finger pounced on the map. The point of her fingernail touched at the lettering, Danville.

"That's the name of the town, all right," George said in amazement. Grant, and Danville. No wonder I got them confused and thought my name was Granville. They gave me a railroad ticket to Manchester and I never went back."

"I lived in Andover, Massachusetts, in 1848," Helen said, tense with excitement. The railroad, this red line on the map shows the railroad. Let's see. Number 20. Up here in the corner it gives the list of railroads. Number twenty's the Boston and Maine! You could have gone on it up to Newton Junction and been kicked off, and then wandered around, winding up in Danville or South Danville where you stayed. Or you could have simply tramped over the country and wound up there."

"IT ALL adds up," George said with finality. "I was the peddler. The stuff that made us immortal was GRANT'S HOME REMEDY."

"Good for making homemade flypaper," Alice said softly.

"Can you remember anything about it now?" Harvey asked.

George shook his head in the negative.

"If we could go back there and I could see Danville I could at least refresh my memory on that," he said. "Maybe, with my name, we could look up records. There might even be a patent giving the formula for the patent medicine, though it isn't likely."

"More than likely," Harvey said, smiling, "you just threw a few things into some sugar syrup and had some fancy labels printed, and hoped the stuff wasn't harmful."

"I might not even remember what I put in it if I could remember doing it," George answered Harvey's smile with one of his own. "At any rate, the four of us alone have reached the end of research project one…"

He looked thoughtfully at Helen.

"I wish I had a mind that worked like yours," he added. "If I had, my subconscious would be starting to work with the clues we've unearthed, and would bridge the connection with the past so that I could at least find out something about it in a dream."

"Perhaps it can, George," Helen said confidently. "The doctor removed that piece of bone that was pressing on your brain. There should be nothing there to stop the bridging of the gap with the past unless the brain tissue itself were damaged permanently."

"It's our only hope," Alice said pleadingly. "We can't travel to New Hampshire. We'd be caught. If we could find out right here what the substance was that gave us immortality, we wouldn't need to run any risks. We could hide away someplace and make that substance and give it to thousands of people in candy bars or something else. In a few years the search for us would drop completely. We could publish the formula and give it to the world. Then nothing could stop us."

"Grant!" Harvey said. "George Grant! Can't that strike even a sensation of familiarity in you, George?"

"Grant's Home Remedy!" Helen said anxiously. "Think about it. Try to grab onto even the faintest whisper of a thought about it. If you can reach into the past and get even one true memory of it you may be able to use that to break down the barrier and remember everything."

George shook his head in bewilderment.

"I'll try," he said.

"If might take weeks," Helen said confidently. "If you keep brooding on it and thinking about it, it'll come."

"There's a lot of things I don't understand about this," George said. "Why, when the operation was performed, did the idiot-George have amnesia? If, as you say, by brooding on this I can find a connecting link with a set of memories that were blocked off by an accident that turned me into an idiot, why can't I also bridge the gap to idiot-George? And why, Harvey, did the doctor say there were no known cases of double amnesia?"

"Yes!" Alice exclaimed, turning to Harvey. "What did the doctor say about that? He must have talked to you about that when I wasn't listening."

"WE talked about that when I was up in Seattle trying to get him to go down and operate," Harvey explained. "What he said, as nearly as I can remember, was that since very little was known about amnesia, and there were so many different causes, probably double amnesia was possible, just as possible as single amnesia. The reason there were no known cases of it was probably because the circumstances in one life leading to amnesia stood about as much chance of being repeated and producing three separate sets of memory as a coin has of standing on edge when thrown into the air and allowed to fall on the floor."

"Oh." Alice said.

"The reason I asked," George said slowly, "is because we have assumed that because I was a village idiot, and got hit on the head and became sensible and intelligent, and became an idiot after being hit on the head. I've always assumed that myself. Yet if that is the case, then why can't I remember?"

He closed the Atlas and leaned on the table.

"Let's assume that I was always an idiot until I got hit on the head in 1905, sixty-nine years ago," he went on. "What evidence is there to support that? First, we have an expert opinion from a brain surgeon that double amnesia is about as probable as it is for a man to play poker for a lifetime without getting anything except straight flushes. Other evidence occurs to me, now that I've thought of that possibility. In cases of amnesia I've read about, the victim forgot his identity and the experiences of his past life, but still was able to speak and to use the vocabulary of that past life. Yet *I had to learn to read and write.* As I recall it now, my vocabulary was very limited. My greatest difficulty was in acquiring a vocabulary that consisted of words a normal person would learn early in life. My landlady used to remark about that."

He gave a humorous chuckle.

"I can still hear her voice as she would exclaim, 'My lands alive, George! One would think before you got the knock on your head that made you a village idiot you hadn't a speck of learning!' And maybe she was right."

The others were staring at him amazed at the startling possibility that seemed more and more probable as they thought it over.

"So you see," George shrugged his shoulders helplessly. "The assumption that I had an early life before I was an idiot has never been anything more than an assumption with nothing to actually prove or support it. I may have had, of course. But it may have been brief. I may have been injured at birth or during my first two or three years of life, so that when I got that hit on the head in Danville that early injury to the brain was repaired. If that's so, how could I recall memories now of those years? Can any of you remember after a century and a half what you knew or what you experienced during your first three years of life?"

They shook their heads mutely. "So," George sighed. "The question comes up in that case—when and how did I get a dose of Grant's Home Remedy?"

THERE was a startled exclamation from Helen. Her eyes were wide and staring as she looked at George. "I remember now," she said in a horrified voice. *"You took the bottle away from me.* You held out your hand and leered at me and mumbled something about giving it to you. I did. It was full of water, but the medicine was thick and a lot of it had stayed in the bottle and you shook up the bottle and drank every bit of it. Then you dropped the bottle and wiped your mouth with your sleeve and went away. I was afraid to move until you were gone. Then I picked up the bottle and ran to the house."

"And thus," George shrugged philosophically. "We see the futility of trying to interpret dreams. That part of your dream wasn't symbolism, based on a memory of me coming from the wreck of my apartment; but a fragment of a true memory, lost in the dim recesses of the storehouse of your mind."

"Brought into the dream," Alice put in wonderingly in a hushed voice, "by that simply wonderful subconscious of yours...Helen...that put two and two together and got four."

"Well," Harvey said bitterly. "There goes our one chance of finding out what went into Grant's Home Remedy. There still remains the question of how you got the name Grant, George."

"Funny thing," George said, a faraway look in his eyes. "I can remember that myself now. You were wearing a white and red checkered dress. A bonnet of the same colors. Your face was awfully white and your eyes were almost perfectly round. The bottle fell on a cluster of buttercups and I felt bad about that. I loved the buttercups."

His eyes seemed to cloud over. Then they snapped back to the present.

"Yes," Helen whispered. "Yes, I can remember that too. That was the dress I was wearing. That was the bonnet."

George was grinning strangely, a wild gleam in his eyes. He gave a short laugh. He repeated it a little louder. It became a frenzied, prolonged laugh that made the chills run. He had both doubled fists resting on the table, his body bent forward, his head bent back. The mad laughter echoed from the walls and rafters of the large room.

The three spectators were as frozen statues, watching.

The mad laughter stopped abruptly. George dropped into the chair just behind him and cupped his head in his arms. His shoulders shook with sobs. He was crying.

Alice came to life. With a look of intense pity she came to him and put her arms on his shaking shoulders and buried her face in the crook of his shoulder and cried with him. Her body seemed frail and small against his huge shoulders.

Helen and Harvey remained motionless, stunned.

The emotional storm ended as abruptly as it had begun. George emitted a long sigh and straightened up.

"I'm all right now," he said wanly. His eyes turned to Alice, a tender look in them. "You loved idiot-George just as much as you do me, didn't you!" he exclaimed.

Alice blushed in confusion.

"I *know*," George said quietly. "You see, I remember everything now."

HE WAITED until full realization of this sunk in. There are some things too great for the human mind to grasp all at once. This was one of those things. Harvey, Helen and Alice had known both Georges well. For them to become one had seemed as impossible as for two different people in different bodies to suddenly become one person, mentally and physically.

It was something too startling to grasp. They knew from experience that a normal person can go into an insane rage, or get drunk, and behave like an utterly different person, though they are still the same person just the same. Abstractly, if they ever thought of it, they must have known that the self of the idiot-George and the mentally alert George were identical, and that the behavior patterns, memories, and reasoning powers of the two were all that distinguished them from each other.

These were no more startlingly different than those of the kind, easygoing gentlemen who under an intense emotional change acts under an entirely different behavior pattern. Such a person, remembering his behavior under such circumstances, might claim he wasn't himself, but he knows that he actually was himself. He might wonder at his behavior when he wasn't "himself." His actions as remembered might seem utterly strange and unreal. They are memories of *his* actions, just the same.

In the same way the flood of memory of the idiot-George had rushed in to become a part of the mass-memory of George. It was an emotional shock. Yet after the first terrible moment had passed it was possible for him to draw on those memories with calmness, and know that they were *his* memories, just as vividly and factually his as were those of the other part of his life.

The alchemy of their blending was not something that could be completed at the same instant it began. It was more analogous to the meeting of two different individuals who, by long hours and days of continual conversational exchange with nothing held back and questions instantly answered at the moment of asking, become completely acquainted with each other and in complete sympathy with each other. Placed on a strictly mental level without need of vocal cords and ears for this exchange, it would be more thorough and rapid. That was the only difference in that one respect.

Already, while George waited for the shock of surprise to fade from the faces of his friends, he was appreciating the behavior, point of view, innocent philosophy, and every other flavor of the memories flooding into consciousness. He was quick to comprehend that idiot-George had been quite a psychologist in his own way, and far from an idiot in many respects. This rapid mental panorama caused smiles to flicker on and off on his face so that perhaps he gave the impression of being more the idiot than the man. It was only by great effort that he kept from chuckling in genuine enjoyment and appreciation of the qualities of his "other" self.

George found himself after a time holding Alice's hand. He found himself talking calmly, too.

Helen and Harvey listened to George's quiet voice. Alice took longer. George had been talking for fully five minutes when she suddenly exclaimed, "Oh, George! I'm sorry. I haven't heard a word you said."

She straightened up and smiled, one hand wiping at the tears of joy that dampened her cheeks.

GEORGE stopped in the middle of a word. His eyes caressed her tenderly.

"I said," he smiled. "That I know how to make Grant's Home Remedy."

Alice struggled off his lap onto her feet and sat down on a chair weakly.

"Go—go on," she whispered.

"I'll begin at the beginning again," George said with an exaggerated sigh of patience.

"All right, George. I'll pay attention this time," Alice said meekly.

"I know how to make Grant's Home Remedy because I used to watch my father make it," he announced calmly.

"Your father?" Alice gasped.

"Yes," George answered. "Alex Potocki, my father."

"Alex Potocki?" Alice exclaimed.

"I'm sorry," George apologized. "Just hang onto your chair, darling. It may come out all mixed up, but I'll tell you everything. You see, as far back as I can remember I was told I didn't have good sense."

His eyes held a faraway, wistful look.

"My mother died when I was somewhere around fifteen, I think. My father always blamed her openly and abusively for my condition. His name in those days was Alfred Grant. My mother's name was Mary.

"As nearly as I can analyze now, my so-called idiocy or lack of good sense consisted basically of a slowness or response between mind and body. Words took too long to register on my mind. After they registered my mind seemed to go into a sort of stuttering paralysis in any attempt to talk or act. As far back as I can remember I can hear my father telling me I didn't have good sense. I came to believe it was true and acted accordingly. Maybe I didn't have. All I can remember of my mother is her thin pale face and her large, dark, tragic eyes. That was the way she always looked, and that's the way she died.

"Paw, as I called Alex, was a very cruel man inside. Outside he was smooth and very suave. He was a ladies' man. He got the idea of selling a patent medicine after my mother died.

"I can remember him bringing home the bottles, it seems now like there were thousands of them, and maybe there were."

George chuckled dryly.

"He was the only person that could ever make me work. He had me out digging up dandelion roots by the bushel for this home remedy. He said he figured they were a good tonic.

"He had gotten hold of a huge hog kettle to make the stuff. After I cleaned the roots to his satisfaction he would dump them in and let them boil and boil. I think we spent a whole day on that.

He wanted the medicine to taste like medicine and be fairly thick so people couldn't say it was nothing but colored water. It took a whole day of boiling to make him realize it wouldn't thicken.

"The next morning he made a screen of cheese cloth and strained the hog kettle full of dandelion soup into a couple of wash tubs. That got rid of the roots. Then he dumped the liquid back in the hog kettle and dumped half a sack of sugar in and cooked it some more. It seemed to satisfy him for thickness when it had boiled for a couple of hours. The taste didn't satisfy him, though.

CHAPTER SIXTEEN

" 'TASTES too good, George, my boy,' he said in high good humor. 'That'll never do in a medicine. Got to have something in it to make it taste bad. But not too bad, though. Otherwise the suspicious souls who insist on a taste before buying will turn it down.' "

"He took a scrap of paper out of his pocket and wrote on it. Then he folded it around a coin and handed it to me.

" 'Run down to the store and get this for me, George,' he ordered sharply. 'Mind you, if you don't run coming and going I'll whip you good with my razor strap! Now get along.'

"He accompanied this with a sharp slap behind that sent me running clumsily. I was back with the sack of white, crystalline lumps, and a feeling of virtue because I had made the trip in the shortest time possible.

"My father took the sack and gave me a couple of sharp looks. I knew he was debating whether he should say I could have made it quicker.

"He reached into the sack and took out one of the lumps. He held it in front of my face.

" 'Alum, George.' he said gloatingly. The stuff that makes your mouth pucker up. But we don't want to overdo it. Can't let it get too bad tasting. Got to put in just one lump at a time and see how it goes.' "

"He dropped the white lump into the hog kettle with an artistic flourish and watched while it sank. I crept up to watch and was sent back with a slap.

" 'I'll tell you when I want you close,' he said mildly.

"He stirred the liquid for several minutes, then took some of it in a teaspoon and tasted it, smacking his lips speculatively over it.

"Three more lumps went into the kettle before he decided it was enough.

" 'That should do it about right,' he finally said. 'But it ought to have something in it to give it some positive effects. Nothing like getting action to convince the people that you have something worth buying again, my boy.'

"I nodded and grinned hopefully. That was one action I could get out quickly enough for it to apply to what had just been said.

" 'Salts!' he exclaimed, holding up his right hand with the index finger extended toward the sky. 'That's what'll give the positive effect the customer wants. Not too much of it or it will give itself away, though.'

"And that's all that went into the concoction. I ran to the store and brought back the salts. My father measured them out as he dumped them in the liquid. I kept my distance from the hog kettle, mindful of my father's too ready hand that could reach out on the slightest pretext and give me a painful slap wherever it happened to land.

"He wouldn't trust me with the job of filling the bottles or pasting on the labels. I tried every way I could to get a taste of what he had made, without success. You see, I didn't have the slightest conception of what he had made. All I knew was that he had gone to a great deal of trouble making it, and it had—a lot of sugar in it.

"He tried to sell it around Boston for awhile without much success.

" 'Too much competition, George, my boy,' was his opinion of Boston. 'We'll have to hit the open road and see the world. There're hundreds of small villages and hamlets where the populace is crying for something that is sweet enough to get down without trouble, and bitter enough to taste like what they think a good medicine should taste like, and with positive enough action to convince them it is doing the work. Think of it, my boy. There are thousands of people dying right this minute who would have lived if they had had something like this to pin their confidence on!"

"THAT KIND of talk, of course, increased my desire to see what it tasted like. I think he wouldn't let me taste it while he was making it just because he liked to exert his authority. After it was bottled it was no longer a liquid to him, but bottled dollars, not to be wasted on the likes of me.

"He managed to get a wagon and a horse somehow. Things like that just happened. The outside world behaved that way to me. There was my own world of interests that consisted of flowers and bugs and an occasional friendly dog. There were my own personal devils, the younger boys, who all reacted in the same way. As soon as they discovered they were much smarter than I would ever be, and that I could be counted on to always run rather than defend myself, they would consistently persecute me.

"I think it gave them a sense of gratifying power to have a human being big enough and strong enough to break their backs whimper like a baby and run from them.

"All that was my personal world. Apart from that was the world of the grownups that I accepted the same way the average person accepts the weather. I couldn't hope to understand the whys and wherefores of it. If punishment descended on my head I merely learned or tried to learn how to avoid it. Otherwise I just ignored it.

"The open country was a revelation to me when we started out one day with the wagon loaded with bottles, a heavy canvas thrown over them. All my life I had known nothing except Boston. I'd been afraid to have kids I knew throw rocks at me and taunt me, but that I feared strangers and strange things.

"Regardless of what sort of man my father was, he was a sanctuary, a star about which my life revolved. So long as he was there in the background of things I found life during that period of wandering a succession of delightful discoveries. I know that, because once when I got lost I degenerated into just a huddling, terrified mass of crying flesh until he found me.

"He became Dr. Grant, the famous Boston physician who had made such a great medicinal discovery that he had given up his very lucrative practice to give it to the world. He passed me off as a ward of his that he had taken under his wing out of the kindness of his heart, and also because he needed a strong back and a weak mind to do the heavy lifting for him.

"I have no idea where we went or how far we traveled from Boston. After awhile it seemed that we had always been living that way. Memories a couple of months old had a way of seeming unreal to me.

"My only really rational world was that of sight. Colors were intensely vivid. Shapes were a poetry of a sort that only an artist can know fully. Colors and shapes were my life. All the rest, words, sounds, muscular control, were things that were extremely difficult to make behave or to understand. I could never explain any of this to anyone, and I suppose that when I saw something particularly delightful like the magic artistry of nature painting a sunset or the strangely wonderful miracle of a carpet of buttercups, to others I was drooling idiotically when in reality I was exclaiming in delight and wonder.

"During all this time I was never once allowed to get a taste of Grant's Home Remedy. The desire to taste it remained and became an obsession.

"More than once when my father was selling I would try to get the cork out of a bottle. My fingers weren't skilled enough to manipulate a corkscrew and the corks were in too far to get a grip on one and pull it without a corkscrew.

"ONCE I broke a bottle over a rock when my father was away, in the hopes that I could salvage some of the liquid inside it. That didn't work. The bottle broke into a dozen pieces and all the contents spilled into the dirt and disappeared before I could get any of it.

"It bothered my conscience so much that I didn't try it again.

"I had lost hope of ever getting a taste of the stuff when one day I was wandering around while my father was selling. At the edge of town there was a row of houses, and in back of them was the ribbon of dense shrubbery and trees that follow a stream of any size.

"I cut through between two houses and started down a path. That was when I saw Helen. She stood there, bent over, with her back to me. She seemed to sense my presence the moment I saw her.

"Standing up, she turned slowly around. In her hand was the open bottle so familiar to me. I wasn't aware she was afraid of me. I don't think it had ever occurred to me that anyone could be afraid of me. I held out my hand pleadingly. I didn't try to say anything. The excitement of seeing an open bottle of the medicine within my grasp had completely paralyzed my vocal cords away.

"She handed me the bottle and I drank every bit of its contents. After that I wandered back into town and found the wagon. An hour or two later my father showed up and we started out for another town.

"That night I got sick for the first time I can ever remember. I was still that way in the morning. Most of the medicine had been sold and there was room enough for me to lay on the wagon bed.

"It took me a week to recover. All that time my father grumbled about having to do all the work of making camp and feeding me. I forgot to say that I had long ago learned that housewives generally took to me. I usually fared better than my father in the way of food, by going to back doors and giving the housewife what I thought was a winning smile and mumbling the one word, 'food'.

"Toward the end I had the feeling that my father was behaving differently toward me. He would squat by his campfire and look at me thoughtfully without saying anything. He seemed to have lost interest in his habit of ordering me around and emphasizing his orders with sharp slaps.

"Then one day in a small town I left him in the morning as usual to wander around and see things. In the late afternoon when I tried to find the wagon where I had left it in the morning it was gone.

"That was the last I saw of my father. I think he had made enough money from the sale of the patent medicine to start in some kind of business. Maybe he went back to Boston. If he did, he didn't have to worry about me ever showing up. I was like a dog or a cat that you take way out in the country and dump. I didn't know how to find my way home. In fact, I think by that time I had completely forgotten about Boston.

"The disappearance of my father was one of those mysterious doings of the grownup world I made no effort to understand. I had gotten over my fear of new places and was I able to keep well fed. In the fall when it would begin to get colder, motherly women would give me warmer clothing. In the spring when it grew too warm for the coats I had worn all winter I would take them off and lose them.

"Life went on much the same, year after year. When one town got tired of me and stopped feeding me I moved on to another. In Danville they never seemed to tire of me. I lived there so long I couldn't remember every having lived any other place.

"The kids and their habit of tormenting me was something I had grown accustomed to. It was like the slappings of my father, just the way a certain section of the rest of humanity acted toward me. I took it stoically, just as I took the food the housewives invariably gave me.

"Then—it happened."

GEORGE stopped talking. The quietness of his talking seemed to persist in the room after the sound of his voice ceased. It was broken finally by Harvey.

"So that's the way it all came about," he said. "Just as simple as that."

"Undoubtedly Alex never realized that you, George Granville, were his half-witted son," Helen said thoughtfully.

"Probably not," George replied. "He never knew I had any of that medicine. When he joined our group he probably realized at once that it was his medicine that had been the cause of our all becoming immortal. He probably recognized enough of us to make that deduction. But he wasn't the type to blurt out all he knew. He gave a fictitious name and kept his mouth shut."

"He had a lot of money when he met up with us," Harvey said. "The research project was his idea. He had something to go on. He knew the ingredients of the original mixture."

"Now that we know them," Alice said brightly. "We can start manufacturing it and making people immortal once more."

"It may not be that simple," George said, frowning. "Did you ever read the story of Jekyll and Hyde? In that story the stuff that caused the transition was some impurity in the chemicals. It may be that way with this. The illness that resulted when we all took some of the stuff may have nothing to do with producing immortality. And when it comes right down to it, how can we know when we do produce immortality. It won't come out for several years, and in some cases not for twenty or thirty years. If we make a lot of Grant's Home Remedy from the formula I remember, we may have nothing at all."

"That's why Alex had to have the research project to find out just what the immortality factor was," Harvey said. "What a diabolical mind. He played along with us so we would bring in all the immortals where he could wipe them out, once he had the identity of the immortality factor, and only he would know what it was."

"But then," Helen spoke up. "Where does my son come in?"

"Tom McCalmont alias Phil Cooger?" George said. "I don't know for sure."

He frowned thoughtfully at the floor.

"I can't see Alex and Cooger working together in this," he finally continued. "If Cooger weren't your son, who at least suspected the existence of the immortals, I might believe he was connected with my father in some way, perhaps as a front while my father was the real mastermind behind his organization. That may even be true. But suppose that Cooger, instead of being in cahoots with Potocki, was actually spying on the whole group of immortals. Suppose that Potocki found the immortality factor beyond question and told no one about it. Suppose Potocki then destroyed Research and all the immortals he could, in an all out surprise move to leave himself in a position to slowly, over the centuries, gain control of the world.

"Cooger, not knowing who did that, would have only the evidence provided by the police and the firemen. He would have a file of pictures and names of all the immortals if he were the least bit thorough. He could show the pictures to witnesses for identification. The firemen or neighbors of mine identified my picture as that of the man who staggered away from the ruins of the apartment house. The hotel people would identify Helen's picture. There would be no picture of Alice yet. Harvey wouldn't be connected with any of it unless he acted suspiciously at the hotel when he asked about Helen, and since his picture wasn't on the front page with ours it seems evident that he was identified then."

"What about those men who followed me?" Harvey asked.

"THE MINUTE the doctor who operated on me reported the location of the lodge they probably sent a plane there," George said. "The plane could have arrived just in time to see your car leave, and get the license number and radio to Olympia to be on the watch for your car. When you reached Olympia they started following you while they waited for instructions. The instructions would be based on the doctor's assertions that there had been four of us. They may have taken in Jerome Dolpin and his wife Martha, your caretakers at the lodge hideout, and given them the third degree or a lie test to find out a few things."

"I see what you mean, George," Harvey said gravely. "Cooger is the political boss of the State of Illinois. It's—"

"Suppose Alex wiped out Research by himself," George took advantage of Harvey's hesitation. "Here's Cooger who has spent a lot of effort in spying on us and knows a lot about us. Maybe a lot more than we think. He would naturally figure immediately that one of the immortals, or a small group of them, wiped out the others for the same reason we figure ourselves. He might not have any indication as to which ones. All he can do is assume that those who were left alive are the guilty ones. He would have every law agency in the country looking for us."

"I see that now," Harvey said. "It casts a different light on the whole thing. If we could get to Cooger and convince him we're innocent we could help him track down Potocki."

"Don't kid yourself on that," George said skeptically. "We can't assume anything like that, at all. If we did we would wind up dead. Even if that is the right answer to what is going on, Cooger would never believe us. If it isn't the right answer, then Cooger and Potocki are together and we would just be playing into their hands."

"Why don't we lay low and work on the medicine formula?" Alice asked. "That's something definite without any risk. In the long run we can get the immortality factor. With luck we might have it in every batch of Grant's Home Remedy we make."

"It would take another Research to find out," George said. "I'll give you a vague idea of the problem the way it stands. First, the stuff was made in a hog kettle, a second hand one. The water used contained impurities we can't know about or duplicate. Such impurities would change in the same source of supply from decade to decade. The substances that made up the iron kettle are unknown and depend on the source of the iron, the past history of the kettle, and a lot of other things. It seems like the sugar, the dandelion roots, the alum, and the salts formed the immortality factor. Alum itself is not a standard chemical, and was less so in 1848. There are alums with no aluminum in them at all. Actually, knowing the formula for the medicine only cuts out a lot of possibilities that would have to be investigated otherwise.

"The immortality factor might not be a chemical with a definite structure. Or if it is, that structure might be so complex we could never analyze the substance. Since it seems obvious Alex found it, we must assume it can be isolated and analyzed. Remember, though; he knew that formula and it took him ten years to isolate the right substance. He had the facilities to eliminate one substance a week, so he must have investigated hundreds."

"We've got to track Alex down and get it from him," Harvey cut in. "There's no other alternative."

"And get caught before we go a hundred miles?" Alice exclaimed.

"We'll have to disguise ourselves carefully," George said. "The best disguise would be age. If we look sixty no one will think we're immortals."

"I think Alice should stay out of this," Helen said. "If she comes along we're putting all our eggs in one basket. If she stays behind and we three get the works, she can devote the rest of her life to searching for IF."

"Nothing doing," Alice said heatedly. "Where George goes I go."

"I think all three of you should stay behind and let me go alone," Harvey said. "I'm officially dead now. If I got killed by Potocki or by the law there would still be the three of you to carry things on."

"We'll all go together," George said quietly. "We four have gone through this much together. We might as well go the rest of the way. I'm sure the future would mean little to any of us if the others were gone for good."

"The four horsemen of the Apocalypse, that's us," Alice said solemnly. She held out her hand, palm down.

With a solemn twinkle in his eyes George placed his under hers. Helen and Harvey placed theirs on top. With the four-way handclasp the bargain was sealed.

CHAPTER SEVENTEEN

AGNES looked from her cards to the face of the man across the table from her. His hair was snow white, combed back carefully. His face had the paleness of one accustomed to living indoors. There was an almost unnoticeable wart on his right cheek just under the eye.

He returned her look with a polite smile, then pursed his lips and looked past her absently.

She dropped her eyes to the stack of chips he had pushed gently into the center of the table a few minutes previously and thought of the many times during the past week he had done the same, and always pulled them back with a stack of her own chips added to them.

Her eyes pulled back to her cards. There were five clubs in her hand. It was draw poker with no limit. She had drawn one card to fill her flush. The man across the table had opened the pot in the first place, and taken three cards on the draw.

She was aware that he must know she had a flush. She knew enough about poker to know that his eyes had analyzed her every move and facial expression. The eagerness with which she must have looked at the card she drew, and the look of satisfaction at finding a club which she was not poker-faced enough to conceal, as far different from the expression she would have shown if she had drawn to two pairs.

She glanced quickly at him once more. His eyes were politely mocking her. Her fingers shook as she counted out the chips to call his bet. When she had them counted out she pushed them into the center quickly before she could change her mind, then spread her hand out face up.

"A flush!" she challenged him, nerves on edge.

She gripped the edge of the table while his eyes coolly inspected her cards.

"So it is," he murmured. "Too bad. I have a full house." He reached across the table and spread his cards beside hers and lazily raked in the chips.

His long, too-white fingers sorted and stacked them neatly before him. His eyes still mocked her in a veiled way. He looked slightly bored.

Agnes bit her lip to hold back the angry words that threatened to come out There were only a few white chips left in front of her.

She shoved back her chair. Clutching her purse with both hands she went across the gambling room to the door marked Office. Her knuckles rapped twice sharply, paused then rapped once more.

Behind her the white haired gentleman had risen and was also crossing the room. He managed to be in a position where he could see into the office as Agnes opened the door.

He had worked a week for this moment. His calm face showed nothing of the emotions beneath. If he made one single suspicious act that would draw the attention of any of the house employees he knew he would never be able to leave the place without being questioned.

That questioning would undoubtedly come around to a close examination of his hair, which would disclose the fact that its whiteness was artificial. From there they would go on until they determined who he was.

The man he saw sitting behind the desk in the office during the brief second Agnes had the door open might even be able to recognize him under his disguise.

IT WAS NOT Phil Cooger, however, that Harvey had waited a week to see. He had seen him many times during that week. It was the inside of that office that he had waited to see, and he was very disappointed.

He continued on toward the doorway leading to the bar. His

going there was very natural. No drinks were served at the table and there was a steady stream of players going to and from the bar out in front.

He sat down on a stool at a vacant section of the ornate bar, a broad-shouldered young man who seemed too young to belong there took the stool next to him.

"Rouell," Harvey said when the barman looked at him briefly. The young man was looking directly at him in the mirror. Harvey pretended not to see this.

"Pretty lucky so far," the young man remarked. His voice sounded casual and friendly. Harvey ignored this for a moment, then did a double take.

"Oh…" he said. "You mean me?"

He returned the young man's smile and shrugged modestly.

"I work here," the young man explained apologetically. "So don't worry about me being another bum who wants to cry on your shoulder."

The barman set a bottle in front of Harvey and the change for his dollar bill.

"Oh?" Harvey said. He poured the rouell beer into the glass, his eyes occupied with the operation.

"Why do you have to pick on Agnes all the time?" the young man said in a mildly complaining tone. "She's a friend of Mr. Cooger's, and he might not like it."

Harvey's pent up nerves relaxed.

"Sorry Mr.—" Harvey hesitated.

"Just call me Schmoe," the young man replied.

"Sorry, Schmoe," Harvey grinned. "I didn't know that."

The young man called Schmoe dropped his legs to the floor and stood up. He laid a friendly hand on Harvey's shoulder.

"You know it now, friend," he said. "By the way, you seemed interested in getting a look at the boss a minute ago. Would you like to meet him?"

Harvey looked at the young man's reflection in the mirror behind the bar without turning. He saw nothing but innocent friendliness in the young man's face.

"You're mistaken about the first," Harvey said disarmingly. "As to wanting to meet him…" He grinned knowingly at the reflection. "If my luck turns on me I'll probably have to do that."

A fleeting expression of disappointment shadowed the young man's smooth features. His hand slid lingeringly from Harvey's shoulder.

"In that case," he said with a casual smile, "let's hope your credit's good." He sounded like a youngster skillfully imitating the mannerisms and talk of an experienced adult.

Harvey's hands felt colder than the glass they were wrapped around. He signaled the barman with his eyes and ordered a cup of black coffee, pushing the rouell beer away.

While he drank the coffee his eyes studied the barroom and the area next to it where there were tables and a small dance floor, with a television set occupying a strategic position.

Alice sat at one of the tables, only it didn't look like Alice. Her face was still beautiful. No amount of disguising could erase that. It was now the face of a woman of fifty-five or sixty who had paid a great deal of money in a futile attempt to make it look young.

THERE could be no better defense for a young lady alone in the CLUB Rouell. A rather handsome man in his late thirties paused at her table and started to sit down, squinted slightly as his eyes looked closer at Alice's skin, then continued on to another table.

Harvey smiled to himself. Then he forgot about the smile and left it hanging on his lips while his mind froze tensely. A profile was reflected in the mirror. It was that of a man who had just entered the club and was walking toward the back rooms.

The man was Alex Potocki! He was walking with the sureness of stride of one who has walked the same path many times and knows just where he is going.

Was he here to play cards? Or was he coming to see Phil Cooger? There was a great deal of difference, and Harvey had to find out.

He knew that Alex would recognize him even through his careful disguise if he took a good look at him. That risk had to be taken for two reasons. One, it was almost imperative that he find out. The other, there was a stack of chips representing almost fifteen hundred dollars on a table in the gambling room that belonged to him, and if he walked out without cashing them in, Schmoe would be suspicious.

Harvey knew just how dangerous it was for him to go back into the card room. One slip and he would be lost.

He would have to tell Alice about Potocki, as she had never seen him and hadn't recognized him as he walked through. He rose abruptly and walked toward the back rooms. Instead of going into the gambling room he turned aside and entered the men's room.

There he wrote a brief note and folded it into a small square. When he left the men's room he went back to the bar. Instead of sitting down he paused and let his eyes survey the tables. The small square of folded paper was cupped in his right palm.

His eyes paused on Alice. To all outward appearances he was just another old man looking for a girl. With his left hand he carefully brushed an imaginary speck off the lapel of his coat and sauntered toward the table where Alice sat.

When he paused in front of her she looked up curiously, as at a stranger. He bent toward her with a charming smile on his lips, placing his right hand on the edge of the table so that the note would drop unnoticed by any watching eyes into her lap.

"Beg pardon miss," he murmured.

"Sorry mister," Alice replied, her voice low, but able to carry to the nearest tables. "You've made a mistake. I'm just in here for a few drinks and to watch the show."

"Please accept my apologies," Harvey said stiffly, his smile vanishing. He straightened up and looked over the room undecidedly, then shrugged his shoulders and returned to the card room. Several pairs of amused eyes followed him until he vanished into the back rooms.

Agnes was back in her seat at the table, he saw. There was another five hundred-dollar stack of chips in front of her. The young man, Schmoe, was slouched against a wall. Alex Potocki was nowhere to be seen. Harvey wanted to be sure. He pretended interest in another table where straight stud was being played. It gave him a vantage point from which he could survey the large room carefully.

Every nerve in his body tingled with suspense. At any moment Alex might appear and recognize him through his disguise.

FINALLY he was sure Alex was nowhere in the room. That meant he had gone to the office, and was therefore tied in with Phil Cooger.

Harvey walked swiftly over to his chair at the draw poker table and picked up his chips.

"Quitting?" Agnes asked.

Harvey smiled politely and nodded.

"What's the matter," Agnes sneered. "Not sporting enough to give the loser a chance?"

Harvey ignored this and continued picking up his chips.

"Just a cheap professional," Agnes said, raising her voice.

Harvey's eyes darted over toward Schmoe. That young man gave his shoulder a gentle push and straightened up. Harvey turned his attention back to Agnes.

"I believe," he said slowly, "that it's a universal house rule that a player may quit when he chooses without recriminations from any other player."

"There's also a rule in this house," Agnes said, her voice even louder than before, "that professionals aren't allowed to fleece the suckers."

Schmoe had stopped beside Harvey by now.

"What's the matter, friend?" he asked.

Harvey shrugged helplessly and nodded his head toward Agnes. He gave Schmoe a knowing look.

"He took my money and won't give me a chance to get it back," Agnes said, still in a loud voice.

"He has a right to quit," Schmoe said pleadingly. "Get it back from the next customer."

"Next customer hell," Agnes shouted angrily. "I've lost enough money in this two-bit joint to buy the place. I say I get it back from him."

"Give her the chance," Schmoe said to Harvey. "It's all right."

Harvey knew what he meant. If he lost the house would pay him to save a fuss.

"How about a cut for high card?" Harvey suggested.

"O.K.," Agnes said, her anger subsiding, replaced by the fire of gambling fever. "Fifteen hundred dollars."

"You only have five hundred in front of you," Harvey objected.

"That's all right," Schmoe said hastily. "She's good for it." He took the card deck and lifted a generous section of it. The card she exposed was a king.

Alarm bells were ringing inside Harvey's skull. His hand trembled slightly in spite of himself as he spilt the meager remains of the deck and turned it over, exposing a king. He smiled slightly.

"All right," he said. "You've had your chance. Should we quit?"

"Yellow?" Agnes sneered. Harvey shrugged resignedly. Schmoe shuffled the cards again.

"You first this time, friend," he said as he set the deck down.

Harvey split a thin half dozen cards off the deck and turned over a three.

Agnes' grin was foolish as she took half the remainder of the deck and turned it over. Her card was a deuce. Harvey took advantage of her stunned condition to turn away from the table and start toward the cashier's window.

Phil Cooger stood in his path. Behind him stood Alex Potocki.

THE ALARM bells were sounding violently inside Harvey's skull now. But, as in the thick of battle, his nerves were dead. Not by a flicker of an eye did he betray recognition of Alex.

He said nothing, pausing in his stride to wait for Cooger to step aside.

Over the shoulders of the two men Harvey could see Alice standing in the doorway looking at him. And suddenly, he could feel the weight of the flat gun cradled against his ribs. He had grown so used to it during the past week that he had almost forgotten it.

Alex Potocki was staring at him. Phil Cooger, a cigar in his mouth, was looking at him closely, his face inscrutable.

A strange thought intruded itself into Harvey's mind. How could a man who had killed some seven hundred people in cold blood still look human?

Alice had backed out of sight at the doorway. The alarm bells were subsiding.

"Would you mind stepping into my office?" Phil Cooger said past his cigar.

Without answering, Harvey looked past him to the office door as though seeing it for the first time. He looked back into Cooger's face and nodded.

Cooger and Potocki stepped aside. Harvey walked past them to the office door.

He paused while Phil Cooger stepped past him and inserted the key and opened the door. He stepped across the room and dropped his handful of chips on the bare desk, his eyes darting around the room as he heard the door close at his back.

The balance hung by such a slender thread now. If both Alex and Cooger believed him to be dead, killed in the Seattle hospital while trying to escape, they wouldn't look at him too closely. Alex wouldn't bother about the similarity of his voice to someone he believed dead. They had no reason to believe otherwise than that he was dead.

He turned with naturalness and looked questioningly at Cooger.

The gang boss counted the chips on his desk by nudging them with his finger and tipping them over.

"Seventeen hundred dollars in chips and fifteen hundred coming on that cut," he said admiringly. "Thirty-two hundred and fifty dollars!"

Harvey still said nothing. He fixed an expressionless smile on his face.

Phil pulled out a fat billfold and extracted a thick bundle of currency. He counted out six five hundred dollar bills, two hundreds and a fifty.

Harvey picked them up and shoved them carelessly in his pocket. He turned toward the door. He could feel his heart pounding violently now. His legs felt like they were wading through thick oil.

The street door seemed hopelessly far away. If he got out of his office he still had to brave the stares of a hundred people. His movements were jerky, mechanical. At least they felt that way. There were needles at the nape of his neck where cold eyes were boring in.

"Well, I might as well be going Phil. Drop up to my office sometime the next few days. Forty-one-oh-six in the Copper Building."

"O.K., Alex. I'll do that."

Harvey's fingers froze on the doorknob. The first sound of Alex's voice had stopped his heart for a brief, terrible instant. The meanings of the words, the natural and easy conversational tone, it penetrated slowly to him that he was not under suspicion. To these two men he was no more than a customer of the CLUB Rouell who had had a lucky night.

The door lock buzzed open. Harvey turned the knob and went out. Agnes was sitting in the same seat at the draw table she had had all night. She didn't look up.

He started toward the exit to the front of the club. The young man, Schmoe, caught his eye and nodded cheerful though casual congratulations.

Alex Potocki brushed past him just before he reached the doorway to the bar. Less than a minute later Harvey stepped out onto the sidewalk and turned his face into the cool night breeze and took a deep breath of relief.

A taxi pulled up before him. Alice signaled to him from inside. He opened the door and settled back beside her as the cab moved away from the curb.

CHAPTER EIGHTEEN

HARVEY and Helen stepped out of the elevator and turned to the right. They were followed by George and Alice. The four of them appeared to be two old couples in their sixties who carried their age very well.

They paused at a door carrying the legend, "4106, Alex Potocki, consulting biochemist."

Harvey opened the door with his left hand. Inside was a reception room with nicely upholstered plastic and chrome furniture. A very attractive young lady sat behind a small desk. She smiled a welcome to the four dignified old people.

Harvey advanced to the desk with a disarming smile and laid a card before her. The card said, "Andover Chemical Co." in the lower left hand corner in finer print it said, "C.G. Cortry, Pres."

"Do you have an appointment?" the young lady asked.

"No," Harvey replied. "You see, my regular consulting chemist just died recently, and I'm looking for another. In fact," he turned and included the other three with a smile. "My partner and I sort of combined pleasure with business on this trip to Chicago. Besides seeing all the sights we are looking for another consulting chemist."

He took the stance of a self-important businessman.

"I rather think Mr. Potocki will see us," he said pompously.

Helen and Alice had taken seats on opposite sides of the reception room. Each had opened her vanity case and seemed intent on inspecting its contents. George stood casually by the hall door, in such a position that if it opened he would be behind it. He held his right hand in his coat pocket.

The receptionist flicked a toggle switch on the base of her phone and spoke into it.

"There's a Mr. Cortry to see you, Mr. Potocki," she said sweetly. "On business."

She hung up and smiled at Harvey politely.

The door to the inner office opened and Alex stepped into view.

Then several things happened. George reached over and turned the bolt that locked the outer door. Helen and Alice each took a small automatic out of their vanity cases and pointed them at the office girl. Harvey pulled a larger automatic from his own pocket and pointed it at Alex.

George slowly brought his own gun into sight.

Alex froze for one brief instant and then jumped back into the inner office and tried to close the door. Harvey hit it with his shoulder. It flew open to reveal Alex staggering backwards.

He caught himself at the edge of the ornate desk and stared with wide eyes at the advancing figures of Harvey and George.

"What is this?" he demanded angrily.

"You still don't recognize us?" Harvey asked, amazed.

Alex licked his lips and looked from Harvey to George, dawning recognition and a growing terror on his face.

"Take off your coat and vest," George said coldly. "And do it slowly, with no sudden moves."

Alex obeyed.

"Now the shirt," George commanded. "Then go over and face the wall."

HARVEY took a flat case from his breast pocket and opened it on the desk. He fixed a hollow needle onto a glass tube with a plunger inside. Then he shoved the needle through the thin rubber cover of a small bottle and pulled the plunger out slowly, drawing the pale yellow fluid into the glass tube.

Alex had watched this over his shoulder. He was trembling visibly.

"Don't move," George warned. "This isn't going to kill you."

Harvey jabbed the needle into Alex's left shoulder, being careful to keep out of the line of fire and ready to spring back.

"Careful, Harvey," George said tensely. "Be sure it isn't in a vein."

"It isn't," Harvey said calmly.

He shoved the plunger in slowly. When it had gone as far as it could he jerked the needle free and held his finger over the puncture until he was sure the liquid wouldn't drain out.

"That's just to put you to sleep so we can take you out to the car," he said encouragingly.

"You can turn around now," George said. "Better go over and sit down on your davenport until it takes effect."

"If you think you can carry me out of here," Alex said desperately, "you're crazy."

He went over and sat down. He was already beginning to look drowsy. In three minutes he closed his eyes and rested quietly.

Harvey straightened him out flat on the davenport.

George went over and closed the door to the reception room and came back.

"What is your name?" he asked suddenly.

"Alex Potocki," came the answer, mouthy and mumbled from the drug.

George frowned. The truth drug was one developed in World War III, and was said to be invariably perfect. It was supposed to be impossible to tell a lie within two minutes after the prescribed injection. Its only drawback was that it also kept the mind from making those slight conjectures that are nearly always necessary in answering any except a very simple question.

He repeated the question and got the same answer.

"Well, Harvey," George said with a shrug. "Either he's immune to the drug or his real name is Alex Potocki."

"My real name is Alex Potocki," came the drugged answer.

"Have you ever used another name?" Harvey asked.

"Yes."

"What name were you using in 1848?" George asked quickly.

"Alfred Grant."

Harvey and George smiled at each other triumphantly. Then they stopped grinning. Each saw in the other's eyes that the moment had come.

It was George who asked:

"What is the equation for the immortality factor?"

The answer came as had the others, slowly and drugged.

"I don't know."

THEY HAD come all the way for this. They had risked their lives constantly, suffered privations and hardships, gone through the tightest police net in the world, knowing that one slip meant death for them all only to have Alex say he didn't know the answer.

"He *has* to know!" Harvey said desperately.

"I—don't—know," Alex repeated tonelessly.

"Do you know how to isolate it?"

"Yes."

"Then it's one of those substances that can't be analyzed?" George asked.

"Yes."

Harvey went over to a chair and sank into it weakly.

He listened while George asked the few remaining questions that confirmed what they had surmised. That Grant's Home Remedy was the answer.

There were additional questions that brought out the method of extracting the immortality factor from the remedy, its physical appearance, the dosage, and what function it performed in the body.

It seemed that nearly every cycle in the body's metabolism was a degenerating cycle. The highly complex molecules of immortality factor seemed able to take on a thousand different tasks at will. Not only that, they could never pass from the body with any of the wastes. They entered into every cycle and completed it perfectly.

The reason they could not be analyzed was because they seemed to be a complex of different molecules with shifting molecular patterns. In research the complex had exhibited almost intelligence, so uncanny was its power to settle into any metabolic cycle and solve its imperfections.

Further questioning brought out the fact that the immortality substance could not be simply produced by making the mixture according to the original formula.

That was the reason Research had taken so many years to isolate it. It had one of the properties of life itself. Some of it had to be already present before any more of it could be produced.

By some freakish cosmic accident there had been present in the original mixture made in the spring of 1848 a minute quantity of IF. There was none present in the batch Alex made up for Research. At first he had concluded that IF must be due to some impurity in the original mixture. It had taken a long time for him to get around to re-examining the original mixture, made with a half pint of his own blood added to the dandelion roots in the first brewing.

THERE WAS A SIX-OUNCE BOTTLE OF THE PURE SUBSTANCE IN HIS DESK.

Harvey searched Alex's pockets and found the key to the desk and opened the drawer that contained the bottle. It was not labeled.

He and George looked at the innocent appearing white crystals that filled the bottle with a mixture of feelings. It was enough of

IF to make a hundred thousand people live forever. It was the end product of Research. It was—IF!

"Let's go, George," Harvey said in a subdued voice.

"What about Alex?" George asked.

"The longer we stay here the greater the chances of our being caught," Harvey said. "We can kill him right now or leave him as he is. He should be killed."

"I don't think I could do it," George said.

"Neither could I," Harvey agreed.

They went into the outer office. It took only a few moments to tie and gag the receptionist.

"Potocki will wake up in a few hours," Harvey assured the girl.

THE TIRES made a humming noise on the metal grid of the bridge. Dubuque was just ahead.

"I still can't believe it," Helen exclaimed in semi-hysterical relief. "We got away without any trouble. We're out of the state. Our worries are over. Every second you were in that inner office with Alex I expected someone to try to come into the office."

"We aren't out of the woods yet," George laughed. We've a long hard program ahead of us. We're going to have to make tons of this stuff and see that everyone all over the world gets some."

"I—I still can't believe it," Helen said. "It seems like we're trying to go against nature in some way, and that some Power will prevent us from doing that. It wasn't intended for the human race to become immortal."

"It does seem hard to swallow all at once," Harvey admitted.

"It doesn't seem right for us to do this," Helen went on. "What of the population problem? If no one dies except by accident, in a hundred years the world will be too small for the population."

"There are other worlds," Alice said. "Man will have to expand now."

"But how do we know it will all work out?" Helen said. "It's like a river flowing through a valley. I mean the human race is like that. To block the gates of death is like damming the river. The waters will back up and fill the valley and flood everything."

Harvey tooled the car smoothly through the traffic of

downtown Dubuque.

"Your analogy is very good," George said after a while. "There's one thing we must remember through all our doubts. We can't sit down and solve all the problems that will come up before we do anything.

"Suppose we started out with the idea that we should give IF to only those people who proved worthy of it? Who would they be? The Einsteins and Newtons and the great statesmen? Maybe! Then what of the man who could have become greater than any of those in a hundred years more?"

"Not only that," Harvey said as he speeded the car up again on the open highway west of Dubuque. "I think we've ignored the main issue. Old age is a disease. We have the cure. Where would the medical profession have gone if it had decided that for the good of the race women who couldn't have normal births should be forced to die in childbirth? Where would it have wound up if it had decided that since the tendency to cancer is inheritable, all potentially cancerous people should be sterilized? There are strong arguments in favor of such things. Survival of the fittest keeps the race strong. But a doctor can't take on himself the problems of race survival. His patient is in need of help he can give. That help might contribute slightly to the decadence of the race in a few thousand years, but the doctor can only think of the immediate welfare of his patient. The overall problem must work itself out, and if in the long run the race dies out entirely due to preservation of the physically unfit by the medical profession, it is just too bad.

"I think we should look at it the same way. We should give everybody immortality, since we can. The problems that rise up when that is an accomplished fact are for the human race to solve, not us."

THE MILES sped by swiftly. Helen thought of the other time they had covered these same miles. George had been the idiot-George. Harvey had been at the wheel then, too.

She turned around and looked in back. George was sitting much as he had sat then, with Alice's head resting against his huge shoulder and seeming so small.

She thought of all that had happened since then—and all that was yet to come in the future.

"Problems have a way of working themselves out if you let them," Harvey was saying. "Take Alex, for example. He is a ruthless murderer, and plans on becoming dictator of the world. His plans hinge on everyone else and then out through the gates of death. If those gates are closed he will never accomplish his aims. If he lives, in a few centuries at the most he will get over that and learn to fit in.

"Take Phil Cooger. He's a master organizer and politician. If his talents were turned into legitimate channels, as they would be eventually, he could become a great force for good.

"All those problems are just too big to bother about. We have a simple job to do. We have to make a few hundred thousand people immortal whether they want to be or not. We have to make sure the whole world knows how to become immortal, so that no legislation can stop it."

"And then?" Helen asked softly, a wistful look in her eyes.

Harvey took his eyes off the road to glance at her briefly.

"And then," he smiled. "We'll take a vacation of a couple of centuries in a little cottage on the shore of the Pacific and watch the waves beat against the rocks and wear them away. About once every ten years we'll turn on a news broadcast and find out what is going on in the world."

"I know what I would like to do," Alice spoke up from the back seat. "George and I will have a cabin just around the bend from yours. I'm going to take about a dozen alley cats and the same number of plain old mongrel dogs and give them immortality. I'm going to see how far they can advance in those two centuries."

"I know what I'm going to do," George said with a sly grin.

"I'll bet I won't like it," Harvey grinned back at him through the rear view mirror.

"I'm going to get a rooster," George said. "And make him immortal. When he gets to be a hundred I'm going to invite you and Helen over to a chicken dinner."

…And that's just what he did.

THE END

If you've enjoyed this book, you will not want to miss these terrific titles…

ARMCHAIR SCI-FI, FANTASY, & HORROR DOUBLE NOVELS, $12.95 each

D-1   **THE GALAXY RAIDERS** by William P. McGivern
             SPACE STATION #1 by Frank Belknap Long

D-2   **THE PROGRAMMED PEOPLE** by Jack Sharkey
             SLAVES OF THE CRYSTAL BRAIN by William Carter Sawtelle

D-3   **YOU'RE ALL ALONE** by Fritz Leiber
             THE LIQUID MAN by Bernard C. Gilford

D-4   **CITADEL OF THE STAR LORDS** by Edmund Hamilton
             VOYAGE TO ETERNITY by Milton Lesser

D-5   **IRON MEN OF VENUS** by Don Wilcox
             THE MAN WITH ABSOLUTE MOTION by Noel Loomis

D-6   **WHO SOWS THE WIND…** by Rog Phillips
             THE PUZZLE PLANET by Robert A. W. Lowndes

D-7   **PLANET OF DREAD** by Murray Leinster
             TWICE UPON A TIME by Charles L. Fontenay

D-8   **THE TERROR OUT OF SPACE** by Dwight V. Swain
             QUEST OF THE GOLDEN APE by Ivar Jorgensen and Adam Chase

D-9   **SECRET OF MARRACOTT DEEP** by Henry Slesar
             PAWN OF THE BLACK FLEET by Mark Clifton.

D-10   **BEYOND THE RINGS OF SATURN** by Robert Moore Williams
             A MAN OBSESSED by Alan E. Nourse

ARMCHAIR SCIENCE FICTION CLASSICS, $12.95 each

C-1   **THE GREEN MAN**
             by Harold M. Sherman

C-2   **A TRACE OF MEMORY**
             By Keith Laumer

ARMCHAIR MASTERS OF SCIENCE FICTION SERIES, $16.95 each

M-1   **MASTERS OF SCIENCE FICTION, Vol. One**
             Bryce Walton—"Dark of the Moon" and other tales

M-2   **MASTERS OF SCIENCE FICTION, Vol. Two**
             Jerome Bixby: "One Way Street" and other tales

If you've enjoyed this book, you will not want to miss these terrific titles...

ARMCHAIR SCI-FI & HORROR DOUBLE NOVELS, $12.95 each

D-11   **PERIL OF THE STARMEN** by Kris Neville
THE STRANGE INVASION by Murray Leinster

D-12   **THE STAR LORD** by Boyd Ellanby
CAPTIVES OF THE FLAME by Samuel R. Delaney

D-13   **MEN OF THE MORNING STAR** by Edmund Hamilton
PLANET FOR PLUNDER by Hal Clement and Sam Merwin, Jr.

D-14   **ICE CITY OF THE GORGON** by Chester S. Geier and Richard S. Shaver
WHEN THE WORLD TOTTERED by Lester Del Rey

D-15   **WORLDS WITHOUT END** by Clifford D. Simak
THE LAVENDER VINE OF DEATH by Don Wilcox

D-16   **SHADOW ON THE MOON** by Joe Gibson
ARMAGEDDON EARTH by Geoff St. Reynard

D-17   **THE GIRL WHO LOVED DEATH** by Paul W. Fairman
SLAVE PLANET by Laurence M. Janifer

D-18   **SECOND CHANCE** by J. F. Bone
MISSION TO A DISTANT STAR by Frank Belknap Long

D-19   **THE SYNDIC** by C. M. Kornbluth
FLIGHT TO FOREVER by Poul Anderson

D-20   **SOMEWHERE I'LL FIND YOU** by Milton Lesser
THE TIME ARMADA by Fox B. Holden

ARMCHAIR SCIENCE FICTION CLASSICS, $12.95 each

C-3   **INTO PLUTONIAN DEPTHS**
by Stanton A. Coblentz

C-4   **CORPUS EARTHLING**
by Louis Charbonneau

C-5   **THE TIME DISSOLVER**
by Jerry Sohl

C-6   **WEST OF THE SUN**
by Edgar Pangborn

ARMCHAIR SCIENCE FICTION & HORROR GEMS SERIES, $12.95 each

G-1   **SCIENCE FICTION GEMS, Vol. One**
Isaac Asimov and others

G-2   **HORROR GEMS, Vol. One**
Carl Jacobi and others

If you've enjoyed this book, you will not want to miss these terrific titles...

ARMCHAIR SCI-FI, FANTASY, & HORROR DOUBLE NOVELS, $12.95 each

D-21   **EMPIRE OF EVIL** by Robert Arnette
THE SIGN OF THE TIGER by Alan E. Nourse & J. A. Meyer

D-22   **OPERATION SQUARE PEG** by Frank Belknap Long
ENCHANTRESS OF VENUS by Leigh Brackett

D-23   **THE LIFE WATCH** by Lester Del Rey
CREATURES OF THE ABYSS by Murray Leinster

D-24   **LEGION OF LAZARUS** by Edmond Hamilton
STAR HUNTER by Andre Norton

D-25   **EMPIRE OF WOMEN** by John Fletcher
ONE OF OUR CITIES IS MISSING by Irving Cox

D-26   **THE WRONG SIDE OF PARADISE** by Raymond F. Jones
THE INVOLUNTARY IMMORTALS by Rog Phillips

D-27   **EARTH QUARTER** by Damon Knight
ENVOY TO NEW WORLDS by Keith Laumer

D-28   **SLAVES TO THE METAL HORDE** by Milton Lesser
HUNTERS OUT OF TIME by Joseph E. Kelleam

D-29   **RX JUPITER SAVE US** by Ward Moore
BEWARE THE USURPERS by Geoff St. Reynard

D-30   **SECRET OF THE SERPENT** by Don Wilcox
CRUSADE ACROSS THE VOID by Dwight V. Swain

ARMCHAIR SCIENCE FICTION CLASSICS, $12.95 each

C-7   **THE SHAVER MYSTERY, pt. 1**
by Richard S. Shaver

C-8   **THE SHAVER MYSTERY, pt. 2**
by Richard S. Shaver

C-9   **MURDER IN SPACE**
by David V. Reed

ARMCHAIR MASTERS OF SCIENCE FICTION SERIES, $16.95 each

M-3   **MASTERS OF SCIENCE FICTION, Vol. Three**
Robert Sheckley, "The Perfect Woman" and other stories

M-4   **MASTERS OF SCIENCE FICTION, Vol. Four**
Mack Reynolds, part one, "Stowaway" and other stories.